Vampire Embrace

Vic Brown

High Tide Publications, Inc.
Deltaville, Virginia 23043

High Tide Publications, Inc.
1000 Bland Point
Deltaville, Virginia 23043
www. Hightidepublications. Com

Publisher's Note: Names, characters, businesses, places, events and incidents are either the products of the author's imagination or used for atmospheric purposes. Any resemblance to actual persons, living or dead, or to businesses, companies, institutions, actual events or locales is purely coincidental.

ISBN: 978-1945990113

Printed in the United States of American

Vampire Embrace is dedicated to

Jeanne Johansen, CEO of High Tide Publications, Inc.

She raised me from a writer to a published author, fulfilling a lifelong dream.

Vampire Embrace
Major Characters

Lamar Bradford
> Wealthy owner of Coleson Manor

Morgan Summers Bradford
> 325-year-old vampire born in Old Salem Village

Robert Diamond
> Gentleman's gentleman to Lamar Bradford

Dr. James R. Heller
> Dean of Harvard's Faculty of Arts and Sciences and Director of Harvard's Genetics Laboratory

Dr. Florence Senger
> Director of Human Resources at Harvard U. Called "Flossie"

Judeland Bundaeker
> Vampire. Out to kill Lamar, Morgan, and Dr. Heller

Jennifer Marsh
> Lamar's former colleague and lover

Dr. Wallace Gibson   ("Wally")
> Director of Operations at Harvard's Genetics Laboratory

Chief Inspector Cordell Peyton
> Cambridge Police Department

Colonel Johann Solento
> Commander of the Pontifical Swiss Guard at the Vatican

Cardinal Santoro Manlocara
> Vatican Treasurer, President of the Fabbrica, and head of the OVFS (Order of the Vampire Final Solution)

Father Ed Hemming
        Priest at Saint Paul Catholic Church
Harold Stone
        Chief of Harvard's Campus Police Department
Charlotte Rhodes
        Former Saint Paul's secretary
Dr. Glenn Ellen Martin
        President of Harvard University
Gretta the Blind
        Raised Morgan Summers in Old Salem Village after Morgan's mother, Marta Sorrel, was pressed to death as a witch
Nancy Worthington
        Manager of MaidPro Housecleaning and Maid Service
Dr. Jene Claude Vompre, cum Andre Suroccan
        750-year Vampire extraordinaire and genetic scientist
Number Three (Imre Sandar)
        Gun for hire. Member of the OVFS. Former East German intelligence officer

Prologue

Coleson Manor's library served as her sanctuary—more like a womb, Morgan thought. The smell of leather, musty books, the hint of pipe smoke, and the wood fire created an aroma that cloaked her with a sense of security and comfort. She'd rarely known those qualities during her 325 years as a vampire. That was behind her, thank all the gods. Or was it?

Restless, she sprang from the sofa, propelling Calvin onto the thick carpet. The cat's angry retort was muted, absorbed by the floor to ceiling drapes, the countless volumes on shelves, the top half accessible only with the use of a rolling staircase, and the faint crackle and hiss of the fire. Morgan faced herself in the massive gilded mirror over the mantle, canted down so she could see her reflection. Her blood chilled.

As a vampire Morgan had different color eyes—one green, one amber. After her gene-editing process (Project Resurrection), both eyes were amber. But somehow her right eye had reversed to green, as it had been for over 325 years. She felt cold and couldn't control her trembling. She bit her lower lip upon sensing the aroma of Absinthe. When a vampire was startled, frightened, angry, sexually aroused, deeply curious, and upon rousing from sleep, he or she exuded the liquorish scent of Absinthe. Normally only another vampire could detect the scent, but sometimes normal mortals could if the vampire's reaction was especially strong.

The fetus! Had to be. It was pulling her back. Back into the piteous reality of vampirism. It was re-altering her genetic makeup. She hadn't told Lamar she was pregnant, because she devoutly wanted to get rid of the fetus. She couldn't bring herself to refer to it by any other name.

Obviously she couldn't have an abortion at a clinic; they would do blood work on her, and the results would cause a medical firestorm. Dr. Wally Gibson, Director of Operations at Harvard's genetic lab, was a Roman Catholic and would never perform an abortion. The only other alternative was abhorrent. Andre Suroccan. He had been a vampire for over 750 years and claimed he could rid her of the fetus . . . for a price. Sex with Morgan. But then he would have power over her for as long as Morgan lived. Three options—but all of them dead ends.

Four if you included suicide.

1 - Andre Suroccan, Mercurial Vampire
February 2013

Behold the vampire in his lair
Who courts yon mortals young and fair
Beseeches them: Come join my fold,
And spend eternity but ne'er grow old
Too late they pound on Truth's stern door
For once passed through they can love no more
Hear their heartless hearts beat in blood-quenched fury
The lords of Hell their judge and jury.

Suroccan pushed through the throng of Harvard students waiting for their lattes in Simon's Coffee Emporium. The pungent smell of coffee beans, the babble of voices, chiming computer tablets, and clatter of utensils almost overpowered his senses. Glaring lights and the garish orange walls hurt his eyes. His nostrils flared, and his lips pursed. A single, short braid of silver hair hung over the back of his starched clerical collar. From his hat to his Florsheims he was dressed in black. Tall, lean to gaunt, his unkempt silver and black eyebrows almost met over the bridge of his nose. Deep-set, feral eyes swept the coffee shop, quickly settling on a woman who sat at a small table in the back corner drumming her fingers. He threaded his way to her and stood like a specter.

Slender, with a striking figure, she combined good looks with a sense of grace and strength, though she looked careworn and tense. "Mrs. Bradford, I presume?"

She had watched him from the moment he walked in. "Morgan. Please sit, Mr. Suroccan. Or should I call you Father?" she asked, her voice edged with sarcasm. "Would you care for a coffee?" She glanced at her latte, the spoon still leaning in the cup. Deep in thought, she had been stirring it mindlessly since it was delivered, a habit borrowed from her husband, Lamar.

"Thank you, Morgan. Please call me Andre. I'll skip the coffee. I am dressed as a cleric, because I've found it just a bit easier to get past the immigration authorities as Father Suroccan. This is a ghastly place." He waved a hand to indicate the coffee house. "Why did you choose it?" The momentary smile on his thin lips never reached his eyes.

"In your letter you mentioned leather goods. Are you familiar with that market?" Morgan asked.

"I think we can dispense with the James Bond part of this interview. I have visited La Boutique Cuir in the Parisian Flea Market on several occasions since the mid-19th century. I spoke with the Countess Amberglass only last month. She extends her regards and begs you to return to Paris and renew your friendships. It was there I learned of your capability to transform members of our kind. Your reply to my letter was most gracious and timely." He reached across the table and removed the spoon from her cup. As his hand touched hers she was enveloped by a torpid blend of dank grave, a coppery taste, and a cloying sense of danger. The faint aroma of Absinthe hovered over their table.

Morgan was wrenched from Andre's mesmerism by the sounds of a mug smashing on the floor and accompanying screech from a coed who leaped up, frantically wiping the front of her sweater. The co-ed was rewarded by a round of raucous applause and a cry of "Take it off." Morgan looked back at Andre; his focus had never wavered. She cleared her throat. "You have no doubt given our offer considerable thought," Morgan said. "Let's start with why you want to experience resurrection. As I mentioned in the letter, it will take total commitment to succeed." The neon sign over Morgan's head lit; order fifty-two was ready for pickup.

Andre folded his hands, interlocking his impossibly long, bleached fingers, made longer by fingernails that could serve as weapons, and nodded, taking a deep breath. "When did you first discover you were one of us, Morgan?"

She frowned. "In the early 1700s, why do you ask?"

"Hmmm. So you've lived in the shadows for well over three centuries, and for most of that time, I strongly suspect, you were searching for the way out, am I right?"

Morgan nodded almost imperceptibly. He was interrogating her. It was supposed to be the other way around. She had to regain control of this interview.

"You have but to search your own memory my dear, your own experiences, and there you will find the answer to your question."

Andre slumped back into his chair, exhaling as if for the first time since he sat down.

Morgan shook her head. "Are you suggesting that all candidates for resurrection come for the same reasons?"

"No, but I sensed what your reasons were, and I share them. I am weary. My special powers have long since given me no pleasure. I have helped no few mortals learn the secrets of death . . . including the fear of it. But that wisdom is denied me, and those are the last secrets about which I care. You offer my only hope of piercing them."

"There are a few brethren of the dark who have chosen death," Morgan said. "I helped two of them while I lived near the Parisian Flea Market in the mid-19th century. You are no doubt familiar with the death rites of the Serpent of Charna?"

"Of course. But choosing that path would be going from living death to final death without having experienced mortal life, with its fear of death. The Vampire Resurrection Project promises a middle path. Oh, and like you, I am fascinated with the prospect of bringing a new creature into being."

"Creature?" Morgan gasped, unable to control her surprise. How in the name of all the denizens of the Underworld could he have known she was pregnant? She wasn't showing yet. This one is a master vampire, no doubt, and dangerous. Her hands, lying on the table, closed into fists, and she glared at him.

"We require total commitment to resurrection," she began, and we offer no absolute guarantees. There will be a fee, one commensurate with your current financial status. Our work is performed in a cocoon of total secrecy. Keeping our secrets will be just one of your life-long—or life short—commitments. It may take up to a year for you to become ready for resurrection. We will judge your progress and decide when you are ready. You will be one of a chosen few who will pursue the goal of resurrection together as a group. You will be expected to help your fellow classmates achieve the goal common to all of you—mortality. In effect, you must completely discard your previous lives and build a new one to replace them. You may encounter hardships and setbacks. Even danger if you fail to follow the program exactly. Are we clear on all that?"

CჳꙄꙉ

Morgan picked up her spoon and began stirring her cold latte. She might well have been stirring her intuition, for it was whispering that she should be wary of Suroccan. More than wary. Why would he, an extraordinary vampire with highly developed and refined powers, want to become mortal? What did he really want? Could he possibly be working against Project Resurrection?

He may be ready.

But was she?

2 - Cambridge: The "Wild East" Town

"It is easy to see why each man kills the things he loves. To know a living thing is to kill it . . . To try to know a living thing is to try to suck the life out of that being. The temptation of the vampire fiend, is this knowledge. The desirous consciousness, the spirit, is a vampire."

D. H. Lawrence,

Famous Vampire Quotes

Morgan slumped at her desk in the small classroom on the third floor of Harvard's Science Center. Leaning on her elbows, face buried in her hands, she squeezed her eyes shut against the tears that fought for release. She was sick of her tears, her lack of control, and mortally tired of the constant ache in her heart since Jamie Junior's suicide. Lamar had done everything, said everything he could think of to convince her she was not responsible for JJ's death. But he was wrong. She *was* responsible. She knew the boy was despondent, knew he was aware of the gun locker in the library, had watched him withdraw, spending too much time alone in Coleson Manor, Lamar's mansion in West Cambridge's Brattle Street District.

JJ's father, Dr. James R. Heller, Dean of Harvard's Faculty of Arts and Sciences and Director of the Genetics Lab, didn't blame her, he blamed himself. After JJ had been the lab's first success in its top secret Vampire Resurrection Project, Dr. Heller ("Jamie") had ignored his son in his zeal to replicate the lab's success.

The first two operations had been ghastly failures, however. A married vampire couple, whose replacement genetic material had been sabotaged by a lab technician, since murdered, had led to the condition of "radical unwinding." The two victims experienced a slow, progressive cellular degeneration; all of their body parts were disintegrating, but they did not die. Until Morgan, who had been taught the ancient technique for the ritual slaying of a vampire, agreed to undertake that grisly task.

Morgan shuddered as she recalled the ritual killings. She had driven an aspen stake into their hearts. After decapitation, their bodies—what there was left of them—were secretly buried in the Saint Paul Catholic Church Cemetery in Cambridge. Their heads had been smuggled into the marble cornerstone of the new Lady Chapel under construction at the church. Morgan wondered if Father Hemming ever suspected the dark shadows that would forever cling to that cornerstone.

For several months during early autumn through the end of December of last year, Cambridge had become a "Wild East" town, as the *Globe* had called it. Morgan remembered some of the headlines:

> *Waitress Kidnapped from Harvard Faculty Club*
> *Hauled off by Fake Rescue Squad*
> *Hotel Shootout: Second OK Corral*
> *Car Bomb Detonates on Campus.*
> *Bomber Probably Killed*
> *Assailant Shoots Valet in Tory Row Mansion*
> *Valet Wounds Assailant*
> *Harvard Employee Attacks Boss with Butcher Knife*
> *Shot Point-blank but Disappears*
> *Catholic Church Scene of Christmas Eve Gunfight*
> *Priest Badly Wounded—Secretary Kidnapped*
> *FBI Called In*
> *Cambridge Under Lockdown?*

During Cambridge's "Reign of Terror" Dr. Heller and his GenLab staff tried desperately to keep their real mission shrouded. While they were partially successful, too many outsiders were drawn into the vortex of Project Vampire Resurrection, including the chief of campus security, the university's HR director, and finally Harvard's President, Dr. Glenn Ellen Martin.

Vampires? Dr. Martin was stunned, incredulous, and outraged in turn, her first impulse being to shut down the GenLab. But the research was showing great promise against a variety of high priority diseases, even if vampirism had secretly become the GenLab's primary focus when its director, Dr. Heller, discovered his son carried the latent gene for that disease. Dr. Martin, against her better angels, agreed to keep the grants flowing, but demanded that Dr. Heller not slight the "open" side of his GenLab's assignment—progress on such diseases as lupus, hemophilia, leukemia, and AIDS. She warned Dr. Heller that if the vampire project were to leak, the pillars of Harvard would crumble.

Morgan sighed, pulled her feet out of her shoes, and leaned back in her chair, propping her heels on the desk, ankles crossed. She had come a long way since that night in 1692 when the Old Salem villagers came for her mother, Marta Sorrel. Had her mother really been a witch? Why not? Her daughter turned out to be a vampire. She could still smell the rancid fat from the torches, hear the chant from the Salem Village crones: "*witch, witch, witch.*"

When her mother had been pressed to death, Blind Gretta hobbled over to Morgan. "You will come with me, child. I will take you home."

"Let her go," the elder crone said. "They deserve each other. A miserable klatch be Blind Gretta, her mangy cat, and the witch's daughter. Best if they starve or freeze this winter—all of 'em."

Calvin—who was not mangy—followed them back to Gretta's two-room thatched hovel behind the gaol, where they could hear the coughing and moaning and screaming from the fifty confessed and eight condemned. Even some of the ninety-two suspects awaiting trial were crammed into the packed gaol. Another two hundred names had been entered into court documents as "under suspicion."

Morgan became Gretta's eyes, and Gretta became Morgan's heart.

Morgan fled the village at age thirteen, the day after Blind Gretta died. She took Calvin, her real mum's wooden cross, some food and wine, and little else.

CR80

Morgan was jarred out of the past as her door opened. "Hey, dear heart. Uh, you look a bit down." Lamar moved quickly to her side and kissed her on the forehead. "You've been working too hard. No, let me guess. You've been thinking too hard. *Remembering* too hard. Am I right?"

She liked it when he called her "dear heart," and smiled wanly. "I guess you could say 'E, all the above.'"

Lamar pulled over a beat-up chair and sat beside her. "So, how did the other three interviews go? I hope they went better than the one with what's-his-name, Sarochan."

"Suroccan." Morgan put her feet on the floor but not in her shoes. "Yeah, they did, but why do almost all the vampires I've ever met the past 325 years turn out to be 33rd degree weirdos? You excepted of course."

"There's a relief."

"You were just a nerd, not a weirdo." She smiled and patted his knee.

"Whew. You really know how to buck up a guy." Lamar returned her smile.

"Ummm. You bucked up quite nicely last night."

"Well, it was okay, of course, but not like—"

She glared at him. "Are you suggesting I was better in bed when I was a vampire?"

Lamar took a deep breath. "Nope, you brought all those skills with you through resurrection. And I love you, dear heart, with or without your vampire wings. But remember, you said we're not supposed to talk about sex during working hours." He tapped his wrist watch.

"I was born to break the rules. You should know that by now." She patted his knee again and left her hand on it. They had only been married a month, though they had been sleeping together the previous eight months. Morgan became aware of the tightness in her belly and frowned.

Lamar groaned and shook his head. "Somebody help me, I married a monster. I'm getting older. I'll be forty in just under three years. How am I going to keep up with you?"

Morgan tapped on her watch as if to say that it was still working hours, and now *he* was talking about sex.

"Anything new in the search for Judeland Bundaeker?" she asked, pulling her hand back.

"Nothing, I'm afraid. I made the rounds. Talked to Hal this morning and had coffee with Cordell. The campus police and the Cambridge detectives are at full stall. It's as if Judeland flew off to Mars or something. Even the FBI is stumped although they won't admit it. Same with the other members of the Order of the Vampire Final Solution (OVFS). At least the Vatican has shut down that organization, or that's what Father Hemming said after he came back from Rome. It wouldn't surprise me if the cardinals just whitewashed the whole issue, though. The Vatican never came right out and admitted there ever was such an organization." Lamar drummed his fingers on Morgan's desk. "If the OVFS had averaged killing one vampire per year, they would have bagged about 87 by now, though they may have had some stand-downs, like World War II for instance. The Vampire Resurrection Project only has three successes and one of those. . . ."

Lamar looked down as Morgan cringed. "Sorry, I didn't think." Lamar reached for her hand and squeezed it. She squeezed back.

"For a nerd, you sure learned how to make a vampire weak in the knees." Morgan's voice was soft, and breathy. Lamar wasn't quite six feet and had obstreperous eyebrows graced with a few gray hairs, along with a turned-up nose, which gave him an understated impish look.

"Not to mention a stray mortal or two," Lamar said. "When it comes to knees, I make 'em all weak."

"I think I liked you better as a nerd." But the reference to JJ had spoiled the moment, as it had so many others during the seven months since his death. Still, she smiled at her husband and stood up, causing her chair to squeak as it rolled back.

Andre Suroccan moved away from the door, his steps soundless, his acute hearing having missed nothing.

3 - Vampire Classmates

The dawn of time and space and light
Echoes the Cosmic proclamation
Life is not all there is, my friend;
Have ye nay heard of the Vampire Nation?

Robert was a gentleman's gentleman. A formal man. Though born and raised in Cheltenham, England, he possessed a perfect blend of the old English and the new American styles. At sixty he was surprisingly agile, could pass for fifty despite a slight paunch and receding hairline. Butler, valet, chef, nurse, tutor, estate manager, he did everything but pee for Lamar. The darkness of vampirism enveloped Coleson Manor like a storm front after Robert found Lamar in that alley last year. Lamar had taken on a hard edge as he began to evolve into a vampire, and Robert was troubled by other changes as well. With Morgan becoming part of Lamar's life, shielding Lamar from the worst of his new condition had become that much more complicated.

On a dead cold winter evening Robert served Lamar and Morgan one of Lamar's favorite dinners: sautéed quail with Shiitake port sauce reduction and a 2005 Domaine de la Collonge Pouilly-Fuisse´. Happy hour had begun with escargot and the venerable Side Car—a drink first popularized in the 1920s and practically forgotten the past four decades.

Morgan wanted to dine in the library. The fire warmed and cheered them, while five candles in a sterling silver candelabra created a romantic glow. Oxnard, Lamar's cat, weaved around their feet, hoping for a handout. But Calvin, originally Blind Gretta's cat, slept on the piano bench. Calvin had been with Morgan since she fled Old Salem, having somehow become immortal like its mistress.

"Lamar, have you noticed how badly Calvin has aged since we went through resurrection? I think, just like us, he has lost his immortality, and it scares me. I've lived with that cat since 1692 when Gretta took me in. I'm going to ask Dr. Gibson if his team could do a kind of reverse engineering on him. I'd like him to last at least as long as I do. If they can remove vampire DNA from a human, couldn't they insert it in an animal?"

Lamar stopped eating, frowned, and rubbed the back of his neck. "That is an interesting concept. And a bit frightening. Think about it. Look through the other end of the telescope. The implication is that you could create vampirism as well as cure it. Suppose it worked? In the wrong hands, that means that not only animals but possibly people could be injected with vampire DNA. We could end up with the power to create more vampires, hypothetically speaking, than we cure. But what if someone found out about that? He or she might pay millions for the formula. Maybe it's not true that every man has his price, but some do for sure. Do you think it's worth the risk of creating a reverse vampire protocol?"

Morgan sat silent for a long moment. "I'll have to think about that." Oxnard purred loudly and brushed up against her leg. Calvin remained silent and motionless but watched them through slitted eyes.

"So tell me about the other three vampires you interviewed for the first class of Resurrection 201," Lamar said.

"I'm not sure you want to know. The first one is an ex-hooker, and I'm not that sure about the 'ex' part. Her name is Evelyn Guard; at least that's what she's using now. Former pole dancer, call girl, member of the Radio City Music Hall Rockettes in 1948, Playboy bunny, and an extra in a half-dozen Hollywood B-grade movies. I suspect her abilities on a casting couch exceeded her acting talent. Along with a centerfold figure, she is bipolar, admits to two former husbands, and has been an active vampire since 1966, although she was born in 1936. She has struggled to hide her identity for almost a half century. She admits to killing two men in separate incidents—they wouldn't take 'No' for an answer—leaving their bodies in their cars, shriveled and nearly bloodless, baffling two forensic pathologists. It had been in the papers. She claims to have become masterful at hasty departures.

"Then there is the professor. Goes by Benjamin Dizzraeli, spelled with a double "z." Full beard, mostly white, admits to being gay, born in 1901, an active vampire since about 1920, the year his maid threatened to make public his homosexuality. Said he had to kill her, but other than animals, she was the only one . . . if you don't count one young boy.

"And finally there is the kid. I feel sorry for him. Alton Ribb is twenty-two and just out of college. Majored in English. He's the only survivor of a car crash his senior year that killed his best buddy and their two girlfriends. They'd been drinking. After the crash he went active—ate most of the family dog. He heard about us from Evelyn Guard. One night he caught her act at some clip joint in Boston, and they started talking and drinking. Ended up in bed together, and somehow, during the night, she told him about resurrection." Morgan pushed the rest of her dinner away and walked over to the fire. Her shoulders drooped, and she sighed. "Why does everything have to be so hard?"

Lamar shook his head and smiled. "Don't forget all the good stuff. We have each other, this mausol—uh, grand old house—lots of money, and good jobs at Harvard. Most people would kill for half that."

"Ummm. You know, I just don't believe that the Order of the Vampire Final Solution is dead and buried. With Judeland Bundaeker out there somewhere, it doubles the odds that she or the OVFS will come after us again. I feel like this is the calm before another storm. And we better be making some emergency preparations, or we are going to get swept away by it." She looked at Lamar and raised her eyebrows.

Lamar gave her a wonderful back rub, no sex, and then promptly fell asleep. But she didn't. Why hadn't she told him about their child? She asked herself for the hundredth time. Morgan refused to admit she was scared. She wasn't sure when she'd conceived. If it was before resurrection there was no doubt; she would birth an active vampire, not just an infant with dormant vampirism DNA. She couldn't go to an OB/GYN doctor. The first thing he'd want to do is run blood tests. And even though she had been resurrected, her blood—and the fetus's blood—would reveal serious discrepancies.

Vampires rarely ever get pregnant. Why me? A sudden chill coursed through her. She'd been pregnant for about five months and still not showing, but that would change soon. She had to tell Lamar. "Lords of the Universe," she intoned, "help me." She desperately wished she could talk to Gretta.

You can. The words seized her, and she sat up, shaking. She turned on the bedside lamp. Nothing. No one. I'm losing it.

She felt wet and looked down.

Blood had spread on the sheet between her legs.

4 - Rebirth of the OVFS

Double, double toil and trouble;
Fire burn, and cauldron bubble,
Fate is baking in the mists, where
vampires circle the quick and dead
Let mortal man lay down with dread
For immortality makes a dreadful bed.
Upon which lies, the vampire's spawn—
here today but never gone
The reek of Absinthe fills the air, its cloying
scent a promiscuous dare
As mortal life you bid adieu, come now to our
cauldron . . . we are waiting for you.

First two lines from Macbeth; balance from author

Cardinal Santoro Manlocara crumpled the note into a tight ball and hissed over his lower teeth, glaring at the acolyte who had delivered it. The young man bowed low, then darted out of the cardinal's residence, which, until recently, had belonged to the missing Cardinal Alfonso Loconi. The 18th century tall case clock, which showed the phases of the moon, chimed ten times. Another dreary morning at the Vatican. As usual, the clock was twelve minutes fast. He had twice asked Ludwig Oechslin, master clockmaker, to come and fix it.

In 1978 Ludwig made his reputation by successfully repairing the Vatican's 18th century Farnese clock, a one-of-a-kind astronomical, pendulum-driven mechanism. He had no records or drawings of the clock from which to work. Ludwig sent word to Cardinal Manlocara that he had added the cardinal's most recent request to his list.

"A pox on your list," Manlocara growled. "I should have you excommunicated." He hissed again, opening the wadded, handwritten note. Just the two words: *Resurrections successful.* It was signed "Father S." La mierda! Andre Suroccan is no more a priest than Winston Churchill was a fascist. But Heller's success portends more vampire conversions—or resurrections as they call them. The OVFS must come out of hibernation. Heller's lab must be terminated. Vampires must be eradicated like smallpox, not given new life.

He sighed. Suroccan is more mercurial than Dickens's third ghost. I don't trust him. At least we have someone inside Heller's laboratory again. Well, almost inside. He wondered how Suroccan had managed the penetration. Damn the man, I should be kept informed.

My predecessor made some bad choices when he recruited for the OVFS in North America. The Bundaeker woman, especially. I can't conceive of Loconi hiring a *vampire* as part of the team, but she was well placed, and her reports were quite professional. She informed us of the radical unwinding, the ritual killings, the burials in Saint Paul's Cemetery, and the secreting of the two vampire heads into the cornerstone of Saint Paul's new Lady Chapel. Considerably more information than Suroccan has ever provided.

And now she's gone rogue. Killed and ate part of the lab tech who had successfully doomed the first resurrection. Killed one of Dr. Heller's housekeepers, abducted Heller's son, and attacked the director of the university's HR department. We must find Bundaeker and add her head to the others in our vault. I wonder how much room we have left in it? I shall have to visit it one day . . . maybe discover why Alfonso spent so much time down there.

That poor idiot Father Hemming. Came all the way from America to demand the Holy See investigate the *non-existent* OVFS. How I would love to tell him he has two headless vampires buried in holy ground at Saint Paul's Cemetery, not to mention their heads in the cornerstone of Hemming's new Lady Chapel, one largely financed by the Vatican. But I rather like the irony of it all. Maybe I should try to place more vampire heads in church cornerstones. Ah, no, too risky. When the OVFS resumes its work, we shall have to reopen the head vault—the one now guarded by the bones of our dear Cardinal Loconi. Perhaps I should create a shrine for his bones. After all, he was Number Two, the head of the OVFS during the happy days after World War II. Still, it was the late Number One who put the organization together and ran it for the first twenty-two years.

Cardinal Manlocara looked around. He was still not used to living in Alfonso's former residence. Even though he'd removed all of Alfonso's furnishings and brought in his own, it still didn't feel right. He'd kept only the tall case clock and the copy of the Mona Lisa done by one of

Leonardo's students and all but indistinguishable from the original that hung in the Louvre. A single, pale yellow spotlight illumined her smile. Or was it a smile? Ah well, some mysteries are not meant to be resolved. He glanced at the tall case clock. That damnable Commander of the Pontifical Swiss Guard had better be on time.

Heaving his substantial bulk from what he called his "apostolic chair," the cardinal walked gingerly to an ornate, gilded mirror. With customary vanity, he performed his morning comb-over before donning his red biretta, which helped keep his gray hair, what little remained, in place. Overfed and cherubic, he could posture as a disarmingly simple man. Aside from his gray hair, only the crow's-feet around his eyes suggested he was over seventy. Colorless darting eyes—small, round, and quick—glinted when he was angry or about to squash the argument of a fellow cardinal. He felt the familiar cold pain in his stomach and rummaged in a bedside drawer for an antacid. Whose stomach wouldn't be crotchety on a day like this? Three stories below, that pompous ass, Colonel Solento, would soon be opening the sealed vault in the necropolis that contained the OVFS collection of vampire heads. Fifty-some-odd at last count. Cardinal Manlocara smiled. He would ask the colonel for details of Cardinal Loconi's death after being sealed alive in the vault with naught but the grisly collection of heads for company.

Yes, it would be fitting to create a shrine in the vault featuring the cardinal's bones.

⋘⋙

The necropolis's passageways were suffused with faint emanations from the long dead, along with the ethereal scent of their decay, a scent which itself had endured the trackless passage of the millennia, such that it had evolved into something like a fine perfume, cloying in a way that triggered mankind's pre-historic fears. To be in the necropolis was to live in the moment of one's own fleeting mortality.

The colonel had temporarily sealed off one section of passageways under the ruse that it was to be checked for the buildup of certain unspecified toxic vapors. The electric power had been extinguished as well.

Colonel Solento had no intention of performing any manual labor despite the cardinal's strict injunction against exposing anyone else to the vault. Minuette, a day laborer the colonel had hired from the Via di Casel Demerode, one of Rome's many slums, carried an oil lantern, a large burlap sack, and a pick. The colonel led, carrying the other lantern.

Cardinal Manlocara had mandated that Johann, himself, do the labor required to tear down the brick wall he had erected to seal the vault, with the late Cardinal Loconi inside. It had been imperative to eliminate Loconi, of course, Johann thought. He would have cracked during the Papal investigation requested by that idiot American priest, and the OVFS would have been taken down. But he, Commander of the Pontifical Swiss Guard, was not about to soil himself tearing down the entrance. It had been bad enough laying the bricks that were to be torn out. But the rewards—promotion to colonel and commander of the guard—had made the indignity tolerable.

The newly-made colonel was long inured to the grandeur of Saint Peter's Basilica, and he despised the necropolis. Tall, all but emaciated, with sunken cheeks, lined forehead, dark eyes set too close together and divided by a classic if thin Roman nose, he looked like the perpetual bearer of bad news. He rather liked that effect. The labored breathing behind him interrupted his thoughts.

The hapless Minuette—such a delicate name for a hulking buffoon—tromped warily behind the colonel through a maze of dimly lit passageways. The laborer would never be able to find the vault on his own, especially after they got to the section where the electricity had been turned off. He would be paid handsomely and threatened with excommunication if he ever breathed a word to anyone about the task he was about to undertake. Shortly after passing Mausoleum C, the colonel spotted the alcove where deep shadows hid the walled vault. It looked as if workers from a previous millennium had begun a passage and then abandoned it about twelve feet into the rock, leaving piles of brick originally intended to line the passages hewn out of the rock.

It took just over an hour for Minuette to tear out the brick wall and reveal the well-disguised door behind it. Johann led his slum worker out of the catacombs, backtracking several times to make it more than certain he could never again find his way to the vault. He paid the man in cash, along with a generous tip, and promised additional work if he behaved, heaping dire threats upon him if he did not. "You will be watched," he told Minuette. The laborer vowed to keep his lips sealed and said he looked forward to any future work the colonel might offer.

After Solento led Minuette out of the necropolis the colonel retraced his steps and stood at the vault entrance, breathing heavily. He did not relish cleaning up the remains of the late cardinal and grimaced at the burlap sack at his feet. He wondered if the door would still work after almost a year. It was an ingenious design, one borrowed from medieval times, based on a clock mechanism. Steeling himself, he pulled the slightly offset brick, sixteen rows up from the tiled floor. The door opened part way and stopped. He pushed. It grated and screeched but finally swung half way open. He wedged it open with several bricks from the wall Minuette had dismantled. He had no intention of joining Cardinal Loconi in an eternal vigil of the heads.

Colonel Solento could feel his face and stomach tighten. The vault huffed, as if breathing out at long last, and the colonel chocked at the acrid smell. Death's smell lingers, hovering, protecting its mortal remains before finally dissipating into the ether like a departing soul. Had he heard the faint sound of dissipation upon entering? Had Loconi's soul been trapped somehow? That breath upon his cheek, that momentary oily feel on his skin. Heart hammering, he crossed himself.

The colonel shuddered as he looked upon the rows of heads sealed in thick cylindrical glass containers, afloat in the "brine of antiquity," as Cardinal Loconi had called it. The ancient Egyptian formula for embalming, lost to the world but preserved by the Vatican, among its many other arcane secrets from the ages, served as the preservative. Fifty-seven vampire heads, the first dating from the mid-nineteen twenties, sat in rows on wooden shelves. The early heads had darkened, but the features were still clear: fear, horror, anguish, anger, disbelief, confusion, and more. Each had been killed according to the ancient ritual: an aspen stake driven through the heart, followed immediately by decapitation, with body and head buried in separate, preferably distant, places.

The last canister—the fifty-eighth—was empty, a mocking tribute to a singular OVFS failure. The name on the brass plaque was Morgan Summers, December 2011. The plaque had been affixed when Loconi had been told that the Summers woman had been killed and her head shipped to the Vatican. The body had been secreted into an open grave in Cambridge's Mount Auburn Cemetery, awaiting a burial the following day. But the OVFS had abducted and killed the wrong woman, and the cardinal's deep remorse was all-consuming, causing him to lose his grip on the North American division of the organization. "Thank God Cardinal Manlocara is putting it back together," Johann muttered.

He blanched as he walked past the rows of heads. A grisly bit of business. Why did the OVFS want to keep the heads? he wondered. Probably only the true believers knew the answer. He wasn't going to question the practice, nor the collection of a swatch of hair from each vampire for mounting in a scrap book, along with a report on the capture and killing of each. At least it paid well. With his salary as Commander of the Pontifical Swiss Guard, and several times that from the OVFS, the colonel's finances had become a source of great pride, though he wasn't permitted to spend his OVFS income until he retired. Well, not much of it anyway. He looked forward to a handsome retirement. He should soon be formally designated "Number Two" if the North American operation was favorably resolved, and that would surely carry another increase in his income. Cardinal Manlocara had assumed the rank of "Number One."

He almost tripped over a pair of feet in the next aisle. "Madre di Dio." Soft, red slippers protruded from an ankle-length black robe trimmed in gold. Johann froze, starring, then crossed himself again. Loconi. Skeletal fingers seemed to rake at his stomach. Yellowed shards of skin hung from the hands, and shrunken eyes leered at him, shrouded by furred eyebrows. His jaw had dropped, exposing a shriveled, grayish tongue.

Had he starved? More likely died of thirst. What must it have been like when he first realized the door had been sealed from the outside? The burlap bag fell from Johann's trembling hand.

5 - Judeland

A mortal born, a fetus warm, how innocent he lay
By morning light the gods took flight from the evil of this day
What hope had she, could she ever be, the child of
sunlight gleaming?
'No, not ever,' shrieked the Valkyries of Charna, as they pawed
through entrails steaming
'Your fate be sealed,' the denizens revealed, as the
night winds lent their storming
With life and love foresworn, and hearts all shorn oh bitter tastes
the morning

Judeland looked around the table and groaned. Seventeenth century British press gangs did better, she thought. The dingy roadside tavern she'd picked was called *Pirates Rock* and boasted several advantages: it was cheap, served the working class—what few customers they had— and was relatively secure. The *Rock* had a back room, one that smelled of stale beer, cigarette smoke, cat pee, and Pinesol. Forty-watt bulbs in badly tarnished brass wall fixtures created a dim candlelit effect that hid the scarred and dirty linoleum floor and cobwebbed corners.

Lynn, Massachusetts, the so-called "city of sin," was ten miles north of Boston. Judeland could just make out Nahant Bay through windows that probably hadn't been cleaned since VJ Day. Not a very auspicious venue for founding an organization dedicated to taking down Dr. Heller, his staff—especially Morgan and Lamar—and the GenLab. Harvard itself! But my day will come, Judeland thought, touching her damaged ear. Morgan will pay for that. While vampires couldn't be killed by a gunshot, the one fired by Morgan in Saint Paul Church had nipped off her left earlobe. The three rounds that hit her chest had done little more than mark her with black welts, which hadn't entirely disappeared.

Judeland Bundaeker had eluded the FBI, the Cambridge Police,

Harvard's Campus Security, and Morgan and Lamar. She had abducted Jamie Heller's son, JJ, from his basement prison where his father had sequestered him since learning of his latent vampirism. Every third-generation offspring from a blood line polluted with vampire DNA would eventually be triggered, causing the individual's vampire genes to become active. She had introduced JJ to active vampirism, killing his friend and guardian, then inducing JJ to feast on his friend's blood. She also initiated the young vampire into the delights of the flesh, their copulation played out on Jamie Heller's bed, bloodying the sheets.

While JJ managed to escape from Judeland, the final outcome was still highly satisfactory. Judeland had become pregnant by JJ, and he had later committed suicide. When she informed Dr. Heller that she was his illegitimate daughter—and a third-generation vampire—pregnant by his son, Heller struggled to hold onto his sanity—with a lot of help from Morgan. Before JJ escaped, Judeland explained in a letter to her father that she would raise his grandchild as a vampire. In a week Heller began to see a psychiatrist. Soon, oh very soon, Judeland proclaimed, he would be seeing a mortician.

Judeland planned to send Morgan and Lamar a dozen black roses on their first anniversary, as she had on their wedding day, with a note: "The Serpent of Charna will welcome you with open arms."

"Are we just going to hang out here all day?" asked the man sitting to Judeland's right. Number Three, formerly employed by the late Cardinal Alfonso Loconi, was a badly-used hulk who chain-smoked foul-smelling Turkish cigarettes. In just over a year and a half he'd worked as a hit man for the Mafia, been recruited by the OVFS as part of a group to take down Morgan and her husband, as well as Harvard's GenLab. When that operation blew up he'd been recruited by Judeland, still using his Cold War "name," Number Three, from his days with the East German Stasi, the Ministry of State Security for the German Democratic Republic. He was usually called "NT."

Next to him sat Monty, an auto mechanic, and his buddy, Jake, a bomb maker, both also formerly employed by the OVFS. Judeland wondered if they were closet gays, not that it mattered. The only other woman, Helen Lott, would be their odd-job-Charlie: forger, driver, spy. Judeland wondered if the woman had ever combed her hair. With the name and the looks she could very well turn into a pillar of salt at some awkward moment. Judeland needed to add one or two new members and get rid of the lightweights. There was always Crazy Charlotte, Father Hemming's former church secretary, who had just been released from the Boston Psychiatric Center in Cambridge.

She thought of the long, hot shower she'd taken the previous night.

Judeland inhaled the scented soap as hot water steamed up the shower stall. How close I came to feasting on Flossie, Harvard's esteemed HR Director, she thought. Screwing and then dismembering Lawrence, the late GenLab technician, was a first—the start of my new life. I shouldn't have killed him though; he'd done a good job sabotaging the first two vampire resurrections, but I needed his blood . . . and the sex. Quite a memorable first night as an active vampire. The sex wasn't all that much, but it was a start. I'd have had sex with Flossie, too—before I killed her—but that damn campus police officer had to show up. At least I sliced Flossie's arm with a butcher knife. Her blood was even better than Larry's. Judeland smiled, but the smile didn't last long as she touched the place where her left earlobe had been and looked down at the three purple welts between her breasts. You can't kill a vampire by shooting it, but in the church Morgan didn't know about me yet. Didn't realize she was dealing with an active vampire.

Ah, Saint Paul Catholic Church. Pinnacle of Cambridge Catholicism. I did a great job turning the church into the second coming of Sodom and Gomorrah until the bitch and her wimp, Lamar, arrived. Did a number on the good Father Hemming, too. He'll walk with a limp the rest of his miserable life. And poor little Miss Charlotte, his secretary, duct taped naked to the life-size wooden cross, with a Jesus wound in her side, leaking blood. Ghastly taste, though, like the blood from all virgins. Who would have thought a thirty-something woman would be a virgin? And Father Hemming, naked, about to have sex with Miss Charlotte—with no little prodding from me and my nine millimeter. If Morgan and Lamar hadn't intervened, that would have been a grand scene, but I'll defeat both of them in my own good time.

First, though, I'll inflict a slow and very painful ending to Daddy Dearest, my bastard *father*, who begot me from that campus whore— my *mother*. Too bad she killed herself; I could have done a much better job on her than a sleeping pill overdose. Yes, Dr. Heller, you will pay with your valuables: your honor, your prestige, your position, and finally with your life.

Too bad about JJ killing himself; he could have helped me found a vampire nation, but at least his suicide sucked most of the life out of his father. And one day I'll finish sucking the life out of you, Dr. Heller. She drew an H on the steamed shower stall glass, then circled it, and made a slash bar through the letter. Her smile was savage.

"Daddy Dearest, you have only made a down payment on your future agony."

The shower hissed in reply.

Everybody ordered another beer except Helen, who was nursing a glass of gin on the rocks. Judeland realized she had better get started before they ran up an even bigger bar tab. "You, my new recruits, are about to be initiated into the 'Order of Harvard's Ultimate Demise—the OHUD.' But to make it easy on us, I hereby nickname you the *Huds*." No one reacted, but all eyes were focused on her.

"First, I'll outline our operation."

"What about our pay?" NT asked.

"Oh, I think Dr. Heller will provide for us quite sufficiently. . . ." Judeland smirked as she sat back and sipped her beer. But she suddenly felt queasy again. This was the third morning in a row. I don't have time to be sick, she thought. The introductions were perfunctory. Helen leaned over and whispered something to Monty, who got a good look at her shapely, bra-less boobs, earning a black look from the leader of the newly-christened Huds.

"We are going to destroy Heller and his GenLab slowly, one step at a time. First, their morale will sag. Then their funding will do the same. Finally, we will provide more clients for Father Hemming's cemetery. Before Heller follows his son down under the sod, his brain will be shredded."

"How?" NT asked, lighting another cigarette with the stub of his last one.

"First, I will—" Judeland was interrupted by a long rumbling coughing spasm.

"Keep on using those things, and you won't last to see our first payday, old man," Jake said, rocking back in his chair.

NT glared at Jake but said nothing. He blew a cloud of smoke over the table. Jake's eyes became reptilian.

"Our first task is to announce ourselves, send a calling card. I will write it, and Helen will deliver it so there will be no postmark. Jake and Monty, I want you two to find us a safe house in Cambridge, one that would be the dead last place the blues would look for us. Monty, can you get me a set of wheels, preferably a van?"

Monty nodded. "You want me to steal one or buy one?"

"Steal one and give it a new VIN." Judeland looked around the table. "Jake, we are going to need some of your calling cards. I want a few smoke bombs. I trust you have some new sources? And we'll need some of the real boomers so start working your supply chain now."

"No sweat," Jake said. He got up and yanked open a window after NT lit yet another cigarette. The previous one lay smoldering in the ash tray, an exceptionally long ash drooping down.

"NT, I want you to sniff around and see if the OVFS is back in the game, or planning to get back in. Is there any chance you could worm your way back into their organization and serve as a double agent?"

NT grunted and waggled his hand as if to suggest the answer was "maybe."

"See what you can do, but be careful. We don't want the Vatican on our tail. Okay, we meet here in a week, same time. Helen, stay put. I'll have the calling card ready for you to deliver in a few minutes. Knock off the gin. We can't have you picked up for a DUI. And go get me some writing paper, an envelope, and a cheap ballpoint." Four chairs scraped, and in a few seconds they were gone. Helen returned and handed the items to Judeland, then drifted out to the bar for some ice.

Daddy Dearest,

I share in your grief. JJ was off to such a good start when he lapped up Hartvig's blood. Sorry for getting so much on the hall rug and on your bed sheets. JJ was such a great cocksman. You should be proud of him. Such stamina. He would have made a delicious sex slave. Ah well, there will be others. Maybe Father Hemming or his previous secretary Charlotte Rhodes (after they let her out of the loony bin). She was fun for a few hours, anyway. The blood of an older virgin tastes terrible though—unless you're really thirsty, as I was that night. Then you can almost ignore the taste. I'm hoping she won't still be a virgin when next I visit her. Could you help me with that, Daddy Dearest?
Oh, I almost forgot. I am carrying your dead son's baby. Yes! It's true. I might even send you a blood sample to prove it. If you promise to behave, of course. I am certain he or she will be a vampire. After all, this is a case where both mother and father were vampires. You might want to check with Dr. Gibson on that point. Together, my babe and I will create a new vampire clan. And in time perhaps a nation. And I think we shall name it "Heller's Angels" in honor of you, Daddy Dearest. Wouldn't that be a fitting tribute?
And one more thing. I will save a copy of this little love

*note. And if you do not fully comply with my wishes, I
shall be forced to send it to your boss, Dr. Martin. You
remember her—President of Harvard?*

*Upon receiving this note I want you to devote all the
energies of the GenLab to legitimate, legal research on
such diseases as Lupus, and AIDS. If I find out that
you are continuing to pursue the Vampire Resurrection
Project, your world will begin to crumble.*

*And never forget, Daddy Dearest, you are a carrier. You
begot JJ and you begot me! It would be best for you and
the world if you were to sever your genitals and inter
them with the vampires you killed and buried in Saint
Paul's Cemetery.*

Do have a nice day, and sweet dreams,

Your Bastard Daughter,
Judeland

6 - Resurrection 201

The time has come," the vampire said, "to speak of many things:
of senses spurned and lessons learned—and angels without wings
And why one's time has gone to rot, whilst the body shirks its
grave. You cannot lay in that happy plot long put aside and saved
for now you bear stigmata of the vampire's immortal calling And
neither consummate love nor the gods above can save you from a
life appalling.

Wind swirled around the bronze figure of John Harvard, as a wet snow found its way into mufflers, and onto eye lashes. While it didn't moan or howl, it attacked in intermittent gusts. Weather forecasters trumpeted their warnings, the lucky ones from within heated broadcast studios, the frozen chosen standing out in the grip of the Nor'easter, gamely trying to smile as they shivered, speaking stiffly through lips turning blue.

The WBZ Channel 4 crew huddled around the famous campus statue in the Old Yard just outside of University Hall, waiting for their seventy-five seconds of air time. None of the four TV crew members noticed the old man, bent at the waist as he clutched his black muffler tightly around his turned-up collar. His rimless glasses, old round-brimmed parson's hat, and close-cropped beard made him look like a nineteenth century Jesuit priest, a standout even among the many students who tried hard to be and look different. Instead, they became part of the campus herd. But not Suroccan. He looked disdainfully at the coed a few feet ahead of him, marching stoically in her miniskirt, legs bright red.

Why hadn't Morgan canceled her class in such bitter weather? So little sanity in the world these days, he thought.

CRANGE

"The scene you just watched is from a current TV drama about vampires," Morgan said. "It featured the old 'bite-you-on-the-neck' routine first made popular by Bram Stoker in his famous 1897 novel. But did you know that vampires were known to the people of Britain long before they were popularized by Mr. Stoker? Can any of you tell me who the Father of Vampirism is?" None of her four students raised a hand.

Evelyn Guard was staring out the window. Benjamin Dizzraeli was hunched over his iPad. The youngest, Alton Ribb, was, as usual, withdrawn, eyes hooded, pressed back in his seat as if he were standing on the brakes. Andre Suroccan reminded Morgan of a cobra rising out of a basket, eyes quick, tongue darting, darting, darting. They all looked at her, but no one spoke.

"Got to be Bram, right?" Morgan asked.

Alton nodded his assent.

"Wrong! The Father of Vampirism is the Serpent of Charna. Have you heard of him?"

Suroccan smiled faintly and nodded once.

"Andre, would you enlighten your younger brethren about this serpent fellow?" Morgan perched on the corner of her oak desk, a careworn throwback to the early 1930s.

Andre strained his throat and sat ramrod straight. Everybody was momentarily distracted by a wave of sleet that raked the windows. "You may want to consider adjourning early, given the Nor'easter," Andre said, his voice a low velvet.

"Let's discuss the weather after we hear what you have to say about the Father of Vampirism."

Andre paused until everyone was looking at him. "The tale has been passed to vampires down through the ages. As different branches of early man—hominine—branched out, including the Australopithecus, Homo erectus, Neanderthal, and others, they spread across Africa and Asia. All but the Homo sapiens ultimately died out. What archaeologists and or clerics have disdained to consider, or admit, is that amongst all branches of man, a select few were vampires. It remains a mystery as to the fate of the few vampires in the branches that ceased to exist. They may have slipped away and joined with strains that continued to evolve.

"In the ancient of times, early man was riven with fear. And they practiced all manner of occult rites to ward off evil spirits. At some point the coalescing of their fears and the practice of the rites gave the breath of life to an entity that came to be called The Serpent of Charna. No one knows why or how it came to be, or how the Father of Vampirism was named. He—or it?—was supposed to have selected one or two members of each early man hunting group to become active vampires while others remained latent, some never expressing their genetic vampire heritage. Today, vampires are divided in their beliefs: some don't believe in the serpent at all; others cling to him as Christians cling to Jesus.

"Now, Ms. Bradford, I suggest we slink back to our coffins before the weather makes bunk mates of us all." Andre projected less emotion than the bronze likeness of John Harvard.

Morgan shook her head and sighed as she walked to one of the two windows and stared out at the morning gloom. Again, sleet rattled against the frosted panes. She watched a handful of students scurrying across the Yard. "Class dismissed. Check the university weather code tomorrow morning. If it's red, stay home. Otherwise, I'll expect to see you in class at the usual time." They were gone in less than a minute.

CƷ৪০

Dr. Wallace Gibson, Director of Operations for the GenLab, frowned as he carefully hung up the phone. He walked out to the admin area and stood, patiently waiting for his secretary, Virginia, to finish the paragraph she was working on.

"Sorry, Doctor Gibson. I didn't see you standing there." He knew that wasn't true. She started to get up, but he waved her back to her seat.

"Just wanted you to know that Morgan Bradford is coming over. Show her right in, and bring us some coffee if there's any left."

"She's a game lady coming in this weather. It's Bristol cold in the Yard and sleeting, but I'll have fresh coffee for you in a jiff."

Wally, which is what most people called him, wandered back into his office and plopped down at his desk with a sardonic smile. Throughout his whole life, whenever it snowed, he found it hard to focus on his work, just as if he were in grade school again. Funny how he'd never gotten over that. He reached for a report from the newest lab tech, the one who had replaced the traitor, Lawrence Ashton. What a price he'd paid. Wally shivered, recalling how the young man had been murdered. Who would have thought the Bundaeker woman had become an active vampire? Ah, well. If she would only submit to the resurrection process. . . .

He stood as Virginia knocked and opened his door, admitting Morgan. "Coffee's on; won't take but two more minutes," she said, as

Morgan entered.

"Thanks for seeing me on such short notice, Dr. Wallace." Morgan pulled off her mittens and blew on her hands, then shrugged out of her lined Burberry trench coat, pulled off her New England Patriots knit cap, and began unwinding her muffler.

"Morgan, you look frozen. And please call me Wally."

Virginia backed in carrying a scarred wooden tray with two university logo mugs filled with coffee, along with packets of creamer and Truvia, and quietly closed the door after her. The strong coffee aroma contrasted with the office's faint musty smell.

"Well, young lady, what brings you over to the Science Building on a day like this?"

Morgan bit her lower lip and glanced around the room. The silence lengthened as she sipped her coffee.

"Wally, I need your good counsel and your help. But first, I need to swear you to secrecy. This can only be between the two of us." Her eyes bored into him, and he straightened, looking concerned.

"We're all pretty good about secrets in the GenLab, as you well know."

"Pretty good won't cut it. I'm talking sealed in a tomb secret. Just between the two of us, even if you decide not to help me."

Wally began to tap the pads of his fingertips together, an unconscious habit he'd developed during his undergrad years, and then he nodded his assent. "Okay, now that's out of the way, best you start at the beginning."

"I'm pregnant." Morgan sat back and watched him.

Wally's eyebrows went up. "Well. Congratulations. But I take it you're not elated?"

"First, Lamar doesn't know. At least I think he doesn't. Something is holding me back from telling him. It's fear. Here's the thing. I don't know whether I got pregnant before or after I went through resurrection. What if I got pregnant when I was still an active vampire? You told me that only the third-generation in a line of carriers of the vampire gene become active vampires. But what if *two* vampires mate and produce an offspring? In fact, I recall, back in the 19th century in Paris, discussing this with the Countess Amberglass, who is sort of the worldwide vampire secretary general. She said the offspring of two vampires who mate will always be born an active vampire, but the question on the flip side of the coin is just as important. What will the offspring be of two *former* vampires turned mortal? Nobody has ever asked that one."

Wally's breath whooshed out. "To answer your question, Morgan, we would have to do a genetic workup on the fetus. That's been done before, but there could be some risks associated. The risk of infection, for one. The risk of someone else finding out about my working on an undeclared project for another."

"Hmmm." Morgan sat on her hands, which were still cold. "Could I go through a second resurrection that would work on my child?"

"Oh, my dear, that would introduce all kinds of wild cards into the deck. I wouldn't hear of it. We have no knowledge about—we've never even inquired—you are asking to go to Mars when we've just invented the jet engine. Morgan, I've never said this, but I think of you like the daughter I could never have. And since Meg died, I've buried myself in this lab, this project . . . and its people. Especially you."

Tears formed in Morgan's eyes, and she tried to blink them back, but a few escaped, and she wiped her face on a sleeve. Wally handed over his handkerchief and looked away. Morgan's voice faltered. "Two nights ago I found blood on the sheets under my pelvis. I was able to cover it and change the sheets as soon as Lamar left the room. And the blood came out in the washing."

"My dear Morgan that could be a sign of something serious. You could be in danger of losing the baby. Have you considered going to an OBGYN?"

"Absolutely not! The first thing an OB would do is all kinds of blood work. Next thing, he or she would do is consult with doctors across the country. I might as well make a video of my lab results and put it on YouTube. I'm asking *you* to do the analysis, Wally."

Wally blew on his coffee, swallowed, and carefully placed it on his desk. He tapped his fingertips together, deep in thought. When he began to speak his voice was so low as to be almost inaudible. "As a scientist I cannot in good conscience do what you're asking. As the man who would be your father, I can't say no."

She reached him in three hurried steps, buried her face on his shoulder, and sobbed. They held and swayed. He asked her to fast for twenty-four hours before he withdrew blood samples from her and the fetus in three days. In the meantime, she was to eat hearty meals, plenty of protein, and red wine would not be amiss. It would take him a week to run all the tests and do his calculations. She was to call him day or night if there were any more bloody sheet episodes or even spotting. They were still hugging and swaying when the door opened just enough for Virginia to look into the office.

"Oh, I'm so sorry. I was going to ask if you, uh, sorry." She withdrew, closing the door quietly.

"Oh, crap," Wally said.

Morgan laughed, dabbing at her tears with his pale blue monogrammed handkerchief.

"Thanks for the coffee, *Dad*," Morgan said as she pulled on her knit cap, donned her coat, and wound her muffler so that it covered all but her eyes, as she blinked back more tears.

"Here, my dear. Don't forget your mittens."

Andre Suroccan waited for her just outside the entrance to the Science Building, the one that housed so many vampire secrets.

7 - Hemlock for Heller—Mandragora for Morgan

O womb awake to lust's keen pressing,
Open thy face to the midnight's blessing
Alchemical joining follows afternoon delights
Beginning a new life according to vampire rites
Though languid will our spawn awake
To find her eternal vampire mate
And open wide like Mommy Dear
To feast on all of mankind's fear.

Jamie Heller leaped up from his chair and backed away from the desk. Wind moaned outside his University Hall window overlooking the old Yard, but that's not what sent a chill through him. His face flushed, and the veins in his neck and forehead pulsed as he gaped at the letter. Soundlessly, his mouth formed the word, no. Icy claws of fear raked through his belly. After months of silence he'd allowed himself a glimmer of hope that Judeland Bundaeker had fallen off some very high cliff and washed out to sea. The undated letter was printed as if by a young grade school child. But it was Judeland. Definitely Judeland. He stared at it as if it were a coiled rattlesnake ready to strike, its dreadful symphony filling his pores.

God's death. She knows where the first two hapless vampires were buried. She knows about the Vampire Resurrection Project's successes and its failures, thanks to that sonofabitch, Lawrence Ashton, may he rot in hell. Dr. Martin warned that if the Vampire Resurrection Project ever leaked, she would shut it down overnight, and deny ever knowing anything about it. The President of Harvard could do that. And she would. What else could she do? He kicked the waste basket half way across his office.

Judeland has to be lying about carrying JJ's child. Doesn't she? Jamie knew he had sinned, God knows, but must he be destroyed for bringing Judeland into this world? She has the bow in her hands. All she'd have to do is loose one shaft, and his life's work would lie in ruins, his name trampled, shunned ever after by genetic science. He felt as if he'd drunk Hemlock. Well, he might become a blood brother with Socrates, but he wouldn't die quite so stoically. By God, no he wouldn't!

Jamie's fear and anger fused into an acid gel, one that would fuel him as he found a way to strike back. He saw himself carving an aspen stake, saw himself driving it through her heart, pictured himself severing her head and holding it up to the sun, her corrupt blood draining down his arm, the stench a balm to his soul, a down payment on his son's redemption. He wouldn't wash off her blood; no, he would wear it with pride.

He would form a team, go after her, not sit back and wait. He would start by calling his old friend, Hal Stone, Chief of Campus Security. And maybe Detective Cordell Payton? He would ask Morgan and Lamar. What better to have than former vampires on the team? At least he would go down swinging.

CBEO

As Morgan was trudging through the snow, Suroccan stepped out from behind a tree.

"What do you want?" Morgan's voice was muffled as her mouth was completely covered.

"I want to help you, my dear." Suroccan held out his gloved hands, palms up. His breath made a fog that seemed to settle all around her as if searching for an opening, a chink in her armor.

"I want you to stop following me." She began walking briskly, looking straight ahead. Suroccan fell in step with her.

"You must hear me out, madam. Our destinies are entwined." His breath seemed to trail after him without dissipating.

"I share no *destiny* with you. I am your instructor, that's all."

"Ah, but if you will hear me out you will learn how the arcs of our lives have crossed, intersecting just at the perfect time. This is the moment when I can be of invaluable assistance to you. I am aware of the acute dilemma you face. But more than that, I am aware of dangers you have yet to recognize. I can be your strength. Your guardian. Your salvation."

"Go peddle that rot to your maidens in waiting, Andre. I'm not buying into your vampire psychobabble. And if you are serious about resurrection you need to do a one-eighty and try to think, act, and feel like a human, like a normal mortal."

"Oh, my dear, is that what you heard—psychobabble? I come not with threats. Not at all. I come with opportunities."

"*Really.* Well, at the first opportunity I'd like you to get lost."

"Surely you don't want me to have this discussion with Lamar. Poor Lamar. He still doesn't know. But Dr. Wally does, and you do . . . and I do." Andre stopped in mid stride. Morgan stopped after two more steps and turned back to face him. Fine white crystals began bouncing off the ground, making a sound like tiny snow crickets.

Morgan's heart began hammering. She *could not* cave in to him. "Vampire Suroccan, you are this far," she held up a thumb and index finger, "from being expelled from the project. You have done nothing yet to convince me that you seriously intend to experience resurrection, to become mortal. Why are you here? No bullshit, answer the question."

Morgan glanced around. A few fraternity boys were having a snowball fight, a campus policeman was making the rounds. An emaciated stray dog, its tail tucked under, was hanging around the front door to the Science Center. Three girls in the distance were laughing as they walked. But no vampires lurked behind the trees. One, however, stood so close she could smell the Absinthe. He was angry now.

"There are forces at work that would destroy you. Do you think the OVFS will never come back? Is that what you think? And the vampire Bundaeker, her heart ablaze with hatred for Heller and all his people, including you? She might be watching us at this very moment."

"We defeated them before," Morgan said, "and we're not blind to the threats."

"You would be a lot less blind if I were on your team. The opposition must be eliminated, ruthlessly. This is not a game your local law enforcement people can play. And you, my dear, are in a somewhat delicate condition—too delicate to play hardball."

"I'm not your dear—"

"Enough! I will no longer stand here in this arctic bone yard and play your silly self-serving word games. You are pregnant. You haven't told Lamar. You don't yet know whether the child you carry will be born a vampire, or whether an infant can be resurrected. You don't know if Lamar will still love you when he finds out you are with child and have been deceiving him. He might even doubt the babe's true paternity. Might you possibly carry some man's sperm since, say, the 18th century, which has only now reawakened, possibly as a result of your passage through resurrection? No, dear lady, you don't even know all the questions that swirl around you like this sleet. And now, Morgan, you must come to me for help. You have rebuffed me. Very well. But the sand in your hourglass is falling faster and faster. For the sake of your unborn child you had better reach out for my help. Or you may need to reserve another space in Father Hemming's cemetery. More than one, in fact."

Andre pivoted and walked swiftly away. He seemed to dissolve among the trees and the darkness settling over the Old Yard. Morgan bent over as if she had been punched in the gut. She began to hyperventilate and staggered over to an iron bench nearby.

There, she felt it again. That thing inside her had kicked.

8 - Jennifer Marsh

I fear not your garlic nor your aspen stake
I fear not your crucifix thrust at my brow
I fear not the dawning as a new day awakes
I fear not the pitchforks of the madding crowd
I fear not evil in its many shapes
I fear not murder, arson and rape
But the one thing I do fear, forever my curse
To live this life everlasting, for naught could be worse

Lamar sat brooding in the Coleson Manor library. Everything had gone wrong: The tall case clock was running erratically, even after the guy from Swiss Watchmaker had been out to fix it. Twice. This morning he'd argued with Robert and with Morgan. Heller had yelled at him over some trivial matter. The Jag was in the shop. Again. The weather had been sloppy all week. He felt old (even if it was just psychological). Well, he was aging now. What could he expect? Morgan lamented daily about Calvin's aging. He pounded a fist on his desk. And what about the pale blue monogrammed handkerchief he'd spotted in Morgan's pocket book. All his were white. His mouth tightened and his eyes narrowed. "Give me a bloody break," he said. The library swallowed his voice.

Lamar found his pipe, filled it with Billy Budd, his special blend from Leavitt & Peirce Tobacco, and lit it. Funny how *after* they got married Morgan decided he should no longer smoke his pipe. Well, the hell with that. He smiled, if grimly, at the cloud of smoke that drifted over his head. Maybe he should take up cigars. That would give her something else to moan about.

Not to mention the sex thing. Or what used to be the sex thing. They had been like wild animals in bed. Now? She'd flipped a switch. For weeks it had been: "Not tonight, dear, I'm just not in the mood."

She'd been in the mood twenty-four/seven before resurrection and even after it for a while. He couldn't remember the last time. Well, maybe he could, but it was a long time ago. She used to parade around in the buff but not anymore. He reached into the bottom left hand drawer and pulled out a half-full bottle of Chivas Regal and an 18th century tavern glass and poured two fingers of the tarnished brass liquid. It was way too early, but he was bloody tired of having everybody ordering him around. Heller, Morgan, Robert, Wally, even Heller's admin assistant, Lenore. Might as well add Calvin to that list, too. Morgan's damn cat was acting just like she was. He wished Cambridge had a bar like *Cheers*, "where everybody knows your name."

And then he smiled, puffed his pipe back to full vigor, poured another two fingers, and knocked it back. He pulled out his iPhone and looked up the number for the Sylphon Nymph, transferring it to his speed dial list. Then he dialed his old office number from memory.

"Good morning. You've reached the Tech Editing Staff. How may I direct your call?"

"Good morning. Is Jennifer in? Tell her it's Lamar Bradford calling."

"Just a moment, sir." The elevator music began.

"Lamar? Hi. I must say I'm surprised. Haven't heard from you in an age. What's up?" Her voice was light and saucy.

"Hi, Jennifer. First, let me apologize big time. It has been way too long. I don't even want to talk about the last time. I've sworn off Beefeaters for life. I was wondering if your frantic schedule might have a gap in it just long enough for me to buy you lunch. I need your wise counsel." There was a long pause.

"When?"

"Either yesterday or today, take your pick."

Jennifer laughed. "Boy, life in the Science Department is doing you a world of good. You're developing a much-needed sense of humor. Okay, how about one o'clock?"

"Unfortunately, my Jag is in the fixit shop. Any chance you could drive? I'll grab a cab and meet you at your parking space at one. That be okay?"

Another pause. "Sure. Is this going to be one of those lunches where you discover you've left your wallet at home?"

"Lord no. That's the dead last—"

"Lamar, I'm kidding. I'll drive, but you'll owe me one more ride in the Jag. You know how I adore that car. It's kind of magical. Almost like the car in Harry Potter."

He wondered who Harry Potter was. "Uh, right. Fine. So I'll see you in about three hours. And thanks for squeezing me in."

"Lamar, you have a special way with words. You're welcome. Bye."

Lamar created a cumulus of Billy Budd around the desk, unaware of having done so. It took him only a minute to book a table for two at the Sylphon Nymph, a twenty-something wine bar that served a surprisingly good lunch. He booked the same table they'd had last time. Then he leaned back in his chair and thought about that night: December 1st, 2011. He was a nerd back then, one who had never had a real date. He didn't count the few fixups during his Harvard undergrad years, or the times he frequented "professional ladies of the evening," as he called them. He couldn't stand the words "prostitute" or "hooker," and "whore" was even worse.

When Lamar was promoted to senior tech editor for the Department of Arts and Sciences, Jennifer Marsh was assigned as his admin assistant, later replacing him as senior editor when he joined the staff of the GenLab. She was tall, slender but well-made, brunette, brown eyes, long bangs, good dresser, and she made him extremely uncomfortable. She was four years older than he was but looked that much younger. She always stood too close, sometimes brushing him with her breasts and would straighten his tie, and bring him coffee. Did a great job decorating his office. On occasion she would rub his neck and shoulders, which were always tight, especially around her.

Lamar smiled, changing from grouch to sly secret-keeper on the instant. December 1st had turned into a cold, windy night, with slanting rain threatening to turn into snow. The snarled traffic and honking horns didn't upset Jennifer; she just snuggled down in the Jag, listening to *Prelude to the Afternoon of a Faun,* unlike Lamar, who tightened up like the E string on a violin.

The Sylphon Nymph was packed. They were featuring a Beaujolais Nouveau that turned out to be quite quaffable. It seemed to Lamar that everybody was talking but him, and they were all ten to fifteen years younger. Finally Jennifer suggested they take the rest of the wine back to her apartment, she would fix snacks, and they would relax and listen to some of her favorite music. By the time they got to her front door, both were soaked. She had to practically pry off his suit coat, tie, shoes, and socks. Then she disappeared for a couple minutes and came back in a purple bathrobe. Lamar felt like that violin string again. While she was gone he had scanned her bookshelves and almost strangled when he saw the two Anne Rice novels: *Interview with the Vampire* and *The Vampire Lestat.*

While she was fixing the hors d' oeuvres she cut her finger, and it bled profusely, which triggered an active vampire response in Lamar. He went after her kitten, Cricket, but Jennifer managed to lock her cat in the laundry room. After a scotch on the rocks she suggested he go take a long hot shower to fully recover from whatever had rattled him so badly, while she ran his clothes through the laundry, pressed his pants, and brushed his shoes.

"Oh My God," Lamar murmured when she stepped into the shower.

"Don't worry, Lamar. I'm not going to bite."

Lamar found Jennifer to be a patient teacher.

CBEO

Lamar was surprised to see her sitting in a brand-new Mustang, the engine idling. "Well, Miss Jennifer, when did you get this?"

"Last November, just before Thanksgiving. Like it? Not a Jaguar, of course."

"Neat. And warm. You didn't have to come down early and warm up the car." Lamar smiled at her.

"You can owe me. So where to?"

"The Sylphon Nymph, ever heard of it?" His eyes looked mischievous.

Jennifer chuckled. "Yeah, kind of. Too bad it isn't dark and raining."

"Next time it's dark and raining I'll call you," Lamar said.

Her eyes widened as did her smile. She backed out and pointed them toward the Nymph. "I'm not sure what they're feeding you over at the Science Center, Lamar, but I like the effect."

Traffic was the usual scrum, but they still arrived five minutes early. "You're a good driver, Jennifer."

"I'm good at a lot of things . . . even editing."

Lamar laughed as they went in. "Not surprised. You pick things up quickly."

"Lamar Bradford. Are you saying I am a quick pickup?"

He laughed again. It felt so good to laugh. There had been few reasons to laugh since JJ had committed suicide. He could feel the tension draining away, and it felt terrific.

"The usual?" she asked, when they were seated.

"What's that?"

"Don't you remember? Beaujolais Nouveau." Jennifer gave him a pouty look.

"What I really remember is the scotch. I think I'll have one of those. How about you?"

"Hmmm. I still have half of that emergency bottle at home. We could save some money if we had a libation or two from that bottle, like we did right after I cut myself. I'm ravenous, though. You at least owe me a salad after dragging me over here. Or . . . we could come back for dinner?" She raised her eyebrows.

The drive to her condo seemed to take forever, especially with Jennifer squeezing his knee and running one hand along the inside of his thigh. She parked in the space behind the condo, and they hurried in. Lamar was surprised when she drifted into the kitchen after a brief kiss and began making a salad. She found a half-full bottle of Pinot Noir, and in a few minutes they were having a particularly sexual salad. It reminded Lamar of the movie, *Tom Jones,* and he wondered if he, too, had been "born to be hung."

"You don't mind if I kick off these shoes? They're fairly new and not broken in yet," Jennifer asked." In fact, if you'll give me just a sec, I'll get my slippers." She didn't wait for an answer and disappeared up the stairs. Lamar fidgeted and pushed his salad around his plate between swallows of wine. As she walked back to the table in the dinette, he noticed she wasn't wearing slippers or stockings. And she had unbuttoned the top two buttons on her white blouse. She leaned over to inspect his plate, giving him an inspection opportunity of his own. Shoes and stockings were not the only clothing deposited upstairs.

"I like to get comfortable after work, don't you?"

"Sure." He noticed she had redone her lipstick and added a few touches of perfume. It wouldn't take a rocket scientist to figure out where she had applied the last few touches. He smiled again.

"What? "Jennifer raised her eyebrows.

"Can't a guy just smile?"

"I always try to make a guy smile, and it looks like I'm succeeding. You'd smile even more without that tie on. Here, let me do it." She sat in his lap and began pulling the knot out. He could detect the perfume better now, and he also noticed two protrusions in the front of her blouse. His mouth went dry, but not for long. She leaned in and kissed him. It was a gentle, lingering, almost-but-not-quite chaste kiss, ending with her tongue moistening his lips. He began to unbutton the last three buttons on her blouse, pushing both halves aside. He rested his palms gently on her nipples, barely grazing the contours of her breasts, eliciting a long, low moan.

"I'll give you all afternoon to cut that out."

"What a delightful idea." Lamar leaned into her neck and began tonguing it as Jennifer pulled off her blouse.

She focused on his shirt buttons and soon had his shirt and undershirt on the floor on top of his tie and her blouse. "Ah. I think we are making some progress, my dear sir, but don't you want to enjoy your salad? I fixed it just for you."

Lamar pulled her closer and began to circle one nipple with his tongue. She moaned again, arched her back, and closed her eyes.

"My goodness, Lamar, where did you go to school?"

"Didn't I read somewhere that men were allowed a few secrets, too?"

She reached down and unhooked his belt, the two hooks under it, and worked the zipper part way down. "Why, Lamar Bradford, I do believe you are still overdressed."

"Then maybe you should do something about that."

Jennifer languidly got up. As she did so, her skirt fell to the floor. Lamar was momentarily surprised. She had shaved, unlike their first time in the shower.

"So. What do you think of the new me?"

"Wow. I'm finding it hard to think at all. You look— uh—really sexy."

She pulled him up, and his trousers slid to the floor. She knelt, pulling off his boxers, and he presented her with the expected flagpole.

"Well," Jennifer said. Whatever you run up that flagpole I'll salute." She took his hand and headed to the staircase. When they got to her bed she pushed him onto it. "I've been wondering when you'd come back to my bed. There are a few positions we still have to try. Give me a sec, I'll be right back. She walked, hips swaying, into the master bathroom.

Lamar? Where are you? I need you.

Lamar sprang up, heart pounding, eyes riveted on the mirror over the dresser. He saw Morgan walking through a dense forest. Her fearful voice trailed off, but she was calling him.

"Jesus, Mary, and—"

"Lamar, what is it? What's the matter?"Jennifer frowned as she looked at Lamar. She looked at their reflections in the mirror and back at Lamar. Reaching up, she gently began to squeeze the back of his neck. "Are you okay?"

"Morgan?" He wanted to follow her, needed to follow her, but she was lost to him in a dense thicket.

"I have to find her," he said, running down the stairs to his pile of clothes. "Call me a cab, would you?"

"Oh shit. I'll drive you."

Jennifer searched for her bra.

9 - Morgan, Where Are You?

"If man were immortal he could be perfectly sure of seeing the day when everything in which he had trusted should betray his trust, and, in short, of coming eventually to hopeless misery. He would break down, at last, as every good fortune, as every dynasty, as every civilization does. In place of this we have death."

Charles Sanders Peirce Bartlett's Familiar Quotations

I n his haste to unlock the door Lamar dropped his keys. "Dammit." As he fumbled to retrieve them, Robert opened the door.

"Do come in, sir. I have made an exceptional clam and oyster soup with French bread, if you will excuse the boast. Found the recipe in an original 1896 version of Fanny Farmer, in our library. I can pair that with an Estate Pinot Grigio. Just what your aging bones need on a day like this." It had started out quite sunny, with small, puffy clouds drifting slowly over Cambridge. In the afternoon the sky had become overcast and sullen, with intermittent wind.

"Is Morgan here? I called her several times on cell, but they all went to her answering service."

"No. I believe she said her class would continue until about four thirty. It's only just half after three. Let me take your coat and muffler. You should be wearing a hat, Mr. Bradford, or you will take a chill. We have discussed that more than once."

Lamar rolled his eyes. "Robert, I am not the same nerd that used to hold onto your hand. And I'm not hungry now, so please save your culinary treat for later."

One eyebrow launched. "As you wish." Robert shoved Lamar's muffler in one sleeve of his coat and hung it up. Then he headed for the kitchen, walking rather stiffly.

Lamar shut the library door behind him and sank into his desk chair. His hands were shaking. *Am I still a mortal, or am I slipping back? I could see and hear her so clearly in the mirror. That had to be some kind of vampire magic. Should I mention it to Morgan? I for damn sure won't mention my near miss with Jennifer.* He felt a mix of relief and regret. *She was one sexy lady, but he didn't really want to cheat on Morgan. Or did he? Jennifer must think I have completely lost it. I need to talk to her and tell her . . . tell her what?*

Dammit, Morgan can take care of herself. I should have stayed.

"Soup is served, sir."

Lamar started; he hadn't heard Robert open the library door. He could hear the tall case clock in the hall; as usual, it sounded ponderous. Without Morgan, the house sagged back into its previous state of fatigue, depression, and lurking secrets well kept. Lamar looked up from his soup, which was as good as promised.

Bloody hell, this is my house. I'm supposed to be the keeper of its secrets. But Robert acts like he's in charge. Always has. And now Morgan. Even the wretched cats. Why should I skulk around? I didn't actually do *anything with Jennifer. Well, maybe getting naked with another woman when you're married is* something, *but in today's world it can't count for much. Can it? Well, there is the thing about intent.*

Would Morgan believe me if I told her the truth? Would anybody? And what about that blue handkerchief? Had to be Wally's. Why did Morgan have it? I wonder how long he's been a widower? Got to be in his late fifties, but I've read that most men have a lot of fire left in the furnace at that age. Maybe she's been feeling guilty about having a bit of a roll in the hay with good ol' Wally. But why did she show up in the mirror earlier today, calling me? And how? How do I get out of this tangle? It felt like he was hacking his way through a dense forest but making no progress.

Morgan, where are you? I need you!

☾☯☽

Her students had left, and Morgan was securing her class notes in a combination safe when she became aware of someone behind her. She whirled. Suroccan had reentered the classroom and shut the door. Morgan heard the lock click. Icy fingers closed around her heart. With a deep breath she began her mantra, the one she had used for centuries to quell her fears. It almost always worked.

Earth, Air, Fire, and Water
Bring me the bounty from your larder
Bestow your peace, your power, your sight
And let me live in your worldly light.

It almost worked this time.

"What do you want?"

His red-flecked eyes impaled her. "Much. I am the ghost of your Christmas past, present, and future. I am here to show you the life that might be, or might never come to pass. And you *will* listen." He reached her, grabbed her arm, and dragged her to a chair, then pulled out a second one facing her.

Lamar? Where are you? I need you. Her thoughts were like laser beams cast out into the ether in search of an elusive target.

She frowned. During the class lunch break she'd called Lamar at the Science Center, University Hall, Coleson Manor, the Jaguar dealership, and the fitness center. She even called the duty officer at the Campus Police. Desperate, she finally called upon the Serpent of Charna.

"He will not hear you. But you will hear me, fair Morgan. I have come with an offer, a quite generous one I think you will agree, so hear me out. First, I can assist you with the child you carry. You have a choice. I can make the babe dematerialize. If that is your desire, it will take the same length of time as it has taken to grow from conception. And since it was conceived by two vampires it will, therefore, without question, become an active vampire at birth. You see, my dear, I am well ahead of Harvard's Genetics Laboratory.

"How do you know about what the Genetics Lab—?"

"My real name is Dr. Jene Claude Vompre, should you wish to research me. I had a close and continuing collaboration with Sir Archibald E. Garrod who died in 1936. He was a prominent physician at St. Bartholomew's Hospital in London, later to be known as the 'Father of Chemical Genetics.' Dr. Garrod formulated the theory of 'metabolic disruption.' But it was I who isolated the morbid blood spore that leads to vampirism. It was I, my dear Morgan, who developed the substance that can both lead to vampirism, and eliminate it. I call it 'JH'—the Jekyll and Hyde potion. I'm sure you are acquainted with the 1886 novel by Robert Louis Stevenson."

Morgan nodded once, slowly, her eyes glazed.

"Who do you think secretly gave the essential plot to Mr. Stevenson, hmmm? Ah, so. Well, if you want some of the potion, you shall have it. I might even arrange a little demonstration for you, should you harbor any continuing doubts about my veracity.

"And, my dear, sooner or later you would have discovered another fact, so I shall enlighten you now, at no additional charge. Your resurrection is not permanent. No, it will wear off. It's doing so now. The inert genes that replaced your vampire genes will at some time in the future—a time different for each individual—become corrupt, which is to say, vampirism will gradually reassert itself. Of course if you had the JH potion, you could quickly, easily, and painlessly prevent you from becoming an active vampire. And each time you needed an extension of your mortal state you would take another measure of the Jekyll potion.

"Oh, and did I mention that your dear husband has already had his first breakthrough? You may wish to call it by some other name. 'Retro' perhaps? That sounds so twenty-first century, don't you think?"

Morgan shuddered and took several deep breaths, staring at her hands, which were trembling. "And what do you ask in return?" Her voice was muted.

"After your child is either dematerialized or birthed, I will have carnal knowledge of you three times . . . before the cock crows, as the good book says." Andre Suroccan threw back his head and laughed; it was the sound of a chain rattling as a coffin was lowered into the ground.

"Ask for anything else, Suroccan. Or Vompre. I am trothed. I am pledged to one man for as long as we both shall live."

"How quaint. My dear, how long do you suppose that will be without my help? That Judeland woman is looming. So is the OVFS. You may surround yourselves with policemen, arm yourselves like an army, hide in a priest hole, but sooner or later they will strike. And then who would raise the babe? Robert? He's too old. Judeland? She would raise the babe as a vixen. The OVFS? They would drive an aspen stake through its little heart and decapitate its tiny little head. Without my help the babe will be born—I promise you that. And it will usurp your powers.

"No, you will consent. Three times of my choosing, and then you are free. You may either tell Lamar or keep it a deep secret between us. I am known somewhat widely on the Continent as an exceptional lover, by the way. Many women would gladly take your place on my couch. I will take you to the stars. You might even ask for more than three assignations. There is so much I can teach you about the fine art of sex."

Morgan slumped in despair.

"Ah. I see you are fatigued. I shall detain you no further, even though there is more to tell. I can protect you against your enemies. Why would I let them harm you with such a delicate prize in the offing? I will give you time to think. But in a fortnight I shall ask you for an answer, and there is only one right answer. You will come to see the truth of that, sooner rather than later."

The room grew still.

When she finally looked up he was gone.

10 - From the Grave to Chairman of the Board - March

"Rough wind, that moanest loud
Grief too sad for song;
Wild wind, when sullen cloud
Knells all the night long;
Sad storm whose tears are vain,
Base woods, whose branches strain,
Deep caves and dreary main,
Wail, for the world's wrong!"

Percy Shelley, *A History of Modern English Literature by Nelson and Thorndike*

Judeland's plan to tunnel into JJ's casket was as bizarre as it was unworkable. NT took the lead in convincing her that it was hopeless Although obviously upset, she was willing to listen.

Over two more rounds of draft beers and half a pack of Turkish Fatimas, they developed a new plan, one with a much higher probability of success. Monty would obtain the form required to disinter a body and have it moved. It would be filled out, dated, and Dr. Heller's signature forged. When the next burial was scheduled in the immediate vicinity of JJ's plot, the Huds would arrive wearing the exact same uniform as the grave diggers that were under contract to Saint Paul Church. Both teams would dig at the same time. JJ's coffin would be spirited into a hearse parked nearby, and the hole would be refilled and made to look as if the site had remained undisturbed.

Judeland would stage a meeting, with JJ as its chairman. The members of the Huds would wear satanic masks and black cloaks, all except JJ, who would be draped in a red cloak. His face, distorted by the bullet that traversed from temple to temple, looked horrific. They would place surveillance equipment in Dr. Heller's home so that Judeland could revel in his reaction to her second letter with the photos. It was a daring plan, she thought, but the results would be worth the risks. She would dismantle Jamie Heller's fine scientific mind piece by piece. It might be better to have him live out his life in the grip of insanity rather than kill him. She nodded to herself, rather relishing that new prospect.

‮ ‬CЖЮ

Pigeons and sightseers swirled in their timeless choreography as the Vatican tour guides struggled to keep order in a dozen languages. It was a metaphor for Cardinal Manlocara's struggles. He had too much work on his plate as the Vatican's treasurer while also handling the missing and unlamented Cardinal Loconi's portfolio as President of the Fabbrica. It was overwhelming, even though he was skilled at delegating. But it left him with too little time for directing the OVFS.

And it was past time to bring in some new vampire heads. Manlocara needed to put his stamp on the organization. And what better way than to bag that Morgan Summers—or Bradford, whatever she called herself. Vampire resurrection is a threat to the OVFS, and a well-conceived one he had to admit. Time to contact that Suroccan fellow and create a plan for adding her head to the others. We need a few more assets in Cambridge. Yet Suroccan might be the key to our success now.

Such a pity the original North American OVFS team scattered to the four winds. He wondered where Number Three had gone. And the bomb maker. And the auto mechanic. Now only two of the originals were still in contact: The Worthington woman—totally untried— and Jill Bonnet, who had proven to be useless. Loconi was an idiot, Manlocara thought. He threatened to kill them if they failed. Well, the failures weren't their fault. Maybe they could be found and brought back into the fold. Suroccan could probably help with that, too. He didn't quite trust the man, however. He had the stench of treachery about him, but sometimes that could be turned to advantage.

CЖЮ

A dense canopy of white summits drifted above Cambridge, creating a light show. The sun beamed down for a matter of seconds before it was covered over again. Blink, blink. Blink blink. Morgan stood at the lectern, uncomfortably aware of the rapid light alterations through the classroom windows. It reminded her of the day in the early 1770s when she first met Jacques, the young French priest. He was not handsome. His black hair was long, stringy, and greasy. His ears stood out too wide, poking through his long hair, and his face bore too many pox scars.

But he had a soft, throaty voice and gentle, expressive hands. Most remarkably, his teeth were flawless. And Morgan seduced him. Three times in one week. Once under the altar.

While he had taken the vow of chastity, she had not had sex for a year. No doubt the lords of the Universe had ordained it—if not blessed them—for it was the closest she had ever felt to mortality. It was as if her vampirism had lifted, if temporarily. Jacques had been married before he took the cloth, but his wife and their one child had died of the pox, and he had nearly succumbed as well.

The first time was urgent, pounding, explosive, but the other two were long, slow, and quite tender. The last time had been best. They had met in a hayfield. The sky was flocked with clouds causing the afternoon to alternate between shadow and sunlight, exactly like it was in Cambridge right now. She wondered what had happened to him. Confession. Penance. Forgiveness. And then, no doubt, he told other young girls not to have sex until they were married. She would never forget him. Could never forget him. He had been the best, until Lamar. Well, there was that fighter pilot in World War Two. That had only lasted a few weeks before he was killed.

She and Lamar had lost the magic, and she wasn't sure they would ever get it back. That was her fault. It was the thing inside her. It didn't want the intrusion and never lost the opportunity to express its displeasure at any sexual activity.

"Do you mind if I go get a beer?" Alton Ribb, the youngest student, took a deep breath and rolled his eyes to the ceiling. "You've just been standing there since class started." He glanced at Evelyn, who was paging through a *Glamour* magazine. The two older men were watching her the way a kid would watch an earthworm as he fried it with a focused beam of sunlight through a magnifying glass.

"I apologize," Morgan said. "I became distracted. It won't happen again. This afternoon's lesson is a grim one, but one we must present, nonetheless. The first two attempts at resurrection were failures. Horrible failures. But they didn't result from an error by the scientists in the GenLab. It was the result of sabotage. A former Harvard employee learned about the lab's secret mission and recruited a GenLab technician to put a toxic substance into the developing stem cells. I won't bore you with the technical details. Our first two vampires—who were married— began to deteriorate just days after their procedures. Dr. Gibson referred to their condition as 'radical unwinding.'

"In a moment I will show you a series of images that graphically portray the impact of their condition over time. They were literally disintegrating, day by day, but could not die. I performed the Vampire

Rites of Death in order to release them from the horrible abyss into which they'd fallen. As you've been told earlier, resurrection is not risk free. The loss of the first two was followed by three successes, however; Lamar and I are two of them. Before your resurrections, you will be given a will to sign giving us permission to perform the Vampire Rites on you in case of radical unwinding. Failure to sign will prevent you from completing the program. Do remember that our failures were the result of sabotage by two people. One is dead, the other driven away." Morgan paused to look at each student. They were listening intently.

"But the more important lesson for you to carry away is this: The success of Vampire Resurrection is entirely dependent on absolute secrecy maintained for as long as you live. The security lapse we suffered in the beginning cost two people their lives." Four if you count the traitorous lab tech and Dr. Heller's son, JJ, who took his own life, Morgan thought. Not to mention the injuries to Father Hemming and Saint Paul's former secretary, Charlotte Rhodes.

"We will call the first vampire, Bill. Here is a photo of him the day after his procedure. The photos follow every two days. Stop me if you have any questions." As the series progressed, all but Suroccan began to squirm and break eye contact.

"God's death," Dizzraeli muttered at photo number twenty-five. Evelyn sobbed. Alton grunted and looked away.

"I'll switch to Mary, Bill's wife." Morgan sped up the viewing as they had already seen the skin become a moist spider web, nearly transparent, draped over the bones. Eyeballs hung loose in their eye sockets. Their hair had grown like kudzu and hung over their foreheads, covering their eyebrows. Bluish-yellow fingernails had grown to half the length of their fingers. Blood pulsed through veins that almost burst through the spider-web skin with every beat of their hearts, and their lungs hissed with every breath.

Suroccan raised his hand.

"Yes, Andre?"

"Would you explain the procedures of the Vampire Death Rites?"

Morgan raised her eyebrows. "I am surprised you, of all people, would need to ask that question. Perhaps *you* would be willing to explain the process to your fellow students?"

Suroccan bowed his head, in part to hide the malicious smile that cracked his usually expressionless features. He began. "As they were practiced in the 19th century, the killing of a vampire required that an aspen stake be driven through the victim's heart, followed immediately by decapitation. The head and body had to be buried separately.

Sometimes either one or the other would be cremated. But part of the dearly departed would be kept as evidence that the vampire had not re-entered the remaining part and regrown the part that was missing. Of course there was a lot of bestiality amongst the peasants in previous centuries, especially as they grappled with the existence of vampirism." Andre sat back, his smile still fixed as if sculpted.

Morgan was angry. "You might have mentioned the prayers from the *Tibetan Book of the Dead*. And the appeal to the Serpent of Charna for safe passage through the Valley of Tears. The blessing of the aspen stakes. You made it sound like the Rites were about as spiritual as changing a flat tire." Her breathing was rapid, her face flushed.

"Ah. I have upset you, my dear. That was not my intention. I do humbly beg your pardon." Suroccan bowed his head once again, disengaging the smile and replacing it with a look of concern.

Morgan could detect the faint aroma of Absinthe as it drifted toward the lectern. "If any of you wish further detail on the Vampire Death Rites, please make an appointment with me after class is over. She looked up just as a cloud shielded the sunlight.

She could feel the chill of the GenLab's cold room, see the two vampires on their gurneys, feel the aspen stake in her left hand, the maul in her right. She could hear the two vampires clicking to one another, having lost the power of speech, saying their final good-byes, pledging to meet in the Valley of Tears. She placed the stake over his heart. The maul flashed down. Blood spattered over her surgical gown, mask, and gloves. She heard the maul driving the stake deeper. Heard his wife grunting her goodbye. And finally, she heard the sound of the laser saw as Morgan cut off his head.

Morgan touched the gold band once worn by the vampire Rena, now signifying her trothal to Lamar. It had been worn by Rena until moments before the aspen stake split her heart. Rena had raised her left hand and grunted urgently to Morgan just before the maul would make its fatal descent. And Morgan understood. Gently, she removed the ring and placed it on the ring finger of her right hand. She promised Rena to return it to her when Morgan made her own journey to whatever lay ahead as her final destination. And she promised Rena she would wear it as her own wedding ring.

A sob squeezed from her chest. Moments later she could sense light beyond her closed eyes. As she opened them sunlight streamed into the classroom—empty except for Andre Suroccan. It grew dark again.

He stood before her at the lectern as if cast in bronze. His voice sounded hollow. "I will have my answer one week from today, Mrs.

Bradford."

Morgan closed her eyes, and her head sagged. When she opened them again, the room was truly empty, except for the light . . . and the lingering hint of Absinthe.

11 - And the Truth Shall Set You Free

*In time of deceit, telling the truth is a
revolutionary act."*

George Orwell, *Bartlett's Familiar Quotations*

Are you coffee'd out?" Dr. Gibson asked Morgan.
"Always good for one more cup, thanks," Morgan answered.
"How's the book coming, Wally?"

"Slowly. I thought I was on the last chapter until I began reading up on the new—relatively new anyway—'synthetic biology.' Can you believe we are on the threshold in genetic engineering of creating entirely new living things, not to mention cloning any kind of cell and then giving it back to the person as a therapy? And that's tossed the whole lot of us into an ethics quagmire that Albert Einstein couldn't have rationalized. Consider the moral implications of creating an embryo from which we can harvest stem cells to grow into whatever it is we need. And destroying mutant embryos. Why even—"

"Whoa. Wally. You had me at a cup of coffee."

"Oh, I'm sorry, my dear. Hang on." He grabbed two Harvard mugs, filled them and asked her if she needed cream or sugar.

"Black is good," Morgan replied, smiling. He never remembered.

"Good girl." They sat in silence for a minute, drinking their coffees.

"Were you able to draw any conclusions from all the tests?" Morgan finally asked. She took a deep breath and held it.

"I'm afraid the news is not what we wanted. You are pregnant, no question. You have a daughter in the making. No question of that either. But it pains me deeply to have to tell you that your fetus carries the mutant gene for vampirism. The news doesn't get any better."

Morgan was stirring her coffee furiously with a wooden stirring stick Wally had handed her. She looked up. "Go ahead, Wally. I can handle it."

"I haven't shared this with anyone else working on the Vampire Resurrection Project, but I've become concerned about the possibility of genetic recidivism."

"Meaning?"

"Meaning that those who have successfully passed through resurrection might eventually slip back into latent or even active vampirism. If that phenomenon should be validated, I would have to believe, as a scientist, that you are at greater risk because you are carrying a latent vampire in utero. We simply don't know the answer to whether a fetus can pass its genetics back to the host—meaning you. It is an entirely unexplored field. Can someone safely go through resurrection more than once? Could we develop a vaccine that would prevent genetic recidivism? Possibly, but we are at ground zero. It could take us years. And we don't have that kind of time in your case." Wally's voice trailed off, and he looked broodingly into his coffee, as if the answers might be floating on the surface.

"Another thing that puzzles me, Morgan, is that you seem to be progressing in the pregnancy at an unprecedentedly slow rate. You have told me that it is difficult for vampires to get pregnant, and when they do, it takes well over a year of gestation to deliver a live birth. You told me that you only ovulate three times a year as best you can tell, and that your flow is no more than two or three teaspoons over the course of two or three days. If all that you have told me is accurate, then you sound to me like you are following the normal gestation progression of a vampire."

"Oh, God, Wally, what can I do?"

"If you are prepared to take some risks, there are some things we could try, but. . . ." Have you told Lamar yet?

"No." Morgan's face tightened, and she looked away, steeling herself for his rebuke.

Wally took both of her hands in his. "Sooner or later you will start to show. You can't hide this forever, even if you are following the vampire profile for birthing a child. This child was almost surely conceived when you were both active vampires. Lamar is a reasonable man. I'm sure he'll understand and support you."

Morgan bit her lip trying to staunch the tears that welled up in her eyes. Wally leaned over and dabbed at them with his handkerchief, which he left in her lap.

"Go to him, Morgan. Tell him about our conversation. Tell him he is to become a father. Come back in a week or ten days, and I'll have a couple of treatment options ready, though there's no way to test them."

Morgan hugged him, shrugged into her coat, and left. It was hard to see; everything was so blurry. And her lower lip wouldn't stop its damn quivering. She pushed through the main exit from the Science Building and was hit by a fierce, gusting wind that bit through her coat, hat, scarf, and gloves. She hunched forward and began walking across the Harvard Yard. Everybody was hunched over against the buffeting wind. Almost everybody.

From behind a large elm, a tall, gaunt man, his face obscured beneath a black muffler, stepped out. He held up a gloved hand, extending three fingers.

"No!" Morgan choked and began to run. The cold seared her lungs, and she was soon out of breath. She glanced back, but he was nowhere in sight. Three more days. Only three. She wondered where the GenLab had obtained the aspen stakes she used on Rena and her husband.

CRBO

Lamar had given Robert the weekend off. He hadn't a clue where Robert went on the rare times he left Coleson Manor but didn't much care. He wanted him gone for what he had to face. He'd ordered Chinese takeout to be delivered and selected a Cakebread Cellars Cabernet Sauvignon 2000, one of their favorites. Way too fine for Chinese takeout, but this was going to be a tough one. He had a sip to insure it was at cellar temperature. Lamar frowned, wondering if they could keep their discussion at cellar temperature as well.

Morgan was upstairs showering. She had been positively brittle when she got home from work. They had been driving separately the past two weeks, and that irritated him. Just one more lump of coal in his stocking. Well, tonight the lumps were going to be dumped out and dealt with.

Lamar had the dinner ready. All he had to do was activate the microwave, light the candles, pour the wine, start the music, his favorite album, *Burnished Brass,* 1958, by George Shearing, and ask her what the hell was going on.

She came down the stairs in a wooly bathrobe, one that looked like a factory reject out of Filenes Basement, circa 1988. Her hair was still wet and she wasn't wearing any makeup. And she was carrying Calvin and Oxnard, both grumpy; neither seemed to want to be carried down the long staircase, especially the aging Calvin. As she walked into the library she dropped her bundle of cats, and both scampered out of sight.

"May I pour you some Cakebread?"

"What's the big occasion? Why waste a great wine for no reason?"

Morgan turned so Lamar couldn't see her face.

The fire, newly lit, was snapping, and the candles flickered. They sat on the sofa, facing the fire. Lamar noticed the space between them. It had never been so wide. "I see you found my old college bathrobe. I thought Robert had thrown that one away."

"Maybe he should have." Morgan sipped her wine and retied the sash.

Lamar arched his back and heard it pop. "Wine okay?"

Morgan nodded and began picking cat hair off the front of the dark gray bathrobe.

"You okay dear heart? You've looked tired a lot lately."

"I'm okay." She took a deep breath, held it, and sighed. The silence lengthened, and she looked down.

Lamar began again. "We haven't been on the same page lately. You know? Hell, I'm not very good at this. No experience at all. This is the first time we've hit a rough patch since we did our resurrections. Something's happened to us, is happening, and I feel like I'm being stretched on the rack. Can we talk and try to find some answers?" He looked over at the fire, then reached for his wine. He extended his glass in her direction. "Here's to the good old days—and the good new ones to come."

She held up her glass, but not quite close enough to clink, and they both swallowed and put the glasses down on the coffee table. Lamar began. "The wine is as good as it's always been. I want our relationship to be like the wine. So what am I doing wrong?"

Morgan stared into the fire. She closed her eyes. This was going to be for all the chips. Her voice was dull, laconic. "I'm pregnant."

Lamar sat, stunned. He failed to notice the cats who crept over to the coffee table, eyeing the cheese. "That's, uh, that's a good thing, isn't it? I'm really surprised. You said it was devilishly hard for a vamp—" The ramifications began to pile up at the front door of his mind. Was their child normal, or . . . not? When was it conceived? Christ on a crutch, was it even *his*? He moved close to her. "Morgan, I love you. We signed up for forever, either as vampires or as mortals. It's okay to be scared; I spent all of my life being scared until I met you. When did you see Dr. Gibson?"

Morgan's head snapped around to face him. "How did you know?"

"Dear heart, who else would you go to see? And you are starting a collection of pale blue monogrammed handkerchiefs with his initials on them. It's okay you didn't ask me to go with you, as long as you tell me everything he said. Give me just a moment first, though." Lamar turned off the music and retrieved the bottle of Chivas Regal and two tavern glasses. "Drink this. You're shaking." It only took them a couple minutes to finish their glasses of scotch. Gradually she began to warm up and relax, her trembling subsiding.

Then she told him everything Wally had said, and that he was working on treatment options for her. Lamar didn't interrupt her. When she finished, he nodded at their wine, and they both took another sip.

"If it turns out that you do a U-turn and become a vampire again, I'll find a way to do the same. But maybe Wally can find a way to prevent that for both of us. And when our daughter is old enough, we can have her pass through resurrection. Morgan, never in all my life did I expect to become a father. I'll need a day or two to get used to the idea. We may be about to enter a foreign land, but we'll do it together." Morgan crumpled into his arms, and she cried hard and long. Lamar stroked her hair and said quieting things.

He only knows the easy half of the story, she thought. In three days I have to decide to keep the baby or not—for starters. Do I give myself to Suroccan *three* times of his choosing? He would hold an axe over my head forever. He could tell Lamar. Or he could tell our enemies, maybe even join forces with them to destroy all that Jamie Heller and Wally Gibson have achieved. If I surrender it will not be for three ugly copulations; it will be forever. He may give us the potion that will eliminate this "genetic recidivism," but then he will surely own me. I would have to become his whore and pray to all the gods in the universe that Lamar never finds out.

Or I could disappear. Morgan stood up, facing Lamar, and sloughed off the ancient bathrobe. She wore nothing underneath it. She would have Lamar for three days. That might have to last her—them—a lifetime. Or an eternity.

Calvin began to purr and was soon joined by Oxnard.

12 - The Undoing of Robert Diamond

The age-old snare, a woman fair, a breach of common sense
A moment stolen from life's should nots
Before the judges' recompense
Undress her now, before you think, whilst passion sears so hot
The still small voice now turned aside
Whilst reason abideth not
As all hope fades, as lust pervades, and wantonness collides
What joy that spasms volcano like
On the morrow shamefacedly hides

Robert's phone buzzed, disturbing his afternoon respite at Coleson Manor. He resented any intrusion in the afternoon. He carefully placed his pipe in Lamar's amber pipe holder, retrieved his iPhone, cleared his throat, and answered: "Coleson Manor, Robert here."

"Hi, Bob. How are you?"

"Who is—" A chill, like an electric shock, seized him. He would rather deal with a vampire than—

"I trust you are still on the line?"

"I am. What may I do for you, Ms. Worthington?"

"Get off it with the Ms. Worthington bit, Bob. It's a little late for that don't you think?"

"As I have stated clearly, our communications should be conducted through your supervisor except when you are on the premises attending to Coleson Manor." Robert thrust out his chin as if she could see him.

"Well, old sock, this *is* about business. And you should be pleased to know that I have been promoted to regional manager. I have a new contract for you to sign. The old one expires in a matter of days, and the new one has some significant differences I need to point out."

"That may as well be, Ms. Worthington. I shall consult my calendar and select a date to come to the MaidPro office and sign a new contract.

I'll arrange that with your secretary."

"No need for that, Bob. I'm sitting in my car just outside your door. It shouldn't take long, and I can't believe you wouldn't enjoy a little company to break up the tedium of your day."

"Tedium! I'll have you know that—" He heard the disconnect. "Hello?" A moment later the door chimes sounded. Robert leapt up, tossed his phone on the chair, and strode out of the library. At the front door he pulled back the two deadbolts and opened it no more than a foot.

Nancy barged in like a pulling guard leading a running back, shoulder lowered. The door put a pronounced scuff mark on one of Robert's highly polished Florsheims.

"See here, young lady—"

"Bob, were you born an old poop, or did you come to Cambridge to learn how to be one?" She had a folder tucked under her left arm, Robert noticed, as she marched to the library door. "Coming?" she asked, raising her eyebrows.

"Bloody hell," Robert muttered. There's no hope for it, he thought, following her into the library and over to the desk, where she had spread out the new contract.

"Oh, I just love the smell of your pipe. You'll have to give me the name of your tobacco and where you get it. Your birthday's not that far off, you know."

Robert delivered a black look, one beneath a scowl and well below a mere frown, adding a proper harrumph.

She grinned at him. "Prices have gone up twelve percent. The rest of it is just mumbo jumbo about HIPPA and privacy, and the new insurance company that covers our girls. You can read it for excitement comes the next big snow.

"By the way, you look nice. It's been way too long since we, uh, could relax a bit. Don't you think?" She walked over to the wingback and turned off his phone, then held it out to him.

Robert's jaw dropped. He grabbed the phone and jammed it into his suit pocket.

"I wish you hadn't let the fire go out, but maybe I can stoke it up and get it crackling again. I can think of something else I'd like to stoke up. Isn't it nice that Morgan and Lamar are going to the fitness center after work?" Nancy walked over to Robert, never breaking eye contact, and unbuttoned his suit coat. She draped it over the back of the chair, then she pulled his arm forward and unfastened a cuff link; repeating the process she placed them in a side pocket of his suit coat.

Robert hissed. It was about the only sound he could manage. His eyes were wide and his breathing shallow as he watched her unbutton her white cotton blouse with the company logo on it. In one fluid motion she handed the blouse to Robert, who stood, staring at it as if it were a poisonous reptile.

"Bob, would you unfasten me, please?" She turned around, presenting her bra's hook-and-eye fitting.

Robert strained his throat, his hands trembling as he unfastened her bra. It fell into her hands and she casually tossed it atop his suit coat. Slowly, she turned around.

"Bob, what are you waiting for?" She pulled her shoulders back and thrust her chest forward. Bob looked down; he couldn't help himself.

She might be forty, but she certainly hides her age well, he thought. His fingertips touched her tentatively, causing her nipples to harden.

"Hmmm. We're still overdressed. Here, let me help you." Nancy was quick, and soon the butler stood in nothing but his black socks, which caused her to giggle. "You got a camera around here?" she asked, stepping out of her slacks, revealing skin-tone bikini panties. Moving into him, she wrapped her arms around him and pulled him close. "Ah. I see we've woken the little bugger up. We'll have to find a place to put him, what do you think?" Her smile was a combination of feigned innocence and outright depravity.

Robert's thoughts were chaotic: What am I doing? I could lose my position. I'm giving up my personal power. She has a bitch of a figure if just a little underfed. Damn, *that* feels good. She should stop that. Now. I should stop this. We need to talk. She can't just waltz into Coleson Manor and start undressing me, it isn't proper. Oh, God. She could get pregnant. Uh, not exactly old sod; don't forget the vasectomy. What about STDs? What about AIDs? What about—

"Bob," she said, "you don't look glad to see me yet. Let's see what we can do about that." And in a moment the tiny bikini panties were gone, and the two all but fell onto the sofa. Both groaned as they joined. "Even better than our first time, Love?" Nancy's smile was genuine.

Coleson Manor's major domo kept his eyes closed but nodded yes. There weren't enough Hail Marys in the world to make up for how good this felt. Besides, he better save some for next time. Next time? Don't kid yourself, *Bob.* He would think about that tomorrow. He began to thrust with more vigor, unaware of the smile that robbed him of his last ounce of dignity and decorum. Unaware that Nancy was watching him and laughing silently. Unaware that the next time would be in just an hour and a half.

Robert watched her drive off with a signed copy of the MaidPro contract. She had acted as if she were subdued, and that he was still the old alpha male, notwithstanding his debauched dress and bearing, which were now vastly below standards. He sighed heavily, and walked into the library where he poured three fingers of Chivas and drank it neat. He would have to buy a new bottle since he and Lamar and Morgan had made some serious inroads into the twenty-five-year-old scotch. He fumbled his pipe back into action and sat, feet up on the footstool, and sighed again. He was drained, mentally, morally, and physically. What is happening to me? That damn woman just snipped the bindings on a packet of feelings and memories he thought he had successfully buried. Right.

Ah, sweet Elisabeth, my only heart's desire, where are you now? They had been lovers in 1973. She was from money, he was from the south side of the tracks as the Americans would say. They had been indiscreet. Hadn't planned to be, it just happened one night. Then his world blew up. She was with child. Her father took her to Switzerland to take care of the problem. That was after her father told him if he ever laid eyes on Mr. Robert Diamond again, one of them would die. And Elisabeth's father was a retired army colonel, well acquainted with firearms. There was little question of who would die in such an encounter. Thus endeth the Canterbury Tale of young Robert D. You couldn't use it in a novel. Too camp. Too cliché. But the event had made him gun-shy about relationships. Not only had it taken the wind out of his sails, it had dismantled the main mast as well.

He swallowed the last of his scotch and decided to have just a wee bit more. He felt good. Damn good, in fact. Sex and scotch go together like—

The door chimes sounded.

"Oh, shit," Robert said aloud. He glanced around after stowing the scotch and his pipe. Everything appeared to be in order. Thank Providence Nancy left an hour ago.

He missed seeing the flesh-toned bikini panties furtively tucked under the sofa, however.

13 - The Body Snatchers

Our birth is but a sleep and a forgetting.

Samuel Taylor Coleridge (1772-1834)
A History of English Literature, page 270

Morgan leaned her forehead against the classroom window. It was cold and made her head ache. She almost welcomed the pain as a distraction from a much larger one. As Suroccan left, he had held up two fingers, which may have looked to others like a victory sign, but Morgan knew what he really meant. Two more days before her fortnight was up, and she would have to decide. True, he could solve some of her problems, but at what cost? She didn't believe he would use her just three times—why would he keep that promise?

She felt a slight movement low in her belly, and her heart constricted. Could she ever love it, this thing inside her? It was destined to become a vampire. For hundreds of years she had longed for a normal life, one with a husband and a baby and a loving home. Maybe it would be better for them to adopt. Maybe not—too much investigation into their backgrounds. She couldn't convince Wally to help her "lose" the fetus: his religion had too strong a hold on him. And—could she do that without telling Lamar? Poor Lamar. He can't understand that the fetus doesn't want him—us—to have sex. By all the gods of the Universe, that thing is already ruling us, and she hasn't even been born. I have no one left to turn to. Morgan pursed her lips and rested her cold forehead on her wrist.

But you do have someone to turn to. The voice sounded so familiar and so real.

Morgan jerked. Was she absolutely losing it? "Who are you?" she murmured, unaware she had spoken aloud.

Blind Gretta, though I not be so blind as before.

"Gretta! Are you real? Are you a ghost?"

Are you real, Morgan? Are you a vampire? Gretta cackled, sounding like a ravaged hen.

Morgan stiffened. That cackle. How could she ever forget it? It was one of the few treasures from her earliest years. "All right, Gretta, what have you come to tell me?" Morgan closed her eyes to better concentrate.

Me? I haven't come to tell you a blessed thing, my sweeting. It be your mum, Marta Sorrel, who stands beside me. She haint got the knack yet for adjusting her voice to be heard by anyone still in body, so she come to me. She know'd I could contact those on your side when the time were right. They hung and pressed all those poor devils back in Old Salem and let the one real witch go free. Gretta's cackle was prolonged, ending in a hollow coughing spasm.

"Mum, are you really there? Can you tell me what to do?" Morgan asked, her voice choked. There was a prolonged silence. "Mum?"

Hush, sweeting. I'm listening to her.

"Cleaning lady," a voice called out behind Morgan. She whirled. "No, get out, get out!" Morgan screamed.

"Lo siento mucho. I am so sorry." The woman backed out of the room pulling her cart, and the door banged shut.

As she turned back to the window Morgan's breath rasped as if she had end-stage pneumonia. She began her calming mantra, then lapsed into stillness. Nothing. "Gretta? Please." The void was filled with etheric noise, the soundlessness of space.

Morgan beat against the glass with her fists, the moaning wind outside damping the sound of her anguish.

CRED

Father Hemming turned on his desk light, glancing out of the window. It was going to rain. Or maybe snow. His hip said so. It had become quite the weather vane since Judeland shot him. Nothing like a little gloom to make my stack of paperwork even more bleak. Best sift through and find the ones I'd rather toss in the trash, and do those first. No doubt the damn building committee will have something to say about why the Lady Chapel is behind schedule. He noticed one odd return address. It was from the State Attorney General. What can they want? he wondered, opening the envelope.

The statement of inquest along with a writ of exhumation for JJ's remains fell from his hands, and he jumped to his feet. "Jesus, Mary, and . . . has Jamie Heller lost his mind?" Why would Jamie want to disinter his son? And without a by-your-leave to me? After all I've done for him?

Father Hemming lunged for his phone and dialed. His first call was to his new clerical intern. He told him where to find JJ's grave, asked him to examine it, and to report back on the dead run. Fifteen minutes later the wide-eyed intern burst through Father Hemming's door without knocking.

"Holy mother of God, Father Hemming, the grave appears to have been dug up. Two of our people saw a crew from Rogers Funeral Home disinter the remains and drive off with them." Hemming gasped and lunged for the phone again. He knew Jamie's phone number as if it were his own.

"I'll see if Dr. Heller can speak to you, if you will please hold the line," Lenore said.

"Tell him it is absolutely urgent that I speak to him *right now*." Ed's voice was harsh.

"Afternoon, Ed," Jamie said. "What's the problem?"

"Why on earth would you do this? This isn't like you. Apparently our friendship doesn't count for very much anymore."

"Wait! Wait! What the hell are you talking about?"

"You know damn well what I'm. . . ." Cold sweat suddenly broke out on Ed's forehead as his anger vanished. What if Jamie didn't know? "Jamie," he choked, "we have a serious problem." Ed's heart was pounding, and his hip began to pound in rhythm with his heart.

"Talk to me, Ed. What's happened? Whatever it is, tell me."

"Did you sign a writ of exhumation for JJ's body?"

"Good God, no! Why do you ask that?" Jamie's voice cracked.

"They came and took him. I just found out about it. They had all the paperwork." Ed stopped. He heard Jamie's receiver bounce off something followed by an anguished cry. Ed hung up and quickly found the phone number for Rogers Funeral Home.

"This is Father Hemming at Saint Paul; may I speak to Mr. Webley. Tell him it's urgent."

In a moment Paul Webley answered. "Father Hemming. Thanks for your call. How can we be of serv—"

"Paul, did you exhume a body from our cemetery today?"

"Absolutely not! I would have been involved. Perhaps some other home? I could call around and let you know. Can you give me any more details?"

"No time. I have to call the police. Make your calls and get back to me quick as you can, please. We have a very serious situation here, but I want you to hold that in confidence. Is there any chance one of your vehicles has gone missing?"

"Odd you should ask that, Father. No missing vehicle, but the plates went missing off of one of ours. We discovered it today, around mid-morning. Chalked it up to a frat prank. We've been promised replacement plates by the end of the day. That of any interest?"

"Hard to say at this point," Ed said. "Got to hang up. Thanks for your willingness to help. It won't go unnoticed."

"Any time. Back to you soonest." Paul Webbley hung up and shook his head, breathed deeply and whistled. He spent the next five minutes looking up the phone numbers of Cambridge funeral homes, and then began his calls.

"George, this is Paul Webbley. No, I've learned my lesson. No more bets. Look, I was wondering if you folks have been involved in an exhumation recently? Yeah, I know. It is off the wall, but have you? Okay, I didn't think so but had to ask. Well, it's under tight wraps, but when I can I'll call back and let you know. Thanks, George. If you hear anything call me. It's important. Yeah, right. You, too." When he finished calling the last three, he dialed Father Hemming.

"Paul, thanks for handling this so promptly. I didn't expect you would get any hits, but I had to try just in case. As soon as I have any definitive word I'll get back to you."

Just as Father Hemming hung up Jamie burst into his office, face red, hair windblown, breathing hard.

"In the name of God, Ed, what the hell is going on? Who took JJ?"

"Sit down, Jamie. I'll get us some fresh coffee. Take off your overcoat."

"Coffee. How can we drink coffee—? Have you called the police?"

Ed shook his head. "We contacted all the other mortuaries in Cambridge, but none were involved in an exhumation." Ed reached for the pot. "You need some coffee, then I'll call Cordell." He added a double shot of brandy from the bottle in a lower desk drawer and handed it to his distraught friend. "Drink that while I call."

"Cordell Peyton, please. Tell him it's Father Hemming, and it's urgent. Yes, I'll hold."

⋘⋙

"Aim the spotlights directly on him," Judeland ordered. Her voice was slightly muffled as she was holding a hand over her nose and mouth. Her people stood in the doorway that led from their meeting room into the bar trying not to breathe.

"She's gone mad," Jake whispered to Monty.

"Tell me if all this is worth what she's paying us. Damn, do I need a beer," Monty whispered back.

"All right," Judeland waved to them. "Put your stage masks on and take your seats. Helen, you sure you know how to work that camera?" The masks looked like they'd come from a wax museum. One looked like Count Dracula, one like the Wolf Man, another like the Hunchback of Notre Dame. Judeland wore a Marilyn Monroe mask.

"I've answered that question twice already," Helen replied, trying not to gag. The corpse of JJ was wired to the chair, but from any distance the fine wire was invisible. He'd been dressed in a bright red cloak with high formal collar, and a black top hat. His hands were clasped on the table in front of him, his lifeless eyes opaque. The others all wore black cloaks and top hats except for Judeland, who wore silver. Five glasses of red wine were set in front of JJ's remains, and the other members of Judeland's group.

"Get going, Helen. I don't know how much longer I can take this," Monty said. The others grumbled their assent.

"Quiet," Judeland commanded. "Hold up your glasses as if in salute to our new leader." Everyone grudgingly held up his or her glass in a surreal toast. Helen took photos from a variety of angles, including close-ups of JJ. His taut, misshapen head, which bulged on its right side just above the ear, was beyond grotesque, with its waxen skin, sagging jaw, and sunken eyes.

"That's it," Helen said, her eyes tearing.

"Leave your costumes on the chair by the door on the way out. Monty and Jake, I want you to put JJ back into the body bag. Follow me to the refrigeration unit I've rented. I shall have our fine corpse stuffed so his presence won't be so offensive henceforth. You all did a good job tonight, and we shall dine at The Tides Restaurant on my nickel."

Monty and Jake loaded JJ into Judeland's van while Helen packed all the costumes. Judeland exhausted a can of air freshener throughout the room, paid the manager of the *Pirates Rock,* and took off.

"Shit." Judeland watched NT drive off in the opposite direction.

CRID

"There's a special delivery guy, uh gal, who wants to personally deliver something to you," Lenore said.

Heller frowned, took off his glasses, laid aside the report he'd been reading, and motioned for the delivery person to come in. It was late afternoon, and Jamie was tired.

"I just need you to sign right here," the uniformed girl said.

Heller scribbled his nearly illegible signature, and she left. The return address was Rogers Funeral Home, and he groaned as he slit the large envelope open. He pulled out four eight-by-ten color glossy photos.

"Jesus Christ on the cross!" Jamie shouted, leaping up, his chair rocketing back and crashing into the wall. His face was red, and the veins in his forehead bulged. One hand went into his trouser pocket and brought out a bottle of Valium, and he popped one into his mouth. The soft knock on his door made him jump. He felt cold and nauseous.

The door pushed open a couple inches. "It's Morgan. May I come in?"

Jamie pulled her into his office and slammed the door, locking it.

"Jamie, what's happened? What's the matter? You look—"

"Sit down," he rasped. Morgan dropped into the chair closest to his desk.

"Look." He motioned toward the pictures of his son and the others.

"Gods of the Universe, who could have—"

"Judeland. Who else?"

"When did you get them?"

"Two minutes before you got here."

"Those people must be demented." Morgan cupped her hands over her eyes as if trying to make the macabre photographs disappear. "When did they stage that grotesque scene?"

"Had to be yesterday," Jamie said.

"Those costumes. Could the police find out where they were rented?"

"Maybe." Jamie pulled a hand through his hair a couple of times. "But if they ever run Judeland to ground she will tell the whole vampire story, and that will be the end of the GenLab and Vampire Resurrection." Jamie groaned. "And us. Maybe even the university."

Morgan got up and hugged him. "We love you, Jamie, and we will get through this together. If I drive you home would you be willing to take a sedative and get some rest? I could stay for a while if you'd like."

They both started at the knock on his door. "Yes?" they said in unison.

"Shall I leave the coffee out here, Dr. Heller, or bring it into your office?" Lenore asked.

"Outside," Jamie said.

"I'll go get my purse and coat. Won't take me a minute."

Jamie hesitated, took a deep breath, and expelled it noisily. "Okay."

"Should we drop those off with Cordell on the way?" Morgan asked.

Jamie reached for his pipe and nodded in the affirmative. "Those photos could be the first step in our undoing, but we have to stop Judeland and her . . . her people. If that's what they are."

∞

Cordell sat at the head of the precinct conference room table, flanked by his two subordinates, Detective Sergeants Blanton McConnell and Ron Logan, who had replaced Jim Larkness. Four others were present: Hal Stone, Ed Hemming, Lamar Bradford, and Jamie Heller. The room was spare, the conference room table scarred from years of constant abuse. Though built with sound abatement materials, the noise from telephones ringing, clunking from vending machines, occasional loud altercations, and the wheezing of the anemic air handlers provided a background symphony. Emotions around the table varied from Cordell's resignation—here we go again—to Dr. Heller's extreme agitation. Hal was watchful and curious, hiding any emotions he might have harbored. Logan and McConnell took their cue from Cordell. Lamar sat rigid, trying to control his emotions. Father Hemming's outrage was evident.

"Now it's body snatching," Cordell said. "Last year we had a hell of a wild ride in this town, and when the media gets their fangs into this one, they'll trot out all the crap that hit the fan last year. They'll ask if this is round two of 'Cambridge, the Wild East Town.'"

"I don't care about that," Dr. Heller blurted, "I want my son's body back."

"We all do, sir," Cordell said. "And we'll do everything we can." He recalled how the governor had almost sacked him last year, had called in the FBI, and later given them credit for stopping the mayhem. He blew on his coffee. "I want to ask for your help and your patience. Whoever did this exercised a great deal of ingenuity, faking a letter of inquest and a writ of exhumation, working side by side with real Saint Paul contract employees who were digging a new grave so they wouldn't look conspicuous, and then doing a damn good job of disappearing.

"We have no motive, no communication claiming responsibility for the act, no decent descriptions of the perps, so we start from ground zero. Do any of you have any thoughts? Dr. Heller?" Cordell nodded at Jamie.

"It's got to be Judeland Bundaeker. Can't you see her claw prints all over it? She's back, and she intends to destroy me . . . and our work at the lab. She's using psychological warfare to unnerve the GenLab employees, but her game is to start with me." Jamie placed his head in his hands, leaning on the table. "We have to find her quickly. Maybe we could force her into resurrection." His voice was muffled as he spoke through his hands. Lamar and Hal stiffened and glanced at one another.

"Ron, get Dr. Heller some strong coffee," Cordell said. "Extra strong."

"On it, Chief." Ron returned in about three minutes and handed the mug to Jamie, who drank half of it and set it before him, both hands wrapped around it as if in supplication.

After a tense pause, Cordell addressed the stricken GenLab Director. "Dr. Heller, could you clarify what you meant by getting Judeland into 'resurrection'? And tell us, sir, if you have received any correspondence from her before the body was stolen." While speaking he fished out his scarred leather notebook and a pen.

Heller lifted his head. He looked like a spent boxer, face puffy, eyes red. He began to cough and reached for his coffee. "Yes. I received a threatening note. She—Judeland—said I was being watched, and that if I didn't do what she directed me to do, there would be dire consequences. She never makes idle threats."

"May we have the note? Our lab technicians might be able to—"

Jamie cut him short. "Do you seriously think someone with the cunning to steal my son's body in broad open daylight would leave her fingerprints on it?" Heller gave Cordell a scathing look. "In a fit of anger I tore it in half, but it may still be in the waste basket, unless my housekeeper tossed it in the trash."

Cordell's knuckles whitened, as he stared at Heller. "It's possible she left some DNA on it. Has she sent any other communications?"

Jamie started to reply but stopped himself and looked away. He wasn't about to reveal anything about the photos.

"Sir, without your complete cooperation our chances of finding your son's remains will be much reduced. I would advise you to—" A uniformed officer opened the door, walked over to Cordell, bent over, and whispered to him. "Would you inform these people as to what you just told me," Cordell said.

"We just received a call from University Security that the fire alarm at the Science Building has been set off. A general evacuation is in process. No sign of any smoke or fire yet, though."

"My God!" Jamie blurted. "If the GenLab is left unattended they will wreck everything."

"Who will wreck—" but Cordell watched, stunned, as Jamie, Lamar, and Hal bolted through the door. "Follow them," he roared at his two subordinates. "Call me with a report as soon as you have anything." He watched McConnell and Logan scramble out of the room.

"Christ on a rubber crutch," he muttered." I need a drink." He watched Father Hemming hurriedly limp out of the conference room, leaning heavily on his cane with each step.

Wonder what the hell Dr. Heller meant by "resurrection"?

14 - To Be or Not to Be

Like one that on a lonesome road
Doth walk in fear and dread,
And having once turned around walks on,
And turns no more his head;
Because he knows a frightful fiend
Doth close behind him tread. . . .

Samuel Taylor Coleridge (1772-1834), *Rime of the Ancient Mariner, A History of English Literature*, page 270

M organ couldn't mask her trembling. How could she finish the class? That thought was overwhelmed by the sudden deafening clamor of the fire alarm.

The sounds of people filling the halls, a few shouting, others laughing, added to the bedlam. What a blessing, Morgan thought, but her relief was short lived. By all the gods, the GenLab! What if the fire is in—

"Class dismissed," she yelled, dashing to the coat closet and grabbing her coat. She was about to leave when Suroccan grabbed her arm. His voice was quiet steel, meant only for her.

"Your time expires at midnight tonight. I shall have your answer then. I will meet you in the Yard at the John Harvard statue. I am stronger than you were as a vampire. But you have forfeited your powers, and you're no match for any one of us." He waved his hand at the vacant classroom. "I offer you my protection. As you may have suspected, Charna has granted me more powers than most. You would do well to shelter in them." He stepped through the door but looked back, his eyes no more than slits, and then disappeared into the throng.

Morgan blinked. Gone. She inhaled. His scent lingered, acrid-sweet, stinging her senses. She leaned against the door jamb, biting her lower lip in a vain attempt to collect herself. She had to get down to the GenLab fast.

☙❧

Jamie fought his way through the mass of students pouring out of the Science Center. Hal followed close behind, as did Cordell's two detectives and Lamar. They hurtled down the stairs to the GenLab and found it unlocked. "Damn fire code," Jamie roared as he flung the door open and raced through the outer office. No one. The fire alarm ceased its ear-bludgeoning noise, causing all five men to stop for a moment. The silence was broken by the faint shuffle of footsteps of the last few students leaving the building and the shouted commands from fire fighters on the floor above. Jamie looked at the door to the inner lab. It was ajar, and a spasm of despair began to uncoil inside his chest. His meltdown was interrupted by a groan.

"That's Morgan," Lamar exclaimed. "Morgan!" While Jamie stood transfixed, the others began looking under desks and behind filing cabinets.

"Here. She's here," Hal said. They converged to pull Morgan out from under a desk in the far corner of the work space.

"Where are you hurt, Morgan?" Lamar asked as he kneeled and held her.

"My head. Slammed me into the wall before I could see him. Feels like my head is in a vice." She groaned again. Detective McConnell returned with a stack of wet towels. While everyone was focused on Morgan Jamie silently slipped into the inner lab. The Cold Room door was still secured, and Jamie almost hyperventilated with relief. Then he saw the envelope taped to the bottom of the door. It was addressed to him in the childish handwriting Judeland had adopted. He tore open the envelope and unfolded the letter:

The First of March

Daddy Dearest,

What an interesting lab you have. Are you making
another round of zombies? No? Are you quite sure?
What if we have added a little spice to your ingredients?
One could surely guess what your final outcome would
be. Radical unwinding, right?

*Did you enjoy the photos of the meeting your son
chaired? He was most articulate and especially glad
to be out of his stuffy coffin. I have more copies of the
photos you've seen. We plan to distribute them to the
provost, the president, and the deans. Who else would
you suggest?
On the other hand, I think we could come to an
accommodation. I'll contact you soon, Daddy Dearest. I
may even offer you a way out. We shall see.
With Undying Affliction,
Your Bastard Daughter,*

JB

Jamie's hands shook, making it hard to re-read Judeland's message. His teeth clenched and his lips drew back exposing the yellowed teeth of a life-long pipe smoker. Detective McConnell startled him.

"What's that?" he asked.

"Nothing. Just an appointment I missed." Jamie folded the letter in half and jammed it into a suit pocket. "It was, uh, is a personal message from an old friend." He coughed as his face reddened. "How is Morgan?" Jamie asked.

"Hell of a headache but hopefully nothing worse," Lamar said. "We should have her looked at to make sure she didn't have a concussion, though."

"Good idea," Jamie said. "Why don't you fellows help her out of here? I'll lock up and stand door guard before we have a horde of firemen trashing the place."

"I'll send a couple of my security people to do that, Jamie," Hal said.

"We should dust the place for prints and look for any DNA they might have left," McConnell said.

"Okay, but let's lock up now. You can come back first thing in the morning," Jamie said. McConnell began grumbling about not following police procedures.

Jamie left for his office, shuffling like an old man.

Finally, Hal broke in. "You're welcome to follow me back to my office and look at the video from the surveillance cameras."

"*Surveillance cameras?*" Detective Logan looked at McConnell. The two detectives began looking around.

Hal smiled. "We just finished installing them about ten days ago. They are well hidden, don't you agree?"

 beginning ornament

Hal restarted the high-resolution color video and played it again. It showed two men wearing ski masks and gloves. One stood guard at the outer door, while the other pasted the envelope on the Cold Room vault door. They were about to leave when Morgan rushed in, only to be slammed against the wall and crumple. The two intruders carried her to the desk farthest from the door and rolled her under it.

Lamar winced as the video showed Morgan's forehead hit the wall. "At least we know they didn't penetrate the Cold Room vault," he said. "Hal, I suggest you put a guard or two back on the GenLab twenty-four/seven. If they have a bomb maker they might blow the vault door next time."

"Not likely. They'd need fifty pounds of C-4 or Semtex plastic explosive to get through that Mossler door. And that would take out one end of the building as well," Hal said.

"With all due respect, I don't believe that note taped on the door was from a colleague," McConnell said. "I got one glimpse at it. The writing looked like it was done by a psychotic. The way Dr. Heller reacted I'd put money on a death threat. Somebody has got an axe over Heller's head. That letter might give us a lead."

"I'll see if Heller will show me the letter," Lamar said. "Tell Cordell I'll get back to him win or lose on that."

ornament

Morgan sat at the kitchen table frequently glancing at her watch. Earlier, Robert had bid her good evening. Apparently, so had the cats. Lamar was off to meet with Jamie. The light seemed too bright, and she shaded her eyes with her hands. She'd glanced at the Seth Thomas clock on the mantle almost as often as her watch. The tall case clock in the hall bonged nine times. She looked at her watch and the mantle clock again. As usual, the old case clock was twelve minutes fast. Damn thing. Every minute was precious now. In less than three hours she would have to meet Andre Suroccan—a cold meeting in more ways than one. I *have* to decide. She poured herself another glass of merlot and wandered into the library, lighting one candle. The fire was no more than a bed of coals as Morgan sagged onto the couch.

Life had been simple as a vampire—life? No, it had been anything but simple. Was it really life at all? She had yearned to return to mortality for over three hundred years. The irony was that life was even harder.

Do I really want this baby? It is already in competition with Lamar. And what's happened to my sex drive? I can feel, even hear, the babe's rejection of sex. If I can't be in charge of her when she's still gestating, how the hell am I going to be alpha after she gets here? I want a normal, mortal baby. Morgan choked down another swallow of wine and leaned her head on the arm of the sofa. But if Suroccan helps me, either way I choose, he's got me in a trap. What would Lamar do if he found out I'd gotten rid of it?

And what would mortal life be like without Lamar? But how can I hold off Suroccan?

My child, my child. You have the power.

Morgan sat up so fast it made her dizzy. That voice. It sounded like— like who?—like Blind Gretta. "Gretta, is that you?"

I am always with you. Have been since they put me neath the sod.

"By all the gods, Gretta, I have created a black hole, and I am about to plunge headlong into it."

You have the power. Call on Charna. Use it.

"But . . . but I gave all that up; I lost my powers when I submitted to resurrection."

Did you now. Have you noticed you are not showing? And you made this child with your man long before you passed through resurrection. Have you noticed how often you smell the scent of a vampire? Do you not think it takes special powers to commune with me? Oh, my dear one, open your eyes. Every day your powers become more acute. Soon you will have no need of that blackguard, nor will you need fear him. He senses that. Why do you think he demands your consent to be under his powers so quickly? Gretta's voice began to fade.

"Gretta, wait. What should I do about the babe?"

Use your power. . . .

The silence was deafening, and she bent double, resting her forehead on her knees. She began to feel lighter, freer than she'd felt in a long time. This was not Andre's time; it was hers. She smiled. The tall case clock intoned the hour: eleven. Morgan laughed. Well, it was a little past the hour. Calvin brushed her ankle.

"How did you get in here, Old Mr. Calvin? Lords of the Universe he has lost so much weight. You are just fur and gristle." A tear fell on the bony one's head. "You're mortal now and soon to leave me." She wiped her eyes. Then a smile slowly spread over her face.

Maybe not.

15 - In the Shadow of John Harvard

I struck a match and from its glow
the meaning of death I came to know
whose endless passages through Destiny's door
led me to love death all the more."

Morgan wore an old topcoat of Lamar's, and an equally ancient fedora, pulled low over her eyebrows, black muffler over her face, gloves with most of the fingers missing, and badly scuffed oversized boots. The cane and limp made her look even more like a senior citizen living on Social Security or a long-forgotten veteran. Her fortnight was up. No doubt Suroccan would come, but she allowed a fleeting hope that he might not. Nonsense.

The night air was cold and still, and it was unusually quiet, she thought, save the sounds of distant tires plowing through slush. The Yard had the smell of a deep wood in winter: hidden acorns, frosted moss, and decaying oak leaves. It was a good smell, reminding her of several long-extinct forests in Britain.

Her stomach muscles pressed into her diaphragm, and she had to remind herself to breath. Her boots crunched on the salt granules that covered the walkways. Stupid university. The chances of slipping on the salt were at least equal to slipping in the snow. She would be about ten minutes early. Better to see him coming than to have him materialize out of the dark.

Despite the old-style lamp posts, too much of the Yard seemed to crouch in shadow, especially John Harvard, who sat, forever silent, forever observing the follies of students, visitors, and vampires. She looked around. Few students were out so late, none near the statue. She studied the nearest trees. Nothing.

"You are early. That's good."

Morgan whirled around. By the wrath of Charna, she thought, as Suroccan appeared from behind the statue.

"Dear me, did I startle you, Mrs. Bradford?"

His smile appeared brittle. Could Picasso have done something with it? she wondered. Or better, a mortuary technician? Morgan stood as if she, too, were cast in bronze, staring at him through the slit between the brim of her fedora and the muffler that covered her nose, almost as if she were peering through a burkha. The silence lengthened.

"I selected this spot and this time because it is not conducive to lengthy conversation. A simple 'yes' or 'no' will conclude our business unless you wish to convey more information." Suroccan bowed slightly. The stark silence was shattered by a falling branch.

"Well?"

"I accept your offer to demonstrate your powers. You do recall making that offer during our first discussion of this, um, issue?"

Suroccan's face hardened. "And just what—"

"My cat, Calvin, is aging, something that began the day after my resurrection. He's been with me for over 325 years. I want you to demonstrate your powers by resuming his immortal life. Oh, and you may include Lamar's cat, Oxnard, in the bargain. If, in the process, any harm comes to either creature that will end of our negotiations."

He made a guttural noise from deep within his throat. "A pox on your *negotiations*, woman. I am not here to negotiate; I am here to collect your decision."

"If you pledged to demonstrate your powers and later revoke that pledge, then I have no basis for trusting anything you have said or will say. Either you demonstrate or the answer is 'no.' I will give you a fortnight to establish feline immortality for both cats. We will meet here, at the same time."

He leaned back against the statue, draping one arm in a manner of studied nonchalance. "Ah, my dear one. You beg for a shard of additional time. All right, you shall have it. Your ravishing will be all the sweeter if delayed. Bring me the cats tomorrow. I will return them in a fortnight, if not sooner."

"I will, of course, need time enough to validate your results—or the lack of them." The strong scent of Absinthe enveloped Morgan, and she smiled. He was really angry now.

"Bosh. All you will have to do is feed them poison. When they don't die, there's your proof."

"I will be the judge of your success or failure." Morgan was startled by a dense mist that swept around the statue, obliterating her vision. Moments later, when the mist cleared, he was gone.

"You are good at parlor tricks, Suroccan," Morgan shouted. She took a deep breath and blew it out, slowly turning back toward the parking area. She had won a reprieve, if only for another fortnight.

"Thank you, Gretta." Her voice was muffled.

16 - A Word from Rome

*Well, right now . . . I'm not dead. But when I am,
it's like . . . I don't know, I guess it's like being inside a book that
nobody's reading . . . . An old one. It's upon a library shelf, so
you're safe and everything, but the book hasn't been checked out for
a long, long time. All you can do is wait. Just hope somebody will
pick it up and start reading.*

Tim O'Brian, *The Things They Carried.*

Cardinal Manlocara had included the OVFS motto at the bottom of his note: "Opus Dei Lamia Eradico." *The work of God to eradicate vampires.* Colonel Solento snorted. Not only do those red hats surround themselves with all the trappings they can think up, they wrap themselves in Latin as if to further sanctify their existence. The day may come when some innocent who wears a golden halo will throw the money changers out of the basilica. Ah, well, we've already waited over two millennia. If patience truly was a virtue, the masses would be virtuous to a fault. The red hats don't want to see the second coming. Who would need them then?

Colonel Solento glanced at himself in the full-length mirror, one of the first pieces of furniture installed when he moved into his predecessor's office. As always, he was perfectly turned out, his uniform as sharp as a stiletto. "Am I aging?" he asked the mirror. No answer. Maybe I should have addressed the bloody thing the old way. "Mirror, mirror on the wall, who's the best-looking officer of them all?" Still nothing. He turned his head. Definitely grayer. He stamped his boot, recalling his performance—or lack of one—last night when he went to visit Tanya. They had feasted. Altogether too much wine. An expensive cigar, and then he fell asleep. He would watch that from now on. He sucked in his gut, but that didn't help either.

He opened the note from the cardinal. It was succinct—and lethal. Veins in his neck began to pulse, and his lips turned white as he sucked them in and bit down. Morgan's head was to be added to the vault within the month. She had been priority one on the OVFS hit list for over two years. He must travel to America and personally control the operation. Failure was not an option.

CR&O

Colonel Solento looked at the red neon letters: *Harvard Street Deli.* The "D" was burned out, and "eli" was fizzing and blinking. He cracked his knuckles, glanced around, and walked in, making a quick survey. When he saw Andre Suroccan it was disgust at first sight. Suroccan was dressed in 19th century clerical garb no doubt from a cheap costume rental shop. Solento looked around with obvious disdain. Suroccan had picked a low-class bistro— "deli" he had called it—packed with students, laborers, and homeless men trying to get warm. No doubt Suroccan had chosen this wretched place to agitate him, as it would any man of impeccable bearing. And it had worked.

The smell was vile, despite the drafts of cold air ushered in with each new customer; he doubted the place had been visited by sanitation inspectors since Waterloo. Solento would try to conduct their business with haste. He had a flight back to Rome in four hours; that was three too many. He sat, stiffly.

"The timetable for Morgan Summers has been moved up," Solento began, just above a whisper. "You have thirty days to have her head in a diplomatic pouch headed for the Vatican. As you know, the OVFS has made several attempts to add her head to its collection, but all have failed. You will not fail. You will be richly rewarded and almost surely promoted after her head joins the others in our vault. You provide the plan, select the place and time. I will insure you have all the supporting manpower and other resources you need, within limits."

"I have killed before without, as you put it, 'supporting manpower and resources.' But what makes you think Mrs. Bradford—Morgan—is still a vampire?"

Solento raised his head and eyes as if in supplication to the one true God. "What makes you think there is anything on the earth or in the heavens such as an ex-vampire?"

"There are more things in heaven and earth, Solento, than are dreamt of in your philosophy." Suroccan's eyes betrayed the mischievous side of his nature.

The colonel shifted in the uncomfortable chair and dropped his gaze. "I did not come here to joust with a poet. You have your orders. Morgan Summers must be dispatched within a month. Any outcome short of that will be dealt with. Severely. Don't tempt the OVFS to substitute your head for hers." Solento stood abruptly. Suroccan kept his seat, squinting at the colonel as he flicked one hand in dismissal.

"I have been threatened before, many times, by men a lot more frightening than you, colonel of the combat-hardened Pontifical Swiss Guard." If that ass knew I was a vampire he'd turn to a pillar of salt.

Solento leaned down until his face almost touched Suroccan's, almost choking on the scent of Absinthe. "You have been given your assignment and a warning. I expect you to succeed." Solento stalked out of the Harvard Street Deli into a cold, blustery day. He needed a drink and a hot shower before his flight left.

CRED

Damn him, Morgan thought, listening to Lamar's soft snoring. When was the last night I got any decent sleep? Unconsciously she twisted the sheet. But how can I sleep? Suroccan will want his pound of flesh, unless— Lamar snorted and rolled over. How can I think with you taking up most of the bed? Crap. She swung her legs onto the floor and reached for her nightgown. She slept in the nude since moving into Coleson Manor, not that that had improved their sex life of late. He knows I'm a wreck but hasn't a clue why. Well, at least now he knows we are going to have a baby. He even raised the prospects it will be a vampire. Prospects? According to Wally it's a dead certainty. According to Suroccan I have several options, but they all come at a price. The same price.

Use your power, Morgan thought. But what power? She'd lost all that during resurrection, right? She wasn't at all sure that Gretta was right about regaining her old powers. The hall floorboards were cold on her bare feet. Where the hell are my slippers? Robert probably put them in my closet. It's strange not having the cats weaving around my ankles. She groped for a brass chamber stick on the hall table. It clanked as she bumped it into another stick. "Dammit." Why don't I just wake up the whole house. She pinched the wick out of habit. Most senior vampires could light a candle that way. "Double damn," she muttered as the candle refused to light. She missed her old laser-like night vision, too, stumbling twice on the way downstairs.

Morgan pulled the cork from the merlot they'd shared with dinner and headed for the library, juggling the chamber stick and the wine bottle. The candle stick sounded like a cannon shot when she sat it on the table. She held her breath, waiting to hear Robert prowling around. The wine tasted good, and she began to feel a bit better. Drinking out of the bottle reminded her of Paris in the early 1700s—her "youth." Red wine was a cheap substitute for blood. Her saliva glands shifted into high gear, and she felt an electrical quiver course up her spine. A muffled noise made her freeze, breath suspended.

The candle suddenly lighted, and the case clock struck two. But it was the meow that made her blood run cold. And the faint aroma of Absinthe.

"Calvin!" By all the gods. How did you—?" The cat jumped into her lap, purring loudly, and began sniffing her as if for the first time. His fur was sleek, eyes more alert, and he'd regained some weight. But he stopped purring, jumped down, tail erect, stalked over to the book shelves, and disappeared. Tears welled in Morgan's eyes. "Did that bad man put a curse on you my old friend? Or on me?" Is he here? she wondered, looking at the lighted candle. She started at the second meow.

Oxnard appeared, wraith-like, a shadowed mix of black, white, and ginger. Taking no notice of Morgan, he started across the library probably intent on joining Calvin. They've rejected me. Morgan's throat closed, and she stifled a sob. I've even lost the cats, she thought. And soon Suroccan will own me . . . for as long as it pleases him.

Use your power. The voice was distant, hollow, but unmistakable.

"Blind Gretta?"

No, I be quite far-sighted now.

"Thank all the gods; I thought I'd lost you. Again."

Only way that can happen is if you declare you don't want me anymore.

"I need you now more than ever, dear Gretta." Morgan gulped more of the red wine. "I wish I could share this with you."

So do I, dear one, so do I.

"Can you tell me what Suroccan has done with the cats?" Morgan tensed. Did she really want the answer?

Just what you asked him to do. They are immortal, but you aren't. You no longer smell like the woman that was Calvin's keeper these past hundreds of years. Best you be thinking who is going to take care of the both of them after you and Lamar have come over to my side.

"I hadn't thought of that."

There be a lot you haven't thought about, my child. And well past time you do the thinking.

"Gretta, my fetus is a vampire. Sometimes it feels like that thing inside me is pulling me back to the old ways. Is that possible?"

How long were you a vampire? Gretta's voice was growing stronger. *Three and a quarter centuries, I make it.*

"Yes. Why?" The electrical charge raced up her backbone, the one that used to signal she was going into the hunting. And the air became fetid with Absinthe. "Gretta, he's here isn't he? Suroccan."

Aye. His power is, anyway. Do ye nay feel its pull? You must use —

A book fell off one of the shelves and thunked on the hardwood floor. Calvin emerged and walked languidly toward her, disappearing under the sofa. In a moment he reappeared with something in his mouth. He dropped it and began batting it across the rug. Morgan's eyes widened. "What the hell," she murmured, picking up a pair of woman's flesh-colored Bikini panties. Her lips pursed, and her eyes became slits. Well, well, Mr. Bradford. Getting a bit careless aren't we? Who—? Jennifer! Who else? I've put him off, and he. . . .

Morgan felt a faint waft of air. The candle guttered and went out. She looked at the door as it opened, slowly. "Gretta, help me," Morgan murmured as she stuffed the panties under a seat cushion. She heard Gretta's last words, but they were ephemeral, an echo from a distant place, too indistinct to be understood.

Robert Diamond beamed a flashlight at her.

17 - At the Feet of John Harvard

Death is nothing to us,
since when we are,
death has not come,
and when death has come,
we are not.

Epicurus 341-270 B. C.

Cold rain pattered across the Harvard Yard. If the Budweiser commercial ever needed a dreary scene, tonight was the night, Morgan thought, as she headed for a tree. She wore a bag lady outfit, with a knit cap, no umbrella, pushing an old wire mesh grocery cart filled with a blanket, some food, a pillow, a pile of clothes, all covered with plastic grocery bags. The cart rattled and squeaked across the soggy ground under the canopy of trees that sheltered the Yard She reached a tree nearest the John Harvard statue. No doubt Suroccan was watching her, even though she was almost thirty minutes early.

The fetus writhed, making Morgan gag. No matter what the cost, she had to get rid of the abomination inside her, for it was actively pulling her back . . . back into vampirism.

She would make him swear an oath upon the heart of the Serpent of Charna that she would owe him no more than three assignations. But she knew he would hold one of those over her forever, or at least for as long as she was granted mortal life. She knew her mortal clock was ticking since she'd gone through resurrection. She wanted a baby but not this, this abomination.

"Excuse me, madam; may I see your university credentials?"

Morgan jerked out of her brooding contemplation. "What did you say? I'm just, uh resting. For just a minute," she stammered.

"I need to see your student identification card or your faculty registration. If you don't have one of those I'll have to escort you out of the Yard."

"That won't be necessary. I have asked this woman to meet me here, and we will be on our way directly." Dressed all in black, a muffler wrapped around his neck high enough to cover his mouth, wide-brimmed hat pulled down over his eyebrows, Suroccan looked like *The Shadow* from the 1930s pulp novels, radio programs, and movies.

The campus security guard suddenly doubled over and grimaced.

"I suspect you will need to visit the nearest necessarium—uh, make that restroom—given the acute state of your gastric distress." Suroccan wrapped an arm around the man, turned him around, gave him directions, and pushed him on his way. The guard was almost running when he disappeared in the gloom. Suroccan turned to Morgan.

"Perhaps we should find somewhere under roof for our talk. Your disguise is quite good, by the way, apart from your boots. Not enough wear and way too expensive."

"I didn't come here to discuss my disguise." Morgan's cart began its usual protest as she pushed away from the tree.

"Which option have you selected, my dear?" Suroccan easily kept pace with her.

"I can't stand this thing in me any longer."

"Ah. You are referring, of course, to the babe that Lamar sired whilst you were both still members of the Family Vampiris. How sad for you and for our world. Doris or Clarissa or whatever you would have called her, would make a great addition to our blood lines. A pure blueblood as it were, the product of two conjugal vampires. A real pity. Doesn't happen very often. Have you considered transferring the fetus to another female vampire? That would be worthy of a sparkling entry in the *Gran Summario del Historia Vampirismo*. You, my dear, could become famous, and probably quite wealthy in your own right."

"Ah. My car," Suroccan nodded. In the pale street light it looked like it belonged in a junkyard. He pointed at it, and the doors unlocked.

"But that's *my* car—Old Oxidation."

"My dear, it *was* your car, but when you sold it, I acquired it. Your mechanic—Monty I believe his name is—did an excellent job making it road worthy while leaving the exterior to look rather like an automotive bag lady." He held the door open for Morgan.

"My grocery cart?"

"It will be here when we return. No one can see it but us." He started Old Oxidation without having a key and drove to Porter Square. As they entered the building he waved at the security system, and the door clicked open, and the elevator doors separated. "Two please," Suroccan said, to no one. The elevator doors closed. In a moment they hissed open.

"This was my building, my studio apartment. You didn't— how—?"

"I thought you might find our conversation easier with your old things at hand. Please sit. Take off that odorous coat and sweater," Suroccan said, unwinding his muffler, pulling off his gloves, and dropping his trench coat and hat over a chair. He sat across from her. "Would you care for some red wine?"

"No. I'm not here to pay a social call."

"I trust you will agree that our contract should be written, dated, and signed, yes?" he said.

Morgan looked down and nodded almost imperceptibly.

"Good. Good. I've prepared a contract. Let me read it aloud. We can make any changes that are agreeable to us as we go. Sure you won't have a glass of red wine with me?"

Morgan kept her eyes on the rug. But her head snapped up when she heard a meow, one that sounded like Calvin. "You have my cat. Where—"

"No, dear lady, your cat is tucked away with his newly immortal friend, Oxnard, in Coleson Manor. I thought you might enjoy hearing his projected voice. Remember? Weren't you able to do that before your resurrection?" He poured merlot into a fluted glass and held it up to the overhead fixture, which dimmed as he frowned at it. "Much better, don't you agree?"

Morgan took a deep breath, held it, then quietly released it. What was much better now? she wondered. Gretta keeps telling me to use my power, but against Suroccan what chance do I have? My cat has more power now than I do. Somehow I have to find out if Suroccan will honor his part of our bargain. He may be gaming me.

"You have no intention of going through resurrection, Andre, do you? So what is your game? Who are you working for? Let me guess; the OVFS, am I right?"

Suroccan scowled. "I am working for you, my dear. I am protecting you from the combined forces of evil from various quadrants of the Zodiac." He held up the wine and squinted. A slow smile unfolded like a cat stretching after a long nap. "This is really quite good."

"So if you really are working for me, why do you put such a high price on your services?"

"High? *High?* Why do you submerge your intellect now that you are human? Can you not sense the danger that is closing around you? Listen to your breathing. It is already restricted. You are warring inside.

You want to be rid of the seed you carry, yet you yearn to be a mother. The gods have favored you, yet you are rejecting them. Can you not feel the consequences of that hovering around you like a pox? How much sand remains in your hourglass? Rather little by my lights." His eyes snapped, projecting tiny sparks that betrayed his frustration.

"And do you think the OVFS has given up? Not to mention this Judeland creature? Which of them will the gods send against you? And who will come to your defense when the ring-pass-not closes around you, eating away at your time and space until you dare not exhale for fear there be no air left for your next breath? Ponder that for a moment while I pour your wine."

He was right. She *could* feel her time and space shrinking. The air felt more dense, and she could feel it pulse with the universal breath of life. How could she fight him? Them? The All in All?

Use Your—

The voiceless whisper was choked off.

"There you are, my dear. Drink. You need to relax." He held fast to the wine, and their hands touched. Hers cooled; his warmed.

"What did you put in the wine, Andre?"

"You stab me in the heart, dear Morgan. Do you really think I need to resort to such chimera as that? No!" he roared, slamming his glass down so hard it shattered, shards of glass flying, wine flowing over the table. One shard nicked Morgan's right hand causing a seam of blood with tiny droplets running around her wrist. Before she could react, he yanked her hand to his lips, and his tongue wiped the wound clean. When he released her hand it bore no trace of the cut.

Suroccan sat back and sighed, eyes closed, mouth open, pulling in the scent of her blood the way a cigarette smoker French-inhaled.

He formed an image of Morgan, nude, wanting him, pleading with her eyes, reaching out to grasp his hands and pull them down to her breasts. The shock from their touch coursed up his arms, through his torso, finally nesting in the genus of his longing. The image vibrated with the intensity of his will . . . and his desire.

Morgan moaned, her eyes fluttering, no longer able to focus. Against her will she felt the sweep of sexual tension engulf her, intensifying with each breath. She wanted him. Now. Urgently. Erasing the world, herself, the writhing fetus in her belly, leaving only the desperate need for him to crash against her shore like the eternal tide of man and beast, and the gods, and the galaxies.

As he picked her up she was jarred by the voice from at least one of the gods. Awaken. Arise. Attend yourself, it seemed to say. Disembodied, she perceived herself lying on the bed, naked, while a specter stood like an obelisk at the foot, looking at her as an artist would study the Mona Lisa.

Use Your Power!

She had one remaining power, one she had pushed down into the depths of her being, before resurrection, believing it would never be needed but unwilling to lose it

She regressed into the perfect stillness wherein lay . . . *the power of Death.*

18 - The Power of Death

A body all crumpled and bleached a stark white
As dry as the Sahara on its driest of nights
Confounds all the gendarmes who evil would fight
No earthly explanation for this most dreadful sight

Suroccan covered his forehead and eyes with one hand in exasperation, stifling a groan. Did she think she could fool him? "You are not the first to fake your own death for my benefit," he seethed. He studied her as if she were a germ under a microscope. No sign of breathing. He snapped his fingers. No reaction to sound. He placed a hand on her breast. Her body temperature was dropping, and the fetus had become lethargic. Her brain waves lapsed. He didn't need a CT scan to read them. "She's flatlined," he murmured. This one is quite good—the best I've seen in over seven centuries. She will have to restart in an hour, two at most. I can wait.

Wait. That's all I've ever done. Just once I wish someone would wait for me, someone without murderous intent. He glared at his clenched fists as if they had betrayed him. "Come to me, Morgan. Want me of your own free will." He'd taken hundreds of women, but few had loved him. He looked at her, mesmerized by her beautiful nakedness. So still, so lifeless. Silhouetted by a single 25-watt bulb in a lamp on the bedside table, she lay in illuminated peaks and shadowed valleys, the faint light accentuating her grace, sculpting her form, sharpening her haunting sensuality.

She is exquisite. Why in the name of all the gods—former, living, and yet to come—does she waste herself on that utter imbecile, Bradford? He doesn't deserve her. I do. He must be a pathetic sex partner. So beautiful. Tears welled in his eyes, and he cracked his teeth together so hard the sound echoed from the dark corners of the room.

What if I were to risk my powers to get her to come to me? If I laid aside all my powers, and we met as equals, could she not see my worth? Suroccan pulled an armless chair up to the bed and sat, heavily. After a long moment of silent meditation, he reached out with the backs of his fingers and lightly brushed her cheek. No reaction. He hadn't expected any. His heart filled with a rush of abject despair.

Take the risk, Andre.

Suroccan yanked his hand away from Morgan's cheek and leaped to his feet, knocking over the chair. He took two quick steps back and summoned his etheric shield, which swirled around him. In a few seconds his acute vision swept the room, finding no sentient being, nor could he detect a non-corporeal entity. The parched laugh sounded like dry leaves shuffling in a gutter.

Take the risk, Andre, the voice repeated. *Lay down your sword and shield. Take away the darkness in her womb, the stain of Charna. Protect her from her enemies. And ask nothing in return.*

Ask for n o t h i n g. . . . The voice faded.

"I must know who you are. Why do you come to me and ask for something in behalf of another?"

In life I were known as Gretta the Blind. The Universe be watching you Master Suroccan. The gods be giving you a rare chance to redeem your soul, to nurture it, and to learn the secrets of love. Bend your knee. Bend your will. It be time for your resurrection. Without surgery. You are offered this one chance. Refuse it, and you will spend eternity pleading to all the gods for another—

The voice stopped abruptly. Morgan's sightless eyes snapped open as a key turned in the front door lock.

"By the wrath of Charna," Suroccan cursed as he hastily pulled a blanket over Morgan and snapped off the bedside lamp. He sensed the apartment door open slowly. His eyes narrowed and his gaze riveted on the bedroom door handle, which began to glow. His senses focused as two men slowly walked through the apartment, finally stopping at the closed door.

Jake yanked his hand back. "*Ahhh, Jesus!* The door knob's hotter than a fucking branding iron." Jake moaned as he headed for the kitchen.

"Where the hell do you think you're going?" the other man asked.

"Run cold water over my hand. I burned the hell out of it."

"You ain't worth the powder to blow yourself a new asshole."

"Well you go right ahead, grab the damn door knob, and just waltz right in. She's probably set another booby trap inside the bedroom. But don't let me stop—"

"Just shut your mouth." Monty aimed at the lock. The gunshot sounded like it could have been heard throughout Cambridge—by the living and the dead. The door swung open about two feet, and his flashlight beam danced around the room.

"Come in." Suroccan's voice sounded like an echo from a crypt.

"Who the hell are you?" Monty spun to his left and caught Suroccan in his flashlight beam.

"I have been called by many names. Dr. Jene Claude Vompre at your service." His black attire was suffused with a faint green luminescence. His piercing eyes appeared to fling off tiny red sparks. "Please turn off that flashlight."

"You gotta be shittin' me." The flashlight dimmed, then went out. "Son of a bitch." Monty knocked the flashlight against his thigh. "What have you done with the girl?"

"And who might you be other than a presumptuous ass?"

"Look, Captain Midnight, if you don't tell me where she is, your fancy jacket and vest are going to be filled with bullet holes. You read me?"

"Reading you is no problem. You smell like oil, grease, gasoline, and rubber. Except for your rudimentary facility with language I'd guess you were an automobile."

"I'll give you to the count of three to tell me where she is. One—" He choked, and began to shake. The automatic fell to the floor. Suroccan smiled and stepped toward him. Monty turned to run, but couldn't move. Two hands fastened on his collarbones sending a violent electrical shock through the terrified man. "NO. *NO—Nooooo.*" His cry ended in a gurgle as he slumped into a formless heap. Suroccan bent over the body.

"You may taste like gas and oil, but it has been so long—so very long—since I tasted human blood." Not quite, he reminded himself, smiling at the taste of Morgan's blood.

Monty's cell phone vibrated, and Suroccan retrieved it. "Yes?"

"I just saw Jake run out of the building. You okay?"

"Never better."

"Who is this?"

"This is Jene. I look forward to making your acquaintance soon. Oh, soon indeed."

The line went dead.

Tires screeched as a car carrying Judeland, Number Three, Jake, and Helen sped away.

"I am served by a pack of fools and idiots," Judeland grumbled.

19 - The Trial

"Love sought is good, but given unsought is better."

Shakespeare: *Twelfth Night*

Morgan gasped and her lungs heaved. Her eyes shut tight as she focused on restarting her life force: heartbeat, breath, body temperature, awareness. She began to shiver. Low at first but building slowly, she sounded the basic earth tone—the musical note that accompanied the creation of the universe—as taught her by Blind Gretta. She opened her eyes, and her vision returned, yet still opaque. She was aware of a ball of yellow light to the right and behind her head and of a presence at her feet. Her awareness sharpened. She felt cold and thirsty. Her head ached. And though naked, she was covered by something. A blanket. Yes, that was it. She loved that blanket, for it shielded her from the predacious eyes of the night.

She wasn't alone. That sifted into her consciousness as a heavy mist seeps beneath an ill-fitted door. Her head felt so heavy; lifting it made her dizzy. She would lie still and collect herself.

"I can get you another blanket."

Morgan frowned. It couldn't hurt to have two, could it? She nodded. A man—yes, definitely a man—placed a blanket over the one that clothed her nakedness. She squinted. His face was famil—Suroccan! And smiling. Was she hallucinating? He pulled up a chair and sat beside her, holding one of her hands. His hand felt warm and his aura pulsed, emitting a faint green hue. "How long have I been like this? Why are you keeping me here? Where am I—?"

"You must take time to fully restore yourself, my dear. Rest and allow that to happen naturally, in its own time. Are you hungry?"

"Thirsty." She heard a clock ticking in another room—a pleasant sound.

"Ah yes, of course. I'll be right back. And I promise to answer all your questions."

There was something different about him. His aura had changed. Not nearly so dark and dense. Quite the opposite she realized. And something else. What? His scent. Not a hint of Absinthe. That's a first. I wonder—

"Here, let me help you to a sitting position."

As Morgan drained the glass of water the blankets drooped, exposing her breasts. Suroccan looked away. Morgan's eyes widened.

"Andre, do I repulse you?"

"Repulse?" he choked on the word. "Of all the goddesses throughout creation thou art the fairest." He reached down and pulled the blankets up around her shoulders. "More water?" She nodded, and he left her again.

She could feel her heart beating stronger, her body heating up, though a strange lassitude settled upon her. How can this be? Suroccan is the most feared vampire in the known world, yet I feel relaxed and, and what—safe? Yes, safe. Did he cast a spell on me, perhaps while I was at death's portal?

"Drink this slowly, my dear. You gulped the last one."

"Andre, why are you being so, uh, so kind to me? You never have before. Is it part of a plan to own me? Have you cast some spell on me that makes me see shades of—"

"Nay, woman. 'Tis I who have fallen under a spell, one assisted by your mentor from the World Unseen. I believe you called her Blind Gretta when she were among the quick."

"Gretta? What kind of hoodman's blind are you playing? I don't believe she would, or could, do that. You have powers beyond almost all others of our kind."

"Ah. You said 'our' kind. But you have experienced resurrection have you not? How can you be of 'our' kind now?"

"You are evading me. Why all this?" she waved her hand to indicate the room, the blankets . . . and her nudity.

"Are you aware that you have called me by my first name? And that my scent is no longer that of a vampire? You see, dear one, I have set aside my sword and shield, as your Gretta put it. I am quite defenseless. I no longer have the power to cast spells."

Morgan shook her head as if trying to clear it. "But why? What has happened to you?"

"Have you any idea how long I've waited, Morgan? Twice as long as you were a vampire and more. Waited to be wanted for who I really am—desperate for that first rare scent of love. Waited for the elixir of life: that combination of love and sensuality. Morgan, I no longer want you if I have to bind you with magic, or force you against your will to submit. The contract I offered you is null and void. I've burned it. I will do your bidding without your pledge of sexual reward."

"The day we met you said you sought resurrection to learn the secrets of death, and the fear of it," Morgan said.

Suroccan scowled. "I said what I thought you wanted to hear, concealing my truth. You are not the naked one now, Morgan, I am. I stand before you self-shorn of the mystical powers I held for over seven centuries." He trembled, and his eyes glistened, but they didn't emit sparks.

Slowly, Morgan sat up and swung her feet to the floor, the blankets falling. As she did, Suroccan stood and pulled the chair out of the way. Standing before him, swaying, her eyes focused on his, she smiled. Time pulsed, its primordial sound filling the room with its breath. Finally she leaned forward and kissed him like a butterfly lighting on an open bud. Then she stepped back. "You can resume breathing, Andre."

His sigh was long, and he blinked furiously to prevent the welling in his eyes to escape as tears. Though he smiled his pain was obvious, and he closed his eyes.

"Do you not choose to gaze upon the form I stand in, Andre?"

He opened his eyes and said, "Do believe me, Morgan, I have etched your every centimeter on the pallet of my memory. Naught could ever erase you."

"You know this body will decay. The beauty you see will sag, wrinkle, stoop. My voice will take on Gretta's timber. Then you will reject me, as will all men."

"Dear Morgan, you have learned the secrets of finding the beauty within the form. Will you not teach me those secrets?"

"Andre, you don't teach that, you learn it. And if you do, you will be able to see the beauty that is Gretta's, the beauty hidden in all mankind."

Andre reached for her. She stood, motionless, smiling, eyes wide, and his arm fell to his side.

"No," he choked, "I have not earned the right to touch you. And if I ever do, it must begin with you touching me."

"Are you ready for resurrection, Andre? Can you see how impossible it is for a human and a vampire to really touch? To really touch? Are you prepared to never again pick up your sword and shield? Are you willing to die to find the love you seek with all your being?"

"Twice before you have asked me for time. Now I ask you for that same grace," he answered. Andre's eyes sought hers. "You shall have my answer in a fortnight" His shoulders slumped, and he appeared drained of the life force.

"During that time, Andre, will you remove the stain of Charna from my womb?"

"Yes. If that be your wish I shall take on my powers again and do as you ask. But is there any hope for me, for us, my dear one? I must know."

"You know I am trothed to another, Andre."

His head sagged.

"But there is always hope," she said, her voice just above a whisper.

Suroccan stared at the blankets draped around her feet like the discarded raiment of a primeval goddess.

"Unless you are a vampire," he murmured.

20 - 1911 Napoleon Grand Reserve Cognac

I bend and bow and weep in despair
the angels watch unending
Our existence is doomed through immortal ages
to all the gods offending
I hear the siren call of love
to my heart the sound is rending
And the immortal drudge of hapless life
beyond the long road's winding
Unblessed by love or death or shame
Oh mortality, where be thy fame?

Judeland was surrounded by her crew at *Pirates Rock*. "Jake, you were in the apartment. Tell me again what happened. And this time don't leave anything out."

Jake was tearing his napkin into confetti and blowing it around the table. He shifted in his chair and cleared his throat. "Not too much to tell. I told it all the first time." As the silence lengthened, he and Helen each lit another cigarette. "It didn't take Monty a minute to open the window," Jake began. "The lights didn't work, and we swithed on our flashlights. We looked in every room till we came to the bedroom. That door was shut." He looked at his bandaged right hand and shook his head. "Fucking door handle was red hot. When I grabbed it, I burnt the shit outta my hand and ran to the kitchen to run water on it. That's when I heard Monty shoot the lock off and kick the door open. I heard him say something to somebody, but couldn't make out what they were saying with the water running.

"I called to him, but he didn't answer. Finally, I walked over to the door and shined my light inside. That's when I saw Monty on the floor all crumpled up. This really weird dude came out of a closet or somewhere and said something or other, and I beat it. That's it."

"You didn't look to see if you could help Monty?" Judeland asked, her voice acid.

"No sense wasting my time, I could tell he was dead." Jake rocked back in his chair.

"Really? How?" Judeland's face was pinched, and she was struggling to control her breathing.

"The way he was all crumpled up. It was like he didn't have a bone in his body."

"And what did you say to the man who appeared?"

"Nothin'. All I wanted to do was get the hell out of there." Jake reached for his cigarettes.

Judeland turned to NT and Helen. "And what do you think of Jake's story?"

Helen reached for her glass of gin. NT blew a cloud of smoke at Judeland, causing her to wave at it and sit back in her chair. She turned to JJ—James R. Heller, Jr.

JJ sat at the head of the table, where he'd been placed by Judeland and Helen. The two men kept their distance from his Styrofoam-filled body. A guy they hired had filled out his face and neck making the late JJ somewhat more natural. He wore a suit and tie, and had an old-style briefcase on the table beside him. An unlit cigarette was wedged between his index and middle finger on his left hand. His face still portrayed a sense of shock, however.

"JJ, let's hear from you. What do you make of Jake's story?" Jake's head snapped up, NT's eyes widened, and Helen choked on her gin. "Come on, speak to us. Just because the others sit mute like the Sphinx, no need for you to be like them." Judeland leaned toward JJ.

"Ah, yes. For those of you who couldn't hear that, he says that Jake should have taken his pulse. And what else?" Again she leaned toward the figure. "Absolutely right. He says you should have retrieved Monty's automatic. He calls you a careless oaf. I'm inclined to agree with him. What's that you say, JJ?" She turned and smirked at the others. "Too bad he doesn't speak to the rest of you, but he says if you perform your assignments to his satisfaction, he will begin to speak to you as well.

"Jake, we will need some fire bombs to take out the GenLab and its staff, maybe even the whole Science Building. When can you procure them?"

Jake looked at his watch. "When do you want 'em?"

CR80

Colonel Johann Solento hated this task more than any other since he had been inducted into the OVFS. Two new vampire heads had come in from field operations: one from Central America, the other from Paris. It was his job to place them in one of the empty canisters reserved for new heads and then to fill it with the ancient brine and seal it. The brass name plates had been ordered. When all was completed, he would screw the plates onto the shelves in front of the canisters and transcribe their histories into the codex. He fingered the iron key to the lock on the weathered chest in the corner of the vault, and thought about the codex inside. The trunk must have sat on the deck of a ship for some years to bleach out to such a silver-gray patina. This would be only the second time he had opened it. He would hold his breath, for it smelled like an opened grave.

Johann paused to look at the two new additions, numbers fifty-nine and sixty. Number fifty-eight was an empty canister but the brass plaque was already in place: *Morgan Summers, 2010*. He glanced at the head of the wrong woman sitting by itself. The OVFS had devoted half its yearly budget trying to acquire Morgan's head, as yet to no avail. According to the records, the OVFS had been tracking her since before the turn of the millennium. Other than Morgan, the longest any of their targets had eluded God's justice was three years. Even with occasional covert help from Interpol, she had survived at least a half-dozen operations—probably more—against her. He wiped his brow. You had to envy her uncanny skill and phenomenal luck. "I wish she were a member of the OVFS," he said aloud.

Johann looked at the newly-finished shrine. With considerable help from Minuette they had boiled the flesh off Loconi's bones except for the head, which had been placed in a brine-filled canister. His bones, laced together in proper order, were housed in a simple wooden coffin propped up in one corner, the lid closed. The top part of the coffin, however, had been fitted with separate hinges to allow it to be fully opened. Resting on a wooden base, the cardinal's head floated in the canister. The hinged cover was always left open to reveal his face.

"Why are you smiling at me, you fool? You are stone dead!" Johann yelled. Loconi's smile seemed to widen as Johann stalked over and grabbed the hinged cover, closed and secured it with the latching pin. He walked back to the table, face flushed, heart racing.

I'll top off and light two more oil lamps so I can see to write, he decided. Opening his attaché case he pulled out a sheaf of papers covered in a neat script—the meticulous hand of Cardinal Manlocara—and groaned. It will take hours to transcribe all that into the codex. As he inserted the iron key into lock, he held his breath and raised the lid, grabbing the codex and slamming the lid in one practiced motion. Even so he couldn't entirely avoid the stench.

Leafing through, he discovered that the late Cardinal Loconi had long ago written much of the story on Morgan, leaving space for the conclusion, her death. Strange, there seems to be a lot more writing after the story on—*Dios en el cielo!*—what is this?

> *Written this, the twenty-fifth day of February in the year of our Lord, 2011, by God's good and faithful servant, Cardinal Alfonso Loconi, President of the Vatican's Fabbrica and Director of the Order of the Vampire Final Solution. I have been murdered at the hand of Cardinal Santoro Manlocara.*
> *I offer this to my creator and savior as my full and final confession of all sins. I provide the names and sins of those who have been a part of the OVFS, for they have been the cause of death and destruction well beyond the confines of delivering mankind from the foul bondage of vampirism.*
> *Let it be known to all men that. . . .*

Johann felt dizzy and nauseous as he lowered his head onto his arms, which encircled the codex. If this confession ever became known outside the chamber there would be a sudden increase in the number of heads on these shelves, starting with his and Manlocara's. What must I do? Think! He could feel his heart thudding, feel his temples pulsing, hear his ragged breath. He had to pull himself together. A slow smile began to crack through the granite face that had but scant practice at smiling, and those few had been contrived. He had the answer, and it was brilliant. It would insure his survival and his prosperity as well. Surely it had been an inspiration from, as Loconi used to say, "The One in whom we live and move and have our being." He closed the codex softly and gave it a paternal pat.

"Thank you, Cardinal Loconi. Thank you."

He glanced at the shrine. The lid that covered Loconi's face was open. The late cardinal was smiling at him. Again.

০৪৪০

Lamar emerged from the Coleson Manor wine cellar carrying a bottle of 1911 Cognac Grande Reserve Napoleon, 44 years old when bottled. Morgan promised him a night he would never forget. Well, he planned to do his part. Robert would be apoplectic to find that Lamar had opened one of only two bottles of the husbanded Napoleon Grande Reserve, but Robert had the weekend off, and it would be at least a few days before he discovered the cognac missing. Well, he could refill the bottle with a cheaper cognac. Good idea, he thought.

The catered dinner had just been delivered, including hoer d' oeuvres and high-end wines. Morgan loved fine dining, especially after her resurrection.

His mind drifted from the dinner they would share to more important delights. Morgan had been indifferent about making love since . . . since when? The last couple of months? Since her resurrection? Or maybe since she learned she was pregnant? That happened to some women, he knew. He'd consulted Google.

Damn. She was always ready—eager!—for sex as a vampire. But now?

Morgan had promised a night to remember. From the feelings he was experiencing as he pictured her lying naked in front of the fireplace, their special night was already under way. He wished he hadn't ordered a fine, catered dinner. A couple of ham sandwiches and some beer after making love would be all they needed.

Upstairs Morgan affixed a red bow to the silver package and nodded. This should rattle my philandering husband. I wonder if they belong to Jennifer? We will settle that little score. Unbidden she thought about Andre Suroccan and the fetus. She wasn't exactly playing fair with Lamar. She could handle her end but strongly suspected that he wasn't up to resisting Jennifer who, rumor has it, is sleeping her way up the ladder at Harvard. Well, Morgan wasn't about to let Jennifer sleep her way up Lamar's ladder.

Glancing in the full-length mirror, she saw the reflection of a Playboy or Penthouse centerfold of the month. She was wearing a flesh-colored string Bikini and bra combination under an almost transparent shoulder to floor negligée. Her nails were painted, hair down, Wine with Everything lipstick, eye makeup, and Euphoria perfume—Lamar's favorite.

She was ready. She would take him apart piece by piece she thought, descending the staircase barefoot.

The candles were lit, the cognac poured, a small fire crackled in the fireplace. Both cats were poised for a shrimp treat. The library door hushed open, and she stood for a moment, striking a pose made famous by Lauren Bacall and perfected by Marilyn Monroe.

"You look smashing Mrs. Bradford. Come sit. Would you like a cube in your Grand Reserve?" Why do I feel so nervous? Lamar wondered.

"No, just neat."

"I like your outfit. Doesn't hide very much, but a figure like yours isn't meant to be hidden. From me, that is." Just out of reach she allowed the negligée to fall to the Persian rug and sat on the edge of the sofa, knees together, deeply inhaling her drink and then sipping it.

"I brought you this." She handed Lamar the silver box.

"Wow. I wasn't expecting a gift."

"Especially not this one."

"Would you care for a mini oysters Rockefeller? I tried one in the kitchen, and they are first class. They served these on the Titanic so the story goes." Morgan shook her head almost imperceptibly. "Is something wrong? It's not like you to be so quiet. And why the gift?"

"Consider them a return on investment. Open it."

The package contained a pair of Bikini panties exactly like the ones Morgan wore.

"I don't get it." Lamar was frowning as he held up the panties.

"When was Jennifer over here, and how did she *come* to lose these?"

Lamar stood abruptly, face flushed. "She's never set foot in Coleson Manor! Look, I don't know what you think happened, but I've never seen those damn pants before. Where did *you* get them?"

The fire crackled, and Calvin yawned. The silence stretched out as the two glared at one another. Finally Morgan spoke.

"Will you swear by the Serpent of Charna that you don't know anything about these panties?"

"Hell yes. I'll swear by any bunch of gods you want to dredge up. Anyway, why are we talking about them?"

"We are talking about them because I found them, or rather my cat did, under the sofa the other day." She pointed. "So would you be so kind as to explain how they got there?"

"Not in a million years, Babe, because I've never seen them, and I really resent not being given the benefit of the doubt. You put on a one-act play about a pair of panties I've never seen. We could have got there in two sentences and then had a damn nice dinner. Well, you eat it. I've lost my appetite. I suggest you pitch those panties in the fire. That would make a fitting end to this charade." In six long strides Lamar was out of the library. She could hear him bounding up the stairs.

"Guess I fucked that one up," she said to Calvin. Morgan sagged onto the sofa, her eyes glistening, while an elegant dinner grew cold. She reached for her cognac, took a sip, and threw the snifter into the fireplace.

"1911 was a shitty year."

21 - The Lusty Month of April

But what of love, my fainting Maid?
Have ye ne're yet thought of that?
You find it scattered round your lair,
It even redeemed your cat
Why then not drink from the lover's cup
And submit to a full embrace?
But I see with pain as you awake
No yearning in your face
I have searched but find no single shred,
Nor even the faintest trace
So with bitter gall I now withdraw
With practiced vampire grace

Father Edward Hemming almost missed the turn onto I-95. It's a mistake to wrestle with your conscience—with the Devil—while driving, he thought. He had long ago forgiven himself for lying to beat a paternity suit back in his undergrad days, and that he'd talked his best friend, Jamie Heller, into covering for him. He'd even forgiven himself for the time he had sex with Flossie Senger during seminary. She had wanted more. They could have made a great couple, but he chose the Church, and eventually she fell for a Navy aviator. She and her pilot were engaged when he botched a carrier landing. She never did get married. Had worked for the university ever since and was the Director of Human Resources now, although still on a medical leave of absence after the attack by Judeland Bundaeker. Flossie told him a long time ago her door was always open for him at any hour, and he knew it still was. "Damn!" That kind of thinking is dangerous.

He'd used that door once, after seminary, to his everlasting regret. Well, semi-regret. He worked hard to regret it, but couldn't make himself totally condemn that weekend, even if God did. As the undergrads say, it was a "peak experience." They were still friends. Good friends. But their past clung to them like fog along a riverbank. The future hovered too, like the first scent of spring. How many times had he dialed her number and then hung up? God must be rather enjoying one of his priests twisting around a dilemma of his own making. It must be harder for him to be a man and a priest than it is for most of the others. Priests joked about it sometimes, but he lived with the fear of falling off the wagon—again.

Flossie had extended her medical leave after she'd recovered from Judeland's attack. *Wonder how Flossie's doing? I've got to call her, maybe take her to lunch.*

His mind wandered, and he pictured how Judeland had hung his secretary, Charlotte Rhodes, on the life-size wooden cross behind the altar in Saint Paul Catholic Church—his church. Charlotte had spent almost a year in McLean Hospital, Harvard's largest psychiatric affiliate. Last week, after her release, she had asked for her old job back. *I'll have to think of some way to put her on the payroll as part of her recovery. My new secretary, Phyllis, is young, energetic, hard-working—she practically runs the place—and not apt to attract a husband any time soon. And I'm not about to let her go; who knows whether Charlotte can keep it together? And who's to blame her if she can't? Hmmm— maybe Flossie could find her something at the university.*

It feels so good to be off on a vacation. Ten days in a cottage at Old Orchard Beach. Haven't had one in way over two years. I can smell the sea, taste the lobster, feel the sand under my feet during my morning jog. Only Phyllis knows how to reach me, and she knows not to try unless it pertains to the Second Coming. I shall go to the movies. Read some books. Have an ice cream cone. Wander around the beach and check out the Bikinis. Uh, no, scratch that last one.

Just ahead he spotted the Maine Welcome Center and pulled in. He fished out his phone and dialed Flossie, suffering a momentary pang that he'd had the number memorized ever since she gave it to him. She answered on the third ring.

"Hi. I owe you a call. Whole bunch of them more like." Ed's chest felt tight, and he reminded himself to breathe. As the silence lengthened he tried to think of something—anything—to say.

"How many do you owe me?" Flossie asked, her voice neutral. "I intend to keep a strict account."

"How about you tell me the number." Ed felt a tremor course through him.

"You can't count that high. And I recall you almost flunked freshman math."

"That was because you sat right in front of me."

"I'd be happy to sit in front of you again. But you've known that since we graduated. Where are you, by the way?" She sounded less neutral.

"A rest stop on Route I-95 about twenty miles from Old Orchard Beach. I've got a cottage rented for ten days. Where are you?"

"Sitting in Logan waiting for a flight to Denver."

"I wish you were waiting for a flight to Old Orchard." He held his breath.

"God, Ed, don't say something like that if you don't mean it."

"The cottage has two bedrooms. If the door locks are broken I'll get them fixed."

"Or not." She laughed. "Text me all your contact data at the beach. Do it the instant you hang up, I don't want you to change your mind. I'll go cancel my flight and book another one."

"Try to get a bus, dear heart. I don't want you to arrive exhausted."

"Trust me, Ed, I won't be too tired. We should stay up all night, uh, talking."

"Sounds super. You go cancel Denver."

I'll be damned, he thought. I forgot to ask her about Charlotte.

೮೩೮೦

Somehow Flossie found the cottage about ten minutes before full dark. She smiled at the porch light, which was swarming with moths. A metaphor for me? she wondered. She slammed the trunk lid after retrieving her suitcase and carryon. Ed opened the door and all but knocked her down grabbing the luggage out of her hands.

"Sorry, Flossie. I wasn't trying to knock you down."

"Pity." Ed's eyebrows rose, and she laughed. "Tell me you didn't trade in your sense of humor for a clerical collar."

"Uh, right. I was worried about you fighting all the traffic."

"Relax. I'm here. Are you ready to show me your cottage, or do we stand out front with all the bugs?"

"Right. Sorry. If you'd open, I'll tote your stuff." The door screeched as Flossie pulled it open, and it slammed behind them.

"How's your supply of WD-40?" she asked.

"I'll get some tomorrow. Promise. You hungry? I am."

"Sure, but could you show me my room first?"

"Oh, sorry."

"Ed, would you give me a big hug, and please stop apologizing?"

He set the two pieces on the frayed hooked rug, took three quick steps into a hug that went from hello, to welcome, to what kept you, to are you sure you want something to eat, to we really need to breathe.

"That was the best hug I've ever had. You need to give me the contact data for the guy that taught you how to—" She silenced him with a kiss, one that started with hello my old friend and progressed to hello my old lover.

"Now you can resume breathing, and show me my bedroom . . . where you think I'm going to sleep." Ed grabbed the two valises and walked to the guest bedroom at the end of the hall.

"This one has the most comfortable bed I think."

Flossie smiled. The living room-dining room was furnished in early attic and late depression. The bed squeaked, the closet had a 25-watt bulb that masked a few spider webs and some dust. As she turned on the shower—the pipes clanked like the engine room of the Titanic after it rammed the iceberg—it produced an anemic stream of beige-colored water. He watched her as she finished a brief inspection of the unkempt cottage.

How could she get to be forty-four (or was it forty-five?) and not have an ounce of fat? He looked down. For an ex-track star he could pinch an inch—maybe more. She had a short hair style; he thought it might be called a page boy, light brown with strands of silver. She was wearing jeans and a tank top with a long turquoise necklace. Her eyes were wide and almond shaped. She had a long but graceful neck. He became aware she was watching him watch her and began to blush.

"Well, did I pass?"

"Flossie, as I recall you've been passing ever since we were undergrads."

"No, my friend, it's you that did the passing."

"You know how to hurt a guy." He grasped both sides of her tank top and raised his eyebrows. Flossie grinned and raised her arms as if to surrender. He pulled it over her head and tossed it on the sofa. He glanced at her arm, the one Judeland had sliced open with a butcher knife. The scar ran the length of her forearm, mostly white and still somewhat raised. She slid the arm behind her.

"Sorry about me being damaged goods. Not much I can do about it."

"Yes. There is." He pulled her arm out and placed his lips on her wrist, slowly kissing all the way to her elbow.

"God, Ed that was so sweet. You can do that again any time."

He straightened. "Well, I've spared no expense to prepare you a gourmet meal. How does pizza, tossed salad, succotash, and your choice of red or white sound?"

She smiled. They looked at each other, not moving, as the sea breeze lifted the curtains. The placid surf hissed and young voices sang and laughed at a distant beach party. Somewhere a dog barked with little enthusiasm. The tang of seaweed and salt air graced the cottage. Early spring flowers in a flower box outside the kitchen window danced in the sea breeze.

"I am so glad you called. I've always wanted us to—"

Placing his fingers on her lips he stilled her voice, then led her over to the sofa. She reached behind her for the hook-and-eye fastening.

Neither heard the camera click from just behind the window box.

CRWD

Morgan plodded toward her classroom. Her heart wasn't in the lessons for today: How to build a new persona. All but the kid, Alton Ribb, had experience fabricating new personalities as they moved on from one lifetime to another. Alton had been an active vampire for about a year, not long enough to experience the desolate sense of loneliness, the absence of love, the constant lack of appetite, going into the hunting, and so many other grinding differences between being human and being a vampire. At first the absence of fear about death was a release. But the stark visage of everlasting existence soon felt like one was trying to swim while wearing a suit of armor. True, some vampires reveled in their special powers, but in time almost all of them became morose. A few, however, were truly creatures of evil, whose perceptions of sanity defined the lowest standard of depravity—and these, like Judeland, were dangerous to man and beast.

She wondered about Suroccan. For so long she thought he was a danger—and maybe he is. But now she was not so sure. Had he really divested himself of all his powers when last they were together? Could she ever trust him? Was the OVFS back in business? And where was Judeland? She felt the fetus squirm. It was as if it knew her thoughts and resented them.

By all the powers of Charna, here I am teaching four vampires how to become human, and I'm slipping back. I'm having the old feelings. My eyesight has become more acute. I find myself looking at animals the way I used to—as potential meals. I *hate* that! It's not happening to Lamar. The other night he pinned me to the bed and, well, it was a bit like rape, but I liked it. How long had it been? I could have flung him off me with ease, though. The old vampire strength has returned. Maybe that's a good thing if I have to go up against Judeland and the OVFS. It's getting harder to focus on love—or even lust—because of the damn fetus, though Lamar knows something's wrong, and he's withdrawing into himself just when I need him to be open and vulnerable—loving.

Gretta, where are you? I need you. Talk to me.

Dead silence.

By the witness of all the gods, I'm losing myself. And Lamar. She felt a kick and scowled, jarred into awareness of her students slouched in their chairs; they'd become used to their instructor zoning out. All but Andre. His look was one of compassion, and he was sitting up, even leaning forward. Was he faking that?

She groaned in relief when the class was over, and the other three students left. Andre stood beside her. "Yes?" Morgan felt exhausted, frustrated, and helpless.

"It is time, Morgan. All but past it, really. Time for you to release the babe back to Charna. You know you are slipping back into vampirism. I can see it. That's because you carry one who will be born an active vampire. If you bear her to full term, you will become her slave. If you think your life before resurrection was desperate, what lies ahead of you will make that seem like child's play. You must surrender the babe before its tentacles become so strong you cannot expel it. And for you to go through resurrection a second time is a gamble. It would require the GenLab to create a new DNA strand for insertion in place of the one that carries the instructions for creating the fetus that you carry. There just isn't time enough to do that. Come with me tonight . . . and finish it."

ଓଞ୍ଚଠ

"Lamar, I won't be home for dinner. Not sure how long I'll be gone. Can't explain it—I'm in a hurry. Just trust me. Will explain when I get home." She heard the line go dead. "Damn you. I could use a little understanding."

Opening her pocketbook, she dropped her cell in it and looked up, her face taught. "Okay, what happens next?"

He led her into the bedroom and told her to undress, lay on the bed under the sheet, and call him. He closed the bedroom door gently on the way out.

"Andre, I'm ready." Am I? she wondered. Oh, Lamar, why aren't you at my side?

He closed his eyes and stood motionless for several minutes, then blew into his hands. A fine silver mist flowed from his hands, slowly settling around Morgan's thighs.

"It's cold," she whimpered.

"You must remain silent. Do not react to what you feel. Keep your eyes closed."

Morgan squeezed her eyes shut, trying not to hear the hollow tones unlike any she had ever heard. She drifted into a reverie broken by a sudden explosive pain in her uterus as the fetus delivered a vicious kick.

Andre began to chant, invoking the presence of the spirit of Charna. The words were unintelligible, derived from a pre-historic language known to only the vampire elders who had become the Charna's grand masters.

Heat began to radiate throughout her lower extremities, and she could feel the fetus begin to writhe.

Andre opened a 19th century black medical bag withdrawing a blunt syringe into which he inserted a vial of clear liquid. "If you would like, I can give you a sedative first so that you are almost unaware of what I'm doing." He raised his eyebrows in question.

Morgan shook her head. "No, I want to be aware of everything."

He nodded and withdrew the sheet. He paused to look at her, then glanced away and strained his throat. "The process is simple, quick, and painless. I will insert this device, and then push the plunger, which will propel the anti-vampirism serum into your uterus. I will put some pillows under your hips to raise you up so the liquid will flow where it's supposed to."

"Side effects?" Morgan eyes bored into Andre's.

"None worthy of mention. If you should have any, please let me know immediately."

"Have you done this before, Andre?" She was unaware she was twisting the sheet.

"Over the centuries, yes. It works to rid a woman of a fetus that was not a vampire as well. Please arch your back while I slide a couple pillows under your hips. There. Are you comfortable?"

"You have to be kidding."

"Ah, well, best we begin and get it over with."

She watched him pick up the syringe and spray it with something from a small bottle.

"What's that?"

"A touch of lubricant, my dear. You can find it in any drug store. Ready?"

She nodded, her face taut. She grunted, her teeth clenched so tight they ached, her breathing fast and shallow.

"Try to relax, Morgan. You will make this procedure more difficult if you stay clenched up."

"Relax? How about we try this on you and see how relaxed you are."

A smile flashed across his face before he could replace it with a look of concern. "This won't take a minute."

Morgan closed her eyes, her breath hissing as she felt the serum invade her body. The fetus began to flail, and Morgan gasped, her eyes widening with fear and pain.

"The fetus will soon be anesthetized. Patience, my dear. Patience."

"You are so full of it," she yelled, twisting her head from side to side. But in another minute she became languid and her breathing slowed and deepened. When the fetus stopped moving Morgan began to float upward. Looking down she saw herself on the table, Andre bending over her, his face a mask of concentration and concern.

Morgan opened her eyes blinking rapidly. She was standing in a shaft of light, the only light in the scriptorium. From a great distance she heard a group of men singing. She could smell ink and parchment, garlic, along with tallow and incense. The monastery! She looked down. Her dress was shabby, brown, with stains under her armpits. Her sandals were worn, held to her feet by grit and sweat. Two arms engulfed her from behind, his fingers pulled her nipples. The kiss on her neck—ah, that was the source of the garlic. Johnathon Coldith, the Jesuit priest she had been laying with the past week. Pox scars made his grin appear a little lopsided, and his breath would repel a charging bull, but by all the gods could he lay a woman in the hay.

It was just days ago that she had killed a man in self-defense—he had a knife to her throat and was raping her. After drinking his blood she had fled. Father Coldith had hidden her from the outraged villagers. Later, he claimed his reward, and she was all too willing to provide it. That was one of the effects of drinking human blood. She couldn't get enough sex, nor could he apparently—the downside of monastery life, she thought. After a fortnight she had to leave. It would not be until World War II that she had sex that good again. But now she was in need. Desperate need. It surged down her legs making them tingle. Her breasts had become super sensitive, nipples taut. But why? She had drunk no blood.

Her eyes fluttered open.

"Are you all right, my dear?" Andre leaned closer to study her face.

Morgan reached for him with both arms and pulled his head onto her breasts. She could feel his lips and tongue and groaned as if in pain. Her hands found his male member; it needed no coaxing to gain its full stature.

"Now, Andre. Now!"

⚇

Morgan's eyes snapped open, her languor vanishing abruptly. She felt betrayed, her anger bordering on rage. What had she done? What had he done? Had he infused her with a strong aphrodisiac or cast a spell on her? He promised he'd never do that. She would have to come to him of her own free will he'd said. *What free will?*

She felt exhausted: mind, body, and soul. The fetus was dormant. She looked up. The water stain on the ceiling grew and then shrank, undulating, its dull brown shape contrasting with the white around it. She felt a strong moral undulation. Wanting Lamar's baby and then willingly rejecting it. Wanting to stay true to him but yielding to an overpowering need for Andre—the man now peering down at her, his forehead creased.

"Are you back," he asked.

"Andre, damn you! You didn't tell me your potion was the world's strongest aphrodisiac." She just couldn't believe he had cast a spell on her. "How could you take me when I was helpless?" Her voice quivered.

"It only happens when the woman is already in love with me whether she realizes it or not. Stop lying to yourself and admit it. There are forces in the cosmos that not even I understand, ones we can't control, ones that defy logic and reason. Becoming mortal didn't erase your passion, my dear. And you will always carry a faint imprint of the vampire."

"Are you saying that us having sex was *my* fault?" Morgan's lower lip quivered.

"Not at all. In no way do I find it to be a fault. It is something we have both been wanting for a long, long time. We shall be good friends. I will make no further intrusions upon you. The fetus will shrink until it becomes a small bit of blood and tissue and will be expelled. Tell Lamar you had a miscarriage. That would be the truth. This miscarriage will in no way interfere with you becoming pregnant again. When the fetus finally dissipates entirely, your residual vampire powers will fade, and you will be as you were right after your resurrection. In the meantime, they are available for you as required. I will reassume my powers to insure your security as well."

Morgan fumbled, then dropped her sweat shirt and stared at her shaking hands. Damn him! I didn't want to make love to Andre—or even have sex. Did I? Why does everything look blurry? Why not? All my life has become a blur. Andre steadied her as he helped her get dressed. Both remained silent.

Coleson Manor breathed out its emptiness in one long, slow, shivering sigh as she closed the front door. She was alone. No Lamar. Robert was obviously asleep. Even the cats did not greet her. No note. She walked into the library and sank into Lamar's desk chair.

How much was she going to tell Lamar? Maybe everything but the part about, about . . . her unfaithfulness. The abortion? No. But she had to tell him *something*. Her concerns were premature, however. Lamar wasn't home. Where could Lamar be?

Oh, no. Not—no, he wouldn't. Couldn't. He was over her. Wasn't he?

〇൫〇

Jennifer had just fallen asleep when her doorbell rang. It was almost eleven thirty. Who the hell. . . ? She reached behind her in the bookcase bed and grabbed her old snub-nosed Colt .38 Detective Special, slipped into her bathrobe and slippers, while the doorbell continued ringing.

"Lamar? Good Lord. It's pouring, and you're soaked. Did the storm knock out your telephone service? Come into the kitchen; I'll switch on the coffee. No umbrella?" Crap, I'm babbling, she thought, as she slipped the revolver into a bathrobe pocket.

After hanging his windbreaker and leather rain hat over a kitchen chair, he sat before a cup of steaming coffee laced with a generous shot of rum. Jennifer sat opposite him. "Speak, oh denizen of the rainy night."

"I shouldn't be here. This doesn't involve you in any way. I seem to have misplaced my wife—or maybe it's the other way around. This isn't making sense; I should go home."

"Lamar, just calm down. Drink some more coffee, take a couple deep breaths, and just start. Sooner or later you'll begin to make sense." She cocked her head and smiled.

Lamar made an inventory of everything in the kitchen except the woman in front of him. "I came home from the fitness center late. Robert had packed it in, and Morgan wasn't there. She called earlier and said she'd be late but didn't say why. She's been gone for hours." He blew on his coffee and hissed in another swallow. "I've called around." He looked down and ran a hand through his hair.

"I couldn't think of anywhere to go or anyone to talk to but you. I know this is a terrible intrusion, but, well, we're friends, right, and I hoped you wouldn't mind, wouldn't mind too much. . . ."

Jennifer reached across and patted his hand. He didn't look at her. "You know, Lamar, if I'm to become your shrink, I'll have to charge you, and double time for visits at midnight. So, do you want to talk or just sit and drink coffee? I could put on some music."

"What I want is a little . . . a little . . . God, I don't know. I can't understand Morgan any more. For the past couple months she's been frigid and won't talk about it. She used to be up for anything any time. Now? Well, it's pretty barren. The last time was almost like rape. It had been so long."

Jennifer poured more coffee in his cup. "Have you guys seen anyone, talked to a professional?"

"No, and that's not likely going to happen either. I've half wondered if she might be seeing some other guy, but I can't imagine who." Oh really? he thought. Stop lying to yourself.

"I doubt it," Jennifer said, "but I can't be all that objective since you and I have a bit of history. You're welcome to have another toddy, take a hot shower, and crash in the guest bedroom. You're always welcome to my humble abode. If there is any way I can help you—both of you—I will."

"I should probably go. Thanks for the coffee and your offer to crash here. Guess I just needed someone to talk to. We could always talk, you and me."

Jennifer smiled. "In the beginning you were a little stiff as I recall. At the office I mean."

"That seems a long time ago." Lamar yawned.

"Look, you are in no shape to drive, especially in this storm. At least take a hot shower before you leave, though I strongly suggest you stay, at least until the storm passes."

⚜

Fatigue, rum, and the hot shower battled against the caffeine. After he wrapped himself in a fresh towel Lamar walked into the guest bedroom, a bit thud-footed. He sat on the edge of the bed frowning at the small lamp on the bedside table. It must have a twenty-five-watt bulb in it, he thought. The door eased open.

"Just came in to say goodnight." She was dressed—if you could call it that—in a sheer thing with poufy ruffles and bows at the shoulders. It hung down just enough, maybe not quite enough. A red sash around her waist held it together. She sat next to him, and he could feel her body heat.

"I like it that you dress up to come and say goodnight," Lamar said. His words sounded careful and slow, and he chuckled. Jennifer crawled up behind him and started massaging his neck and shoulders. "Ummm, I'll give you a week to cut that out." They both laughed.

"I'll take it. Where shall we spend this week? Here or in the Bahamas?"

"Hmmm, I don't even remember where my passport is."

"Well then, looks like we're stuck here. Lay down and Aunt Jennifer will give you a proper backrub." She giggled and pushed him onto the bed face down. "Hold your breath, I have to go get the massage oil"

Aunt Jennifer? She was back in half a minute. She spread out a beach towel on the bed and began applying the oil. "Lord, I think I just died and went to heaven. Who taught you how to massage?"

"If you would hang around a bit more and not bolt out the door at the first guilty thought, you'd learn a lot more about my talents."

"You do know, dear Aunt Jay, that you are working on a card-carrying dork and a married one at that?"

"Better a dork than a Mr. Wall Street stock broker. When I finish your feet we roll you over—no grumbling.

"There. Okay, over you go. Well. It seems my dork spends his spare time at the fitness center. How old did you say you were?"

"Don't ask me questions when you are spreading oil down there." He managed a tight smile. "Ummm, lordy, lordy that feels good. But slow down." He groaned. "Slow . . . down."

"Wow, I can feel your pulse." She squeezed and began counting.

"So what happens when you get to a hundred?" he asked.

"Ask me when I get there."

He pulled her down on top of him and began to massage her back.

"Ummm, how about I give *you* a week to stop that."

"I thought you'd never—" The doorbell jarred them like a bolt of lightning.

"I can't fucking believe it," Jennifer said, grabbing her terrycloth bathrobe. "I'll get rid of whoever that is and be right back. Don't move a muscle." As she padded down the stairs she heard the gusting rain slapping against the windows. She glanced at the illuminated digital clock on the bookcase. Five till one. She opened the door a crack with the safety chain still securing it and squinted.

"What do you want?"

"I want my husband back."

22 - With a Kiss for Andre

When a lovely flame dies . . . smoke gets in your eyes.

From the song, *Smoke Gets in Your Eyes.*
Jerome Kerns

Say something." Morgan's head sagged, and her forehead touched the cold steering wheel, causing a dull pain between her eyebrows. Her hair hung across her face leaking cold rivulets down her neck and under her drenched jacket, sweater, and shirt. Rain rattled against the car in alternating gusts, while smeary light from the nearest streetlamp cast them as two figures in a B-grade horror movie. Her clothes clung to her, and she couldn't stop shaking. Lamar, who had borrowed an umbrella as they dashed from Jennifer's, had stayed somewhat dry as they ran to Morgan's car. But he was shaking too.

"Start the car," his voice rough edged. "You can see your breath in here."

"Tell me why you were with her so late at night." Distant thunder rumbled, and the rain created a constant din.

"That can wait. Start the car and drive. Or I will—you pick."

She started the engine, her face wet from the rain and from her silent tears. The wipers whacked back and forth at top speed, the tires threw off a wake, and the distant continuous thunder and drumming rain filled the rest of the sound space. She glanced at Lamar. He sat, jaws clenched as if rigor mortised. Traffic slithered. Exhausted, she finally turned onto Tory Row and up to his house. Not theirs—*his.*

Morgan followed him as he stomped into the library and yanked the Scotch out of his desk drawer, filled two glasses, and handed one to her. He didn't offer a toast before taking two gulps and coughing. She sipped hers and set it down. She wondered, idly, where the cats were;

they normally were quick to greet them.

Lamar had another swallow and set his glass at the other end of the coffee table. "Okay, Morgan, let's do this chronologically. You go first. Tell me where you were, who you were with, and why I got to sit in here for hours, worried shitless."

His face reminded her of the face of tragedy that typically appeared in the theater opposite the face of comedy. She wanted to be angry, wanted to match his anger, wanted to rise above it to pity him. The almighty Lamar, all of 38 years old, while she had lived 340 years—300 more than he had; she had spent 325 years as a vampire to his one, less a couple months. Poor, dear Lamar. She took a deep breath, then another. Her voice was soft, composed, her eyes dry. She was sick to death of lying. No more of it.

"I had to make a final decision about the fetus. I've told you about my visits to Dr. Wally Gibson. He said there was no hope, that our baby was undoubtedly a vampire, and that the Resurrection process was too new, too untested to try on a baby. He also confirmed what I'd been suspecting for a long time. Vampire regression. The baby is—or was—pulling me back into vampirism, Lamar. My strength has increased substantially, my vision, my interest in animals. I can't stand the idea of reverting. Can't stand the thought of losing you—us. I was nearly out of my mind. Can't you see what I was facing: becoming a vampire again if I birthed this, this thing inside me? I needed an abortion. Wally, a staunch Roman Catholic, would not perform the operation. I couldn't go to any other outside doctor without blowing the cover of Vampire Resurrection. You are well aware of what could happen to the GenLab and Harvard itself if that were to happen."

Lamar's jaw hung open, and he had one hand at the back of his neck, kneading it hard. "Morgan. Morgan? Why didn't you tell me all this before? I . . . I feel like—"

"Hold that thought, husband, there's more. Lots more. I turned to Andre Suroccan, probably the most powerful vampire on the planet. He offered to fix my problem. He—"

"That son-of-a-bitch! All he wants is to jump your bod. He's using you to—"

"No! No he's not. Hear me out. He is a broken man, here (she pointed to her heart) where it counts. He set aside all his powers except the power to rid me of the fetus." As she said that, she doubled over and groaned as the fetus lashed out with every ounce of force it could muster.

"Morgan? What's happening?"

"The anesthesia has worn off. It seems the fetus understands what is going on, what's going to happen. Lamar, why do you think I shut you off from our lovemaking? The fetus, that's why. It was strongly against any man invading its space, but especially you. Don't ask me to explain how I know this, just accept it. Do you think I could enjoy sex with that damn thing kicking and screaming inside me?" Her voice was taut, and she was almost shouting.

"Oh God, oh God," Lamar moaned. "I turned away from you when you needed me most."

"It wasn't your fault. I should have told you everything from the very beginning. When we were first going through resurrection, we were a team. We went through together. But the fetus drove us apart. Neither of us are to blame. Damn," she swore as the tears shimmered in her eyes, and she hugged her belly.

"Andre has administered a potion that will cause the fetus to dissolve in time. But he's not sure how long it will take. In the meantime, I will be half vampire, half human. And you will have to help me get through that. Andre assures me we can have a normal, human child after the remnants of the fetus are expelled. We, we can start over, Lamar. If you want."

"Dear Morgan. Of course I want that." He reached for his glass; she reached for hers. He linked his arm through hers in the European way, and they drank. His head bowed, and he was quiet for a few moments. "Morgan, do you trust Suroccan?"

"Yes."

"What did he ask? What was his 'bride price'?" Lamar's eyes narrowed, and he watched Morgan, unaware of the deep frown that creased his forehead.

"He asked nothing of me. He so desperately wants to experience love that he set aside his powers. I finally saw that he still carried the remnant of a soul, even after well over seven hundred years as a vampire. In fact, it was beginning to grow. It grew a little bit tonight."

"You've been calling him 'Andre.' You've never called him that before. Did he cast any kind of a spell on you? Do you love him?"

"No spell. And yes, in a way I have room in my heart for Andre, just as I have room for Blind Gretta, and Miss Lillian, and Robert. But my dearest Lamar, I waited three centuries to find you. Why do you think I knocked on Jennifer's door tonight? You saw me at my worst, and you saw her at her best. You have known her as a lover, and you have known me that way. So now you must choose."

Lamar was slowly shaking his head. "Dearest Morgan, for all your 340 years you can't read my heart, for if you could you would have never even hinted that there was a choice for me to make. I made it long before we went through resurrection, while we were vampires, before we were married. And I've never wavered. Well, there's the Jennifer thing. I was angry, hurt, confused, and I guess my faith had been shaken. When you knocked on Jennifer's door . . . well, you arrived in the nick of time. Nothing much had happened." *Nothing much?* "But as all the gods are my witness, I haven't the faintest idea how those panties got under the sofa."

They both dissolved into laughter, holding one another and shaking, the irony mixed with love, relief, and wonder. Calvin and Oxnard marched into the library and jumped into their laps.

But there was that one other thing.

She hadn't told him about having sex with Andre. Or was it making love?

23 - The Genetics of Vampirism

A microscopic bit of stuff lies tucked up in its home
A long and stringy ganglia called a human chromosome
It whiles away its time you see, for it has naught else to do
As it waits for the trigger mechanism to summon it anew
That teeny piece of DNA has eternal life to give
But only through Resurrection can the mortal life be lived.

Morgan checked her watch and frowned. It wasn't like Wally to be late. She looked out the dormer window at the ponderous clouds. Another blustery day in Cambridge. Will we ever see the sun? It's April for the gods' sake. She stared at the classroom door as if willing it to open.

Dr. Wallace Gibson tore through the door, unwinding his scarf and pulling off his gloves, dropping them and his hat and overcoat and attaché case on an empty chair. Face red, he blew onto his cupped hands. "Some April, huh?" Morgan's students looked bored except for Andre, who studied the GenLab's Director of Operations as if taking his pulse upon a scale of trust.

"Thank you for fitting us into your busy schedule, Dr. Gibson," Morgan said. "We look forward to your presentation." She smiled. "We have a coffee pot; would you care for a cup?"

"Never turn it down." Pulling his notes out he looked at the wall clock. "And since I'm late—I had an unexpected phone call I couldn't ignore—let's get right to it. As you've read in your syllabus, today we explore the science behind resurrection. I'll try to keep this at layman level. Let's start with a definition from Wikipedia.

"Deoxyribonucleic acid—DNA—is a molecule that carries most of the genetic instructions used in the development, functioning, and reproduction of all known living organisms and many viruses. DNA is the main constituent of chromosomes and is the carrier of genetic information and instructions, often called 'the code.'

"You may dismiss out of hand everything you've read about vampirism starting with Bram Stoker's Dracula, all the Bella Lugosi movies, and the TV serials, as the entire lot is pure bite-'em-on-the-neck Hollywood fiction. A small group of dedicated scientists working in Harvard's genetics laboratory, the GenLab, have discovered a mutant gene that is the real cause of vampirism. Vampirism is a genetic disorder, one caused by what some of our ancestors called 'polluted blood spores.' Any questions thus far?"

Andre raised his chin and one eyebrow. "How do you destroy the mutant gene?"

"Ah. Well, you are leapfrogging over some of my presentation, but yes, I'll address that now." He pulled down his tie, and opened the top shirt button. "We don't destroy anything. We replace the mutant gene with a laboratory-cultured gene, one that will promote the harmonious functioning of all the other instructions carried in the target chromosome with no genetic side effects, assuming our protocol is followed to the letter. And that requires a delicate gene-editing process—in effect genetic surgery—using substance harvested from both live and in the future, synthetically cultured genetic material—think of a cultured pearl—using a complicated surgical gene-editing formula. Any slight variance from our calculations could cause unintended, even catastrophic, consequences."   Dr. Gibson grimaced. "The first resurrection was sabotaged by a rogue lab assistant causing Radical Unwinding. Ghastly! Horrific!" He surveyed the four students. Alton Ribb shifted uncomfortably and looked down. Evelyn Guard chewed her gum harder as she studied her nails, and Benjamin Dizzraeli's eye blink rate speeded up. Suroccan nodded and sat back in his chair, a study in focused attention.

"Would you say that your resurrection process has a parallel with the strange case of *Dr. Jekyll and Mr. Hyde*?" Suroccan asked, his eyes hooded, his lips suggesting a smile.

"You are, as you well know, introducing pure fiction with that question." Gibson frowned.

"Pure fiction, you say, doctor? You might be surprised at how the author developed his story."

"The author, Robert Louis Stephenson, also gave us *Treasure Island* and *Kidnapped,* which hardly qualifies him as an authority of anything beyond the occult. My purpose today is to clarify and enlighten, not muddy the waters with such splendid *fiction* as Stoker and Stephenson have provided."

Suroccan ignored the barb. "Do you have statistics on—"

Morgan interrupted. "I think we should allow Dr. Gibson to continue with his presentation, so please hold your questions until he has finished." Suroccan slouched back in his chair and mumbled something inaudible.

Dr. Gibson flipped forward three pages in his notes, then back one. He pulled out his glasses and put them on, leaning over his notes. Clearing his throat he resumed. "A carrier of the mutant gene for vampirism can go through his complete life cycle without ever becoming symptomatic. Our studies indicate, however, that only the carriers of the mutant vampire gene from every third-generation evolve into active vampirism, unless the offspring is sired by two vampires, in which case the offspring is inevitably fated to become an active vampire at birth. It takes a special circumstance, such as a psychological or a physical shock, to activate the trigger mechanism in those who carry the latent genome, causing the disease to manifest."

"*Disease!*" Suroccan lunged to his feet, almost upsetting his desk chair.

Dr. Gibson stiffened. "And what would you call it, Mr. Suroccan, an *abnormality*?" His voice was laced with sarcasm. The other three students were sitting up, absorbing the moment of drama. The room seemed to quiver in anticipation.

"I do beg your pardon, sir. As Morgan, that is as Ms. Summ—Mrs. Bradford—has stipulated, we should withhold our questions until you are finished." Suroccan sat down, bowed his head, and folded his hands in his lap, willing away the angry tremor that had coursed through him.

Dr. Gibson inhaled deeply and tried to regain his composure but failed. He cleared his throat and resumed. "The task of surgically removing the mutant gene, originally referred to as 'gene splicing,' but more commonly referred to now as 'gene editing,' requires considerable skill. As all of you know—or should—science advances through trial and error. How many people gave their lives in the early days of flight, or even more recently in pursuit of space flight?

"In the interest of time," he glanced at the wall clock and scowled, "I will have to skip the vital subject of the ethics involved in the study and practice of genetic engineering, including such areas as cloning, hybrid food production, synthetic life, and the rest. Perhaps you will invite me back?" Morgan beamed and nodded yes.

"Progress in the field of genetics has already outstripped the need for controlling the process. We have achieved the capacity to eliminate all malaria-carrying mosquito populations, effectively rendering them extinct, and possibly conquering the disease as we have smallpox and polio through the employment of the new 'Gene Drive' protocol." He made quote marks in the air.

"I commend your attention to the ongoing work by the Committee on Gene Drive research in non-human organisms, including viruses. We are very close to a fork in the road for mankind. However, one fork leads to the evolution of vast improvements in eradicating diseases, the other to irreparable harm and unimaginable havoc to the evolution of mankind. Consider the colonization of Africanized bees in North America as an example of what can go wrong.

"My colleague at Harvard's Medical School, Dr. Brandon Chatterton, has recently published an article in the journal *Science* warning of the 'genetic invasion of the planet'—his words—citing the work being done at Berkeley where scientists have created a mutagenic chain reaction in fruit flies. Should they launch their genetic breakthrough, the disease-carrying insects would be eradicated within one year. But at what cost to the world ecology?

"At the very least I hope you have gained some insight into why great care and secrecy is crucial to the success of Project Vampire Resurrection. Thank you for your attention."

"Dr. Gibson, thank you for your comments," Suroccan interjected, "but one last question. What happens to the mutant genes you surgically extract from patients?"

The doctor scowled at Suroccan as he jammed his notes in the attaché case. "Morgan, I'd be happy to come back again and open the floor to more discussion. If any of you wish to consult with me privately, please contact my secretary to set up an appointment."

He hurried out before Morgan could thank him.

Morgan glared at Suroccan.

But her face was etched with pain as she felt a weight pushing from inside.

24 - Evil's Twin: Judeland

*In the extravagance of her evil
she brought shame both on
herself and on all women
who will come after her, even on
one who is virtuous."*

Odyssey, XI, 1. p432

Judeland stood at the door on the third floor of the shabby apartment in a well-worn neighborhood. Apartment 318. The nameplate holder was empty. Half the hallway lights were burned out; two were flickering, creating a hypnotic effect in the heavily shadowed hall. The carpet was ragged and soiled. An ill-fed Siamese cat observed her from the far end, its tail flicking from side to side. Judeland could see a faint light under the door across the hall. The scent of stale pizza, cigarette smoke, and cat urine was cloying. Judeland knocked softly.

She waited, holding her breath. She heard hesitant footsteps inside, but they stopped. The only sound was the distant shrill laughter from young children playing outside at a nearby playground. "Charlotte? Open the door. I need to talk to you."

Silence. Judeland thumped the door again. Nothing. "Charlotte, I have the power to open this door without you unlocking it, so open it, and save yourself some grief." After a long pause Judeland heard a key turn in the door lock and a bolt being drawn back. Carefully she pushed it open. The room was nearly dark. One lamp burned on a side table next to an overstuffed chair, a book was splayed open on the table. The rest of the room was dark; heavy drapes shrouded the sliding glass door that led to a tiny balcony. Judeland pushed the front door open and walked in. The entryway felt like a passage into another dimension to Judeland, and she paused. It could hardly be called an entrance hall. Just inside the door a tiny coat closet was all but hidden. Charlotte stood by her reading chair like the work of a first-year sculptor, exhibiting almost no signs of life, her breath all but stilled.

"Aren't you going to invite me in, Miss Charlotte? I am your guest. We haven't seen one another for over a year. You do remember me I trust, Miss Charlotte. I told you one day I'd come back. Well, this is that one day. Shall we sit down?"

Charlotte exhaled as if she had been holding her breath for a long time. She pointed to the garish sofa, with traces of stuffing coming out of both arm rests. Charlotte shut the door quietly and secured it with the dead bolt. Judeland walked over to the sofa and sat. "How have you been, my dear? I understand you have your old job back at the church. How nice of Father Hemming to have kept your old job open all this time. I trust the doctors at the sanatorium gave you a clean bill of health? Can't imagine Hemming taking you back unless they had. I suspect the Church has him on a tight lead after all the difficulties last year. You do remember our getaway, Miss Charlotte? As I recall it was a bitterly cold evening, and you without a stitch on. Too bad you don't have the face and hair to go with your splendid body. Stand up. Let me look at you. Here, look at me Miss Charlotte—I want to see your eyes. Blue as I recall, yes?"

Charlotte moaned quietly as she looked at Judeland, her eyes dull, and she began to twitch.

"Hmmm. Over dressed for my likes. I'd like to compare your figure with what it was that night we sat on the dead-end street off of Cloverleaf. Undress my dear. Everything."

As if each movement was an agony, Charlotte discarded her sweater, blouse, skirt, and shoes. Judeland nodded for her to continue. Anger and resignation flashed across Charlotte's face as she pulled down her panty hose and kicked them over by her shoes. She stood stock still, looking down.

"Do continue, Miss Charlotte; we don't have all night."

Charlotte reached behind her with trembling hands and unhooked her bra, which she let fall to the floor at her feet. She made a strangled sound and looked away.

"Now that wasn't so hard was it, Miss Charlotte? Do continue. Only one more piece to go."

Charlotte stood motionless for a long moment, her lips tightly pressed, eyes shut, cheeks wet. Finally she hooked her panties on both sides and lowered them to her ankles. She trembled as she stepped out of them.

"Didn't they bother to feed you, Miss Charlotte? You have lost some weight. How much have you lost?"

The young woman stood, mute, goosebumps rising across her trembling flesh.

"I asked you a—"

"Six pounds. I've lost six pounds. More, but I've gained some back these past three months." Her shallow breathing became faster.

"You are one lucky broad. Everyone I know, when they set out to lose weight lose some from their boobs, too. You haven't. Why is that? What's your secret? You might could make some money with it. You know, write a book: How to Lose Weight and Keep Your Boobs. Why, I'd buy the first copy, autographed of course." Judeland cackled and slapped the arm of the sofa. Bits of padding took flight and drifted to the shag rug.

"I don't know." Charlotte's voice was tiny, almost inaudible.

"I have a plan for you. A simple one. Carry it out, and you won't have to worry about me visiting you again." That was a lie of course, and Charlotte shuddered.

"I'm cold. May I please get dressed again?"

"When I've said what I came to say, I don't care what you do. Your part of my plans is simple. I want you to slip this vial of serum into Father Hemming's coffee in the morning. There is nothing lethal in the solution, it will just make him forget a few things." Judeland pulled a small vial out of her purse and laid it on the side table next to her. "This goes into his morning coffee tomorrow. Understood? I don't care how you arrange it—that's for you to figure out. But I want him to drink it early in the morning. I will call you to confirm that he has finished his coffee, the one you will have laced with the contents of that vial. Do you understand? Oh, and keep the empty vial. I want it back."

Charlotte nodded, eyes cast down.

"Good. Do that and wait for my call. I will allow one hour for him to finish the coffee before I call you. As I said, it is not harmful, it's a forgetting potion. Succeed and you will be rid of me. Fail and you will regret it for what's left of your miserable life. Understood?"

Charlotte reached down for her panties.

"Are we clear, Miss Charlotte?"

She nodded and mumbled yes.

"If you ever tell anyone about this I will return . . . and make you pay dearly."

Charlotte nodded again and reached for her bra.

"Just remember, you will be watched. Don't make me come back." Her voice had hardened. She went to the door, opened it, looked back and winked.

Charlotte sagged against the door as she turned the key. Reaching for the door bolt she was jolted.

How had Judeland caused it to close and snap down in the secure position?

25 - Bad Day for a Cardinal, Good Day for a Vampire

From earliest times, when man walked bent
To Earth the Serpent Charna sent
The plague of the vampire to harry your breed
Carried inside of his mating seed.

Federico Cardinal Manlocara, rumored to be appointed the next Dean of the College of Cardinals, straightened the simple gold cross that hung around his thick neck. In his choir dress, with scarlet cassock, white rochet trimmed in lace, and biretta, he looked but did not feel resplendent. The colonel, who as usual was late, caused Manlocara to wonder why the Inquisition was no longer in practice, especially the rack. He knew of several of them that had survived, but all resided in museums. Pity.

"The colonel has arrived, Your Eminence." The badly pocked acolyte hunched rather than bowed.

"Send him in."

Colonel Johann Solento marched in as rigid as a marionette. The hint of a smile ill fit his normally dour countenance. "Good morning, Eminence."

The cardinal studied the colonel as a forensic pathologist might inspect the victim of a gruesome murder. "And what, by all the martyrs in heaven, have you found to be good about this day?"

"Why, to be alive and in good fettle, Cardinal."

"Ah, so you have come to tell me that the two North American vampire heads are in transit? That would go a long way to improving the day," Manlocara snarled. Solento's hinted-at smile vanished. "I gave you thirty days to complete your mission; that was twenty-eight days ago. May I presume you have managed it?" Over the past fifty years Federico

Manlocara had become adept at reading people, especially divining the true from the untrue. He already knew the answer.

"I fear that our special asset has taken it upon himself to create his own timetable for dispatching our targets. He resists taking orders, but I have not lost faith in his ability to conduct the operation leading to a favorable outcome. I fear he has a personal agenda in play that is the root cause of his delay."

"His delay. His root cause. His personal agenda. Tripe! I would have picked a member of the Mafia, but you? You pick a mercurial man without a past who takes our money and dawdles. He doesn't get another euro until there are two new heads in our chamber." Manlocara was practically shouting.

"We pay our North American assets in dollars, Your Eminence."

Manlocara stiffened, took a deep breath, and held it. Veins in his balding head became visible. His eyes were like grappling hooks, and the spare, sallow man in front of him flinched. Cardinal Loconi's final confession—more an expose—nesting in the colonel's attaché case, would soon weigh heavily in the scales of justice . . . and the cardinal would become the colonel's pawn. Or so the colonel hoped. He would likely have to play that card soon. Very soon.

"Get out of my sight. Return with good news. Begin a search to replace that reptile on whom you have squandered our funds. Do those things with haste, and I won't be needing a new commander of the Swiss Guard." Not yet anyway.

"Did I mention finding a curse on the wall above the chest in the chamber?" The colonel smirked.

No hint of fear, Manlocara thought. In fact, he looked dangerous. "What curse did you find?" The cardinal resented having to ask.

"One written in blood. Loconi's blood no doubt. The curse names you."

The cardinal watched the colonel as a stalking cat watches a mouse. Silence. A long silence as the two men, unblinking, looked at each other. Finally the cardinal spoke. "And what did it portend?" Manlocara hated himself for asking the prig who stood before him with all the insolence of the ages clogging his every pore.

The colonel cleared his throat and looked at the copy of the Mona Lisa on Manlocara's bedchamber wall as he searched for the exact words." It was in Latin, of course." Another silence, accented by the ponderous ticking of the 18th century tall case clock across the room.

"And?" The cardinal glowered.

"It read: May the wrath of the vampire follow Manlocara into Perdition."

Manlocara leaned back in his chair and crossed his legs. His eyes widened as if he was kneeling before a guillotine. "What do you make of that curse, Johann?" His voice was soft, his face drawn.

"I, um, fail to see how you would credit my opinion with any worth, Eminence."

Manlocara motioned for the colonel to continue.

"In truth, I hold little regard for the business of formal curses. I doubt there is credible evidence to substantiate any of their effects. Cardinal Loconi was fearful and angry as he faced betrayal and starvation, and he lashed out in the only way available to him. He meant to play on our fears I suspect. What are your feelings about the curse?"

The cardinal's eyes narrowed to slits, and he blurted, "Mind yourself, colonel. You forget your station." In truth, Manlocara was shaken by the news. He had studied the secret histories of the Roman Church, including the use of curses. His scientific mind rejected any reality attached to them. His intuition, however, whispered a different message. Yes, he was aware that curses held only the power given to them by those on the receiving end. People could and did drive themselves crazy, and in a few cases even die. He would never succumb to such behavior. But still. . . .

The threat rested in his gut like a bad cheese. Intuitively, he knew he would need help to purge it. His head sagged.

"Will there be anything else, Your Eminence?"

"Get out. And bring me those heads!"

As Solento closed the door, he permitted a broad and lasting smile to suffuse his sallow face. If the cardinal was concerned, it would weigh little in the scales when measured against the late Cardinal Loconi's final confession. He would be patient. Timing, ever timing.

∞

Andre Suroccan sat in his apartment—the one Morgan owned before she moved in with Lamar—and brooded. On impulse he walked to the battered bookshelf, half empty, that held the few volumes he'd managed to retain over the centuries. Pathetic. Still, he pulled out the worn, author-signed copy of Bram Stoker's Dracula and flipped to the second page. Above the author's signature was the date: 8th November 1897. How many times had he read it? No idea. But each time he'd discovered a previously overlooked nuance, some facet of Count Dracula he hadn't recognized. How he wished Bram were here today to write a novel about "Count Suroccan."

It galled him to realize he felt lonesome. He thought of Lydia. When was that? he wondered. Hmmm. Early 15th century. Was it 1402? Yes, that was it. He lapsed into a reverie. The autographed volume slid to the floor, and he closed his eyes.

∽∝∾

Suroccan's horse needed shoeing. While that was being attended by the village farrier he found an ale house—The Lazy Swann—and ordered a tankard of ale and the daily fare: pork stew and brown bread. Settled in a corner booth, he enjoyed the warmth from the fire and picked at his stew. He had to eat lest he lapse into the deep hunger that led to the hunting. Over the centuries he had become masterful at hunting small game and domesticated animals, but that had become demeaning as well as boring. And it sickened him on those few occasions when a human got in his way and became the hunted. On two occasions he'd had to flee an outraged mob. He couldn't blame them, especially the one time the human happened to be a child. That had awakened a vein of remorse which never healed. Was remorse a sign that his DNA was evolving, or was it an indication that his powers were weakening? he wondered.

Long ago Suroccan had asked himself if his powers were the impediment that kept him from becoming a mortal human. It had taken almost a century to perfect the process of shedding his powers, making himself vulnerable for brief moments before reacquiring them. He had tasted fear during those moments, becoming almost frantic to regain them. But he never tasted love or compassion during the brief interludes when he'd laid them aside. He longed to find the woman who would break through his armor, one who would love him and want him despite his vampire nature.

He thought bitterly of how his quest had become so like that of the Holy Grail . . . and no more productive. He hadn't found it after over half a millennium of searching, although he'd played the voyeur countless times, watching love unfold on the stage and in real life. Charna had "blessed" his brood with endless lust, and many were the men who would trade their fortunes for the sexual prowess of a vampire, but meaningless sex over the centuries had diminished him. Driven by ceaseless urges, he no longer took joy or pride in his sexual accomplishments. At times having sex didn't measure up to the satisfaction derived from a long-delayed piss.

Love wasn't the only emotion denied Clan Vampire. The fear of death, which shaped the lives of all mortal men, was all but absent from his kind. Oh, there was a way to kill a vampire: the aspen stake and decapitation. But very few had been dispatched that way.

Andre was weary. How had he found himself in such a miserable village? The houses were held together by marsh grass and cow dung, and the roads—cattle paths mostly—were frozen ruts. The food tasted like old straw, and the ale was harsh. The locals were hostile as well. Burning peat provided an acrid smell, and the blowing cold mist ate into one's bones. Suroccan was jerked out of his reverie.

"Aleman! Your best table, your best wine, and food fit for a Baroness." A red-faced coachman, dressed in a slightly frayed burnt-orange liveryman's waistcoat, long leather trencher, black boots, top hat and gray scarf yelled as he burst into The Lazy Swann. He held the weathered door open and gestured, "M' Lady."

Andre was stunned. She stood at the threshold, surveying the three villagers hunched over their tankards, her eyes lingering on Andre. "I will sit over there, by the fire." She pointed to a table nearest him.

Andre's pulse began to quicken as he looked at the baroness.

Her eyes were luminescent green with hints of gold. While her hair was quite fair, her eyebrows were coal black. Her face was patrician: pale marble, yet impish. A single pox scar on her forehead was accented with Rossetto, a red sandalwood rouge, which also adorned her cheeks and lips. She wore white leather gloves and matching boots. Her greatcoat did not disguise her impossibly small waist, which gave a certain extra fancy to her demure bodice. Andre breathed deeply of her perfume. She smiled and raised her eyebrows, as if asking his opinion of it. He smiled back and dropped his eyes as a commoner should.

Her wine arrived. She frowned but nodded her assent. The meal that followed included pheasant, boiled potatoes, pickled beets, and white bread soaked in oil and white wine. She began to eat as if she'd been starved the past three days. After a few bites she stopped and looked at Andre. "Won't you join me? I can't possibly finish this, and your meal certainly doesn't look very appetizing. Aleman, another red wine for my dining companion."

Again Andre was stunned. He felt as if his sensory perceptions had been torched. He stood, no more than an automaton, and walked to her table. He bowed, but his eyes never left hers. "You are kind and generous to a fault, Baroness. I could be a common highwayman."

She snorted. "You think I have so little wit, then?"

"What, uh, no, I was only concerned for your safety."

Lydia smiled as her gaze swept the three swarthy men wearing burnt-orange livery who were watching them. "You need not fear for that, sir.

Have you a name?"

"I am called Andre Suroccan. At your service."

"And what service do you perceive I am in want of, Sir Andre?" Her eyes breached every part of him, as a sailor might take the measure of a tavern wench.

"A bit of companionship, mayhap? You did call upon me to attend you."

"And do you find it quite convenient to join me for some spirits and tavern fare?"

"My life was altogether droll until the moment you entered, Baroness."

"Oh ho. You have spent time in the great halls of the royals I take it. Your speech gives you away. Now, tell me what you do to earn your"—she paused to glance at his food and ale left on the other table—"bread and ale?"

"I have served as a tutor, M' Lady."

She studied him and frowned. "While your tongue is brushed with silver, it hangs in chains. Must I find the key that unlocks your tongue such that we may converse as tavern dinner companions do on a cold winter's night?"

"I am not trying to be devious, but you will grant me a measure of caution. I've yet to discover what there could be about me that attracts your attention." Andre nodded at the aleman who set a tavern glass of red wine in front of him. Andre nodded, his smile tight, as a second dinner was placed in front of him.

"So. Where are you bound Andre Suroccan?" She wiped the edges of her lips, as her eyes bored into him.

"Glenwash, Baroness."

"Never heard of it. Is it nearby?"

No, and you never will hear of it as I just made it up, Andre thought. "Not all that far along the post road. Little more than a watering hole for horses."

"Surely you are not walking? I saw no horse tied out front."

"Ah. Well, you see, Posy is at the farrier being reshod."

"Posy!" Lydia shouted, her laugh filling the room. Your horse is named—" She dissolved in laughter. "How come you to call your horse by that name?" She reached for her wine.

"Tis what she were called when I purchased her. She's steady enough." The red wine seemed to taste better.

"So. When will your gallant steed be ready?"

"Come dark I were told, but farriers will always tell you what you want to hear."

"Well, it's too late to make any more leagues this day. I fear we are both stuck in this muck hole. Where would you recommend we seek accommodations?"

"Uh, in truth I hadn't turned my mind to that issue. And having never quartered here I am, alas, unable to provide a suitable answer."

"Well, go and ask the aleman where the best rooms are to be found, and come tell me."

Andre stood, somewhat stiffly, bowed, and headed for the bar. He had forgotten to inscribe a smile on his face.

"The Post House seems to offer the best accommodations, but I doubt if they will suit you, Baroness." Andre looked back at the aleman.

"Where do you intend to stay, kind sir?"

Andre looked down, and his face flushed. His jaws clamped shut, lips pursed at her reference to his apparent financial distress. "I was considering asking the farrier for a place in his hay loft, Madame." His words were clipped, his voice low.

"You may refer to me as Baroness, but I must apologize. Here we were having a delightful dinner, although you seem to be pushing your food around your plate, and I have embarrassed you, which surely wasn't my intent." She reached over and placed her hand over his. The heat radiating from her hand startled Andre, sending an electrical charge through his body . . . and apparently into Lydia, who gasped.

Yanking her hand back she drew a scented cloth from her bosom and inhaled. "You have an extraordinary effect—"

"Do forgive me, Baroness. I suffer from a peculiar chemical imbalance that has plagued me since I were a wee lad. I should have warned, uh, that is I wasn't expecting you to, ummm—"

"Does that happen to everyone who touches you?"

"No, fortunately. It only happens when I am startled." Andre took a bite of his dinner unaware that he frowned as he forced himself to swallow.

"Then I shall warn you next time I plan to touch you."

"That you plan to touch me again warms my heart, Baroness. Being forewarned I shall attempt to tamp down my, uh, unfortunate condition."

The man doth steal my breath away like no other ever, she thought. I feel so open and safe with him, but for all I really know he could be a spy commissioned by My Lord, Baron Rothmell. Yet he be the first man I have yearned to wake up next to. Well, maybe the second. Can these strange feelings be love? Surely not. Lust mayhap? No. Maybe. I've heard the chamber maids talk about love at first sight but put no stock in such tales. And yet . . . and yet. . . .

"Pray don't tamp it down too far, Master Suroccan. I would like you to call me Lydia when we are beyond the hearing of others." Her eyes fairly danced with his.

"As you wish. And if it suits you, please call me Andre."

"We shall share some more of this vapid wine and then repair to the most convenient rooms this village can provide. I shall send my coachman to secure them. I can't have you freezing in a hayloft after such a stimulating—dare I say 'shocking'?—evening." She watched the aleman for a moment as he lit more lanterns, then signaled her coachman and gave him instructions about bedding the coach and horses and securing two rooms in the Post House, then returning to escort her and her new acquaintance.

Both smiled as they clinked their glasses and quaffed the estate claret, though it had little to recommend the title.

☾☽

Andre lay on an uncomfortable horse hair bed with a quilt pulled over him. He had carefully folded his shirt, breeks, hose, cloak, and muffler placing them on the trunk at the foot of the bed. His gloves and hat were placed next to the pile, his boots beside the trunk.

Quivering with fear and anticipation, he had shed more than just his clothing. He had laid aside his powers. He was, at that moment, a doubly naked vampire. The barest hint of light from a sickle moon, intermittently shaded by rushing clouds, lent the small room a ghostly ambiance. Was he supposed to go to her? No, it had to be her choice. He would wait. And shiver. He considered lighting the single candle on the bed stand, but rejected the idea. Time crawled like leeches in a swamp. Would she come?

Watching the door he saw the faint candle light on the floor beneath it and heard a slight scratching noise. He rose and padded across the cold floor, slid the latch back, and pulled the door open.

Her hair hung loosely around her shoulders, and the top three buttons of her shift were open. She smiled and glided past him, lighting his candle and then placing hers on the corner of the chest, well away from his clothes. "Dear Andre. You are shivering. Are you cold? Shall we make our way under your quilt and create enough heat to allay your condition?" Her short laugh sounded like a wind chime, an echo of the wind that moaned around the dormer window.

Andre reached for her pulling her into a tight embrace. Their desire was fed by the timeless need for intimacy and love. A sense of joy and anticipation began to well up in him, unlike any feelings he'd ever experienced. He shivered but not from the cold.

Their first kiss was that of a butterfly landing on a blossom. Then next the pollination of tongues, as his hands released the red sash that secured her shift. In turn, she tugged on his loin cloth and made a cooing sound as she discovered that he was ready. She had no idea how ready he was, after centuries of searching. It took but a moment to arrange the quilt over them. Neither seemed to need any preliminaries, and they both groaned at the joining.

Andre's mind floated on a vapor of bliss, his last cogent thought being: This is truly worth dying for!

ॐ

Baron Rothmell and his companions dismounted with many a stifled groan. They had been riding since first light. Pray God, they all hoped, that the Baroness would be found in this village. The prospects of extending their night ride on no sleep and almost no rations were bleak in the extreme. They rousted out the stable boy and discovered Lydia's coach and horses. For a silver penny, the boy informed the Baron that his wife had taken rooms at the Post House.

Although Andre's vampire powers had been cast aside, his keen senses had not, and he became aware, notwithstanding the wonders of overwhelming bliss, of footsteps, curses, grunts, and pounding from just below his dormer. Alarmed, he leaped from the bed. "Quick! Back to your room. Take your shift and candle. Go! Now!" Andre whispered.

"If we are caught out, do not raise a hand to defend me for that would make it worse for us both," Lydia said before racing back to her room. Andre heard her door close quietly. With haste born of fear, he went into his meditative state. But too much fear and haste pushed his powers out of reach. Grabbing his clothes, he dashed down the hall and found a ladder leading up to a storage loft. Climbing it, he pulled the ladder up, and dropped into place the loft's crude planks that served to cover its entrance. He heard loud arguments below and realized he was likely but a few minutes from discovery. Thunderous footsteps echoed through the Post House. Doors were forced open provoking loud lamentations from surprised boarders.

Andre called on the Serpent of Charna as he had never done before and was blessed. He could feel the presence of his powers wrap around him as he hastily dressed in the cold, musty, and dark storage loft. He would use his powers of invisibility. Or try to. Again, calling on the benefice of Charna, he invoked the sacred vampire magic. He looked at his hands and saw them become pale, diaphanous appendages . . . then nothing.

The bellowing of the irate husband no doubt roused half the population of the village. All of those who had taken rooms in the Post House were more than alarmed. Lydia was marched to her coach, flanked by six of the baron's trusted lancers, pausing only long enough to buy some bread and wine from the distraught owner of the Lazy Swann. The Baron would teach the Baroness never to leave Castle Cambridgeshire without his permission. There were brigands along the road, and men with evil intent frequented the taverns and post houses. But had she left him for an assignation? The four men who had helped her would be hanged in the bailey come daylight the following day. The long journey back would give him ample opportunity to decide Lydia's fate. His smile was venomous.

Andre was destitute. To have found the one he was searching for over centuries, losing himself in the ecstasy of the heart, and then to have her torn from his grasp, thrust him into despair and depression, and he lost all connection with reality. Could he find her again?

He'd never felt so drained, never felt as if his powers lay in shards around his feet. He lacked the strength and the will to pursue her. His brush with love had been a revelation, but he was mired in quicksand as Lydia's husband and lancers rode off with her. Why was he suddenly so weak? He pondered long and deeply, unaware that the sun had made its dull pewter appearance.

☙❧

Lydia's eyes shimmered with tears she fought desperately not to shed. Her ankle ached where the metal clamp had been hammered around it. She was chained to an outsized eye bolt sunk into one wall of the highest room in the castle's keep, its central tower. As she looked around in the dull light that seeped in from two small arrow loops, she decided they'd confined her in a storage bin. Two long bundles were marked "Arrows." Coils of rope lay on the floor in one corner. Two boxes were labeled "Candles." She couldn't read the words on several stacks of boxes close to the door.

Sitting on a crude wooden bench, trembling, for the first time in her life she had been rough handled by the castle guards—the same ones who had been so solicitous until the baron had found her. She had listened to them on the ride back to Cambridgeshire Castle but heard no mention of a man taken at the Post House. Andre, dear Andre. Please make good your escape, my dear one. Come back with a legion and rescue me.

Tired, hungry, dirty, thirsty, and frightened. Did her husband intend to scare her? Well, it was working. If they had found Andre her fate would have been sealed. And even if Baron Rothmell was a harsh and vindictive man, he wouldn't condemn her to the gallows. Would he? She had submitted to him whenever he demanded, though she was without child these past three years, and he held her to account for that. But no few women had the devil's own time getting pregnant. According to chatter amongst the ladies in waiting, some barren women had secretly taken lovers and were convinced their resulting pregnancies were a direct result. Lydia wondered if there might be any chance she now carried Andre's bairn. That would be a mercy. Or maybe not?

She spotted a pan of water with bits of straw floating in it. She blew on the surface to clear a spot from which she could drink. Gagging, she was convinced a mouse must have drowned in it. Across the room lay a moth-eaten horse blanket, but the chain was too short to allow her to reach it.

Thank God and all the prophets Andre couldn't see her now. Her hair was a tangle, and her nails dark with the grime of traveling. And she smelled like overripe fruit. But she pined for him. Oh what heart-pounding love they had shared. For so many years she had protected the battlements of her loins with tenacity. No one had breached them before she married the baron. And then Andre. She had no words to describe how that had happened. But it had. Oh yes, and he felt the same. She could tell, she could feel it in her soul.

Lydia groaned and lay down on the hardwood floor, making a pillow of sorts out of her underskirt. Though riven with fear, suffering painful discomforts, and very hungry, she fell asleep, unmindful of the horrors that the dawn would bring.

CRO

Andre slumped against the cold stone fence that surrounded the chapel tucked up under the south wing of Castle Cambridgeshire. He was dressed as a woodsman and held two leather straps filled with firewood. Guards at the Barbican had merely glanced at him as they rolled the dice at their game of Hazard. He found the iron gate to the cemetery surrounding the chapel. Unlocked and rusty, it squealed as if being tortured when he pushed it. For a few silver denarii the aleman at the Dragon and Dove told him of Lydia's fate and spat. "The baron done her to death, probably these three days past." For two more silver coins the aleman added, "She lies in an unmarked sarcophagus above-ground in the chapel cemetery. Put her there, unshriven, in the dark of night, they did." He spat again.

Walking through the headstones, some cracked, others toppled over, most covered with moss and lichen, Andre finally came to one that caused him to stop in mid-stride and gasp. A single yellow rose in full bloom graced the rough granite lid. He listened, his face composed. Cold. Dangerous. Naught made a sound but the voice of the wind rattling the debris that had collected in the unkempt cemetery. She lay beneath the stone. Cold. Lifeless. He reached for the rose. It seemed to grow warm in his hand. Streaks of sunlight jabbed through the leaden sky as if searching for the newest member of Clan Death. The keening animal sound he made was that of a wolf come upon the stiff carcass of its mate. He slipped the rose beneath his cloak and under his shirt. It felt warm against his chest, smelled like her hair, and seemed to pulse in rhythm with his heart.

"I will find you again, dear Lydia. And we will dance among the white glimmerings of the firmament. And one day I shall affix this rose in your hair." He gently touched it and inhaled it. Her.

◯◯◯

He would die, the baron. A slow sickness that would tear apart his mind as well as his wretched body, casting out his soul to wander the stones in search of all those he'd sent to an early grave. Again Andre touched the stone that housed his Lydia and began invoking the Serpent of Charna. He had done the Invocation of Slow Death twice before, but this time he would revel in the acid joy of revenge.

Sitting before a roaring fire in the great hall, Baron Rothmell began to cough; his throat felt raw. "God-rotted weather," he muttered, reaching for his wine.

◯◯◯

The antique mantle clock chimed seven times, and Andre opened his eyes. He blinked at the light which sliced through the Venetian blinds. His reverie had lasted the night. How could that be? he wondered. Inhaling deeply, he sighed. How beautiful Lydia had been. But it was Morgan's scent that clung to her old apartment. In Morgan he had found another Lydia, and she had become the center of his universe. He would go find her. Claim her. No other option would end his pain, his needs, heal the vampirism that enslaved him every moment. He stood, his face a mask of agony.

"Morgan! Where are you?"

As if in answer the room stilled. He heard a faint crackling sound much like static from an old crystal radio. And a voice struggling to pierce the static. He lurched to his feet, senses keening.

> *It be your time Master Vompre.*
> "You use my original name. Why?"
> *You are known among the living, the non-living, and the living dead.*
> "What have you come to tell me?" *He clenched with such tension that it felt as if he were being stretched on the rack.*
> *You must act now. The time for hiding is over.*
> "But what—?"
> *Find her before it is too late. Go quickly. The sand fair races through her glass.*
> "Who are you?"
> *I am your sand timer. . . .*

Andre felt a stab of fear unlike any he'd ever experienced. But it was not for himself.

26 - All Roads Lead to the Church of St. Paul

Number Three—lit a Turkish Fatima from the burning stub of the previous one. The ash tray was an inverted turtle shell that had been painted white but had turned various shades of gray from long use. Other ash trays were fashioned from the heads of small animals. The owner of *Pirates Rock* was as strange as his collection of ash trays. He grimaced. The beer wasn't very cold. Damn refrigeration must be on the blink again. Jake had been morose since Monty had bought the farm—an old GI phrase for getting oneself killed. NT wondered again if the two were gay, not that it mattered. Monty was the smarter one. Too bad Jake hadn't bought the farm instead.

NT chugged three swallows of his tepid beer and pulled more smoke into his lungs. He and the idiot Monty had been told to wait at the bar while Judeland and Helen filmed the corpse of JJ, as Judeland performed obscenities. He lit another Turkish Fatima, inhaling deeply. He'd collect his pay for the past month and slip out the back, Jack.

The three overhead fans did little more than redistribute the smoke. A burst of laughter from the other end of the bar drew NT's attention. A blonde woman in her late twenties, wearing a red mini-skirt and tight, white tank top, was entertaining two guys sitting on either side admiring the cleavage. The sizzle of burgers on a grill and the hissing of a neon beer sign added to the jumble of sound, and the smoke, stale beer, and Pine Sol made NT scrunch his nose. Thank god the ancient juke box was broken. Shit. All we need is Elvis doing Hound Dog.

Where the hell Jude found a taxidermist willing to stuff a dead body he couldn't imagine. Helen was taking photos of Jude and JJ screwing. Those photos would be slipped to Dr. Heller as part of her plan to drive him crazy. He flicked ashes into the turtle and wiped his eyes with the heel of his hand. He would have to get away from Judeland and the other idiots before they drove him crazy. He took another deep drag on his cigarette.

NT glanced over the bar at the Bud Lite neon sign. Two letters were burned out and one was fizzing and blinking. Judeland couldn't have picked a grungier dive. Helen opened the back-room door and motion the two men to return. With straw for hair, a serious limp, and gin for breakfast, she was the poster child for derelicts. NT groaned. Jake, head down, plodded behind him.

"Hey, guys. You wanna settle up your bar tab?"

໐ຽ໐

Morgan pulled the drapes back so she could see better, not that there was much to see. Gloomy. A steady cold drizzle spattered the library window and ran in rivulets down Coleson Manor's stone siding. Water in the culvert moved with languid grace, but soon would race, gurgling and splashing, out to the street. Robert had lit the fire, but it only provided a little life to the dark library. Calvin placed his front paws on the sill and helped Morgan watch the soggy garden. Oxnard sat on the piano bench doing his housecleaning.

Morgan had been trying all morning to distract herself from a sense that something was off, something needed her attention. But what? She had experienced nausea for three mornings in a row, which made no sense. She thought about a glass of wine, but it was way too early. Her intuition had dulled of late. Suroccan had given her the potion two weeks ago. While she hadn't detected any movement, her breasts had become perpetually sensitive. Last night she and Lamar made love, but that had seemed off, too. He planned to work late at the GenLab. She'd sent him to work saying she felt a bit drained, a bit out of sorts, and would take the day off. Now she wished she'd gone in with him. Maybe after lunch she would put in a half day. Morgan flopped on the sofa and looked at the cats. Had Suroccan restored eternal life to Calvin? Calvin looked and acted much better now. They would have to wait and see if it worked on Oxnard as well.

Her eyes felt heavy. Had they closed? She heard a sound. No, it was a tone, one becoming more intense as she focused on it. All other sensation receded into the stillness.

It be time for you, time to—

"Gretta?Gretta! I lost you. Please try harder."

He needs you. He be in peril.
"Who needs me? I can barely hear you. You must tell me—"
The preacher man. He be needin'... your—
"What? What?I'm having a hard time—"
Father Hemmm— Go to— to hmmm. Naoh.

CR80

Suroccan paced. It was not like him to pace. Where was his vaunted self-control? He reached down and grabbed a pillow off the sofa. How many times had she slept on it? he wondered. And where was she? He'd asked her to call. She hadn't. He had forced himself to stay away for nearly two weeks. He could tell it was costing him, but If he let go of his steely control, he would go into the hunting, something he rarely did any more. That would be a big step backward, especially if he killed a human. How many years since his last kill? Nine? Ten? He felt the familiar pulsing and groaned, remembering his worst kill.

He'd met Dr. Sir Archibald E. Garrod, KCMG, FRS, in Paris in 1932 at a symposium on infectious diseases. At that time Andre was known as Dr. Jene Claude Vompre. Garrod, one of two keynote speakers, a prominent physician at St. Bartholomew's Hospital in London, launched his theory of "Metabolic Disruption" based on genetic abnormalities—and it was a medical bombshell. After his death in 1936 he was recognized by western medical science as the "Father of Chemical Genetics."

While Garrod was studying DNA Andre had achieved an entirely secret but nonetheless stunning breakthrough in his studies of the "Morbid Blood Spore" that causes vampirism. Of even more profound impact, he'd distilled a substance—two substances actually—that could revolutionize life on this earth. The one he called "Dr. Jekyll" could attack the morbid blood spore, whether latent or active, that controlled vampirism. In other words, it could prevent, reverse, and eliminate the dread condition. The other solution, "Mr. Hyde," was the exact opposite when ingested; it would implant the genetic morbid blood spore, causing the recipient to evolve into active vampirism. Of course he couldn't broach his findings without risking exposure. His work was based on developing a correct medical hypothesis and proving it based on experimentation with rats and other small animals. But the real proof, Vompre knew, would be derived from human experimentation.

At first Garrod was reluctant to grant Andre an audience, but by being persistent Andre finally got his meeting. Garrod was entranced. Both

agreed that Andre's course of scientific enquiry would ultimately have
to be subjected to human trials, but the risks were great. Mishandled,
the experimentation could prove disastrous. In a worst-case scenario
a vampire nation could evolve, one which would likely enslave all
mortals. They agreed to form a partnership, with Garrod as the senior
and Vompre as the silent partner. Vompre never informed Garrod that
he—Vompre—was an active vampire.

A year of fruitful theorizing and laboratory testing on animals
reconfirmed Vompre's hypothesis. Their first disagreement, which led to
an abject falling out, burst forth when Vompre proposed to experiment
on himself. Garrod was adamantly opposed.

On a cold winter night in late 1935 Vompre injected himself with
four cc's of the Dr. Jekyll potion. It soon felt like he had removed a
suit of armor, a male chastity belt, and a pair of horse blinders. He
felt giddy, and his emotions exploded like a sun spot arcing into space.
Desperately needing to express his overpowering sense of joy, he walked
to the Crown and Barley, a pub not far from his lodgings, where he
bought several rounds for all his "new friends." Happy, but in his cups,
he left the pub, unaware that several of his new friends followed him.
They set upon and dragged him into Brompton Cemetery, administered
a beating, stole his wallet, tweed jacket, top coat, gloves, hat, and gold
pocket watch that had been his father's. He was discovered the following
morning in shock, soaked, with broken ribs, eyes swollen shut, a broken
nose, missing tooth, and an extremely painful cough that progressed
into pneumonia.

He awoke at St. Bartholomew's Hospital with a most concerned Dr.
Garrod listening to his heart. Six weeks later he was released. All his lab
animals had perished. Filled with anger and hate—and yes, fear—in
haste he administered the antidote to mortal humanity, emerging once
again as a vampire—soon to take on the persona of Andre Suroccan. It
took less than twenty-four hours for him to lapse into the hunting. One
by one his "pub friends" suffered a grisly fate.

This could all be laid directly at the feet of Garrod, Andre reasoned.
Had Garrod not ended our partnership he would not have suffered
this fate. I called him, told him we had to meet, that he had to see
my latest discoveries. Reluctantly he agreed to visit my lab. That night,
overwhelmed by the urge to hunt—and the need for human blood—
he attacked Garrod, rendering him unconscious. He drank Garrod's
blood—just enough to slake his ravenous need but not kill him. With
the help of a cabbie, who was quite willing to accept a twenty pound
note for his services, returned Garrod to his home.

Apparently his heart stopped sometime after they had left him.

His obit appeared in the Times two days later. It contained a coroner's curious finding: "Dr. Garrod was apparently suffering from acute anemia, which fatally weakened his heart." No mention of a puncture wound, nor any other abnormalities. Strange. Maybe the authorities didn't want to unleash another vampire terror among the people. Earlier vampire scares had led to the murder of innocent citizens.

Garrod's death left Andre wretched and deeply depressed. He had killed his only real friend. Finally, he took refuge in his vampirism, returning into the one who observed feelings but personally experienced almost none.

He was, once again, Dr. Jene Claude Vompre, cum Andre Suroccan— vampire!

CR80

Suroccan's throat constricted, and his chest felt tight. The mantle clock chimed, almost as if welcoming Andre back to the apartment that had so recently been Morgan's.

Slowing his breathing he closed his eyes and chanted his mantra:

"Ghost of Charna speak to me, tell me what will set me free. Send me out to find my way. Grant my freedom this very day."

He could feel the winds of Charna stir, lifting him on the black wings of fate. The mists of time thinned, opened, beckoned.

Ye be needed now, Master Andre.

"Who speaks to me from the other side? Were you the woman, Blind Gretta?"

Nay. She asked me to speak for her. She can nay longer match your vibrations. In my last life I were Marta Sorrel, mother to the one you call Morgan Summers. I were put to death as a witch in Old Salem Village back in '92. 1692.

"I was there! You were pressed like Giles Corey. The rest were all hung."

Ye have much to atone for Master Andre.

"That may be as you say, old one, but I never gave false witness during the madness in Old Salem. Why do you come through to me now?"

Morgan and others she cares for be in mortal danger. If the shades that draw near are not altered, the long reach of evil will suffuse the innocent as they did in Old Salem. Save them and the gods may yet favor you with redemption.

"Where should I—"

To the Church of Saint Paul—and make all haste. May the powers you were cursed with become a blessing on this frightful day.

"What kind of peril?" Suroccan felt the vibrations shift. The opening in the mist closed, becoming a shroud, allowing no further sound from the other side.

He shuddered and reached for his clerical collar, his broad-brimmed hat, and his cloak. He muttered a prayer to Charna for help as the apartment door swung open with a wave of his hand, and he walked to the elevator, whose doors opened as he approached them. Old Oxidation, Morgan's former car, sat unlocked, lights on, engine purring. He clashed the gears as he made a jackrabbit start into traffic. Why did anyone still buy cars with a stick shift? he wondered.

೫೮೦

"Are you okay?" Ed Hemming asked, as Charlotte walked into his office carrying two cups of coffee. She was shaking enough to rattle the cups in their saucers. Father Hemming frowned and looked at her searchingly.

"Sorry, Father. I have insomnia. When I don't sleep, I drink too much coffee, and it kind of mangles my nerves." She set the two coffees on the corner of his desk and stood, staring at them as if they might turn into a nest of writhing serpents.

Mangles? "Maybe you should switch to decaf," Father Hemming said as he reached for one of the cups.

Charlotte lunged for the cup and yanked it out of his hand. She drank half the cup, splashing some on her white blouse and matching sweater. She sucked in a mouth full of air, waving a hand at her tongue.

"Charlotte! Are you all right?" He reached for his handkerchief and began dabbing at the stains. She backed away and gulped the rest of the coffee.

"Sorry. I just—I'm a bit rattled this morning. Don't know what's come over me. But I'll be okay. Just my nervies. No sleep. Doctors say I'm doing flashbacks to, you know, when that dreadful woman tied me up on the cross. They say they'll go away, and I'm sure they will, it's just going to take time. I have an appointment next week, you see, and, uh." Her voice dwindled.

Nervies? Jubal? Father Hemming enveloped her in a hug. "Stop talking and take three deep breaths for me." Charlotte took the breaths and tried to smile. It appeared to be a bit lopsided. She trembled and stepped back.

"I, uh, best I guess back to work. Won't get done without I doing it, don't you see." She turned and lurched to the office door. It was closed, which seemed to present a puzzle to her as she fumbled with the door knob.

"Try turning it the other way." Ed shook his head and sighed.

"Oh, yes. Quite. It's my nervies. My nervies, you see." She nodded emphatically and opened the door, took a deep breath, and walked into the door jamb. She stumbled through, leaving his door open.

Poor woman. She's falling apart. I should call her doctor and discuss this. I've never heard her babble before, nor walk out and leave my door open. And why did she grab my cup of coffee? He pulled his ancient Rolodex toward him and flipped it to the letter W. Dr. Walters had handled her case. Dear God, I hope she's not having a stroke. He dialed. "Father Hemming here. Please connect me with Dr. Walters. This is an emergency."

⚬⚬⚬

Dr. Heller was late. Meticulously punctual, he had very rarely ever been late for work. But since the death of his son, JJ, and worse, after the body snatchers had made off with JJ's remains, he had been late all too often. As he was tying his bow tie the front door bell rang. "Dammit, what does somebody want at this hour?"

He heard his housekeeper, Ms. Hartvig, answer the door, but he couldn't make out what she was saying; in a moment she was climbing the stairs. She knocked on the bathroom door.

"Dactoor Heilor, sir, you got special deliver letter. I signid for it."

How long has she lived in the States? he wondered, taking the large brown envelope from her. Special delivery? I thought that went out with the telegram. He ran a finger under the flap and tore it open. Color photos? What—?

"NO! GOD NO!" he screamed, the long nightmarish sound of a soul being rent asunder. Six color photos fell to the floor as he gagged and wretched up his morning coffee, juice, and toast.

Berjit Hartvig, who stood in the bathroom doorway, face ashen, hands covering her mouth, wailed in terror, her gaze riveted on the four photos that had landed right side up.

Shortly after receiving Berjit's hysterical call Lamar pulled into Heller's driveway beside an ambulance. He saw two men loading Heller into the back and winced. One of the first responders approached Lamar.

"My name is Eve. I'm with Cambridge Squad Number Two. And you are?"

"Lamar Coleson. Dr. Heller is my boss at the university," he said, pulling out his Harvard faculty ID card. "What's wrong, and where are you taking him?"

Eve frowned and paused but finally said, "We got a 911 on him. Our instructions are to take him to Mass General. You might want to check on the housekeeper. I could hardly understand a word she said. She was speaking mostly in some foreign language."

"Norwegian," Lamar said.

"Gotta go." She turned and climbed into the ambulance.

Lamar took a deep breath as he watched the ambulance head out, lights flashing. He yanked out his cell phone and called Coleson Manor but got no answer. "Crap." He hurried into the house and found Berjit on the living room sofa, moaning and twisting from side to side.

"Berjit, can you tell me what happened?" She shook her head but reached under a sofa cushion and withdrew a large brown envelope. Lamar opened it.

He sucked in a breath, and his eyes widened. "Son-of-a-bitch. Judeland! She's back. I better call—" He realized he was speaking out loud and that the housekeeper was listening. Lamar strode into the dining room and dialed.

"I need to speak to Harold Stone. This is a balls-to-the-wall emergency." Lamar walked around the dining room table three times. "Hal, is that you? Lamar here. How fast can you get over to Dr. Heller's home? Okay, but cut that by five minutes. The shit has hit the fan big time." Lamar hung up, glanced at his watch, and went in search of the always full coffee pot.

Lamar helped Ms. Hartvig to her room, and put her to bed after giving her two aspirin. He heard a car door slam and raced down the stairs.

"Hal, thanks for coming and for getting here so fast."

"Lay it on me." Hal unbuttoned his trench coat and tossed it on the sofa.

"First, Dr. Heller was carted out of here and taken to Mass General. And this is probably what triggered it." Lamar handed Hal the envelope and sat across from Harold Stone, Chief of Harvard's Campus Security. Hal had spent 34 years with the FBI. Before that he spent four years as an Air Force cryptologist at the National Security Agency. A year after retiring from the Bureau, he accepted the job at the university. Harvard now had one of the best security forces in all of academia, thanks to Harold Stone.

The lines in his face deepened as he studied each of the photos. He flipped them over and found a date on one of them. "These were taken," he looked at his watch, "four days ago. They were delivered to Heller this morning I take it?"

"Yes. The housekeeper signed for them. Said the guy was in uniform and told her it was a special delivery. I thought that had shut down along with telegrams and mailgrams."

"Yeah, it did. Damn. Seeing one's son stuffed and on top, uh . . . Damn!" Hal rubbed his chin and twisted his head.

"Do you have any idea where the Judeland crew hangs out?" Hal reached in his coat pocket for a pipe, a Christmas gift from Jamie.

"Nope."

"Let me know if you object to pipe smoke; Jamie and I have made this our smoking room."

Hal lit the pipe and created a haze of smoke. "Where does the OVFS fit into all this? Didn't Judeland used to work for them?"

"That's the real irony, Hal. All the while she was working for OVFS, back when she was office manager for Flossie Senger, she was evolving into an active vampire. Judeland is Heller's bastard daughter. After JJ's suicide Jamie blamed himself for not watching his son during his post-resurrection struggles. Losing JJ's body and then receiving this second batch of pictures no doubt pushed him over the edge." Lamar scraped the back of his hand over the stubble on his face. "The first responder wouldn't tell me what happened to him"

"What we need to do first," Hal began, "is get some security guys around you, Morgan, and Heller, if he recovers enough to become a target again. You three and the GenLab. Can you provide a few from that private company you used last year? And by the way," Hal continued, "it's past time for us to call a meeting with the boss lady. If we blindside her she just might shut down the GenLab's vampire research, or the whole operation for that matter. We may need to call up the reserves."

"Who are the reserves?"

"Andre Suroccan."

27 - Destiny and the Tree of Life

Have you felt Destiny's long gray arm
As it wraps you in its false embrace
Whose steely fingers cause such alarm
No earthly vampire can find a place
To live in exile from Heaven's grace
In search of the yeast, if just a trace
That causes new growth on the Tree of Life
Free from the burdens of vampire strife

The halls of ivy can sometimes feel like one of Dante's rings, Dr. Glenn Ellen Martin thought as she hung up. Hal's message had been cryptic but all too plain. "Time to revisit the Issue." That could only mean one thing. God's teeth, I have to wrestle with fund raising, student protests, the Federal Government, the ACLU, the budget, and here we go, back to the bloody vampires. It's been over a year. I thought we'd buried that one. She winced. A refrain from one of her favorite old university songs drifted through her mind: *Oh we love the halls of ivy that surround us here today. And we will not forget though we be far, far away.* I wish I were far, far away, like at the fishing camp in Minnesota.

She sighed as she called her secretary to set up the meeting. Who ought to attend? Hal, of course. Morgan and Lamar. Dr. Wally Gibson in the absence of Jamie Heller. I have to go see Heller. At least they say he has recovered movement in all his limbs, but the left side of his face is still affected. I wonder where Flossie Senger is? Maybe still in an FBI safe house? Pray whatever Hal is going to tell me hasn't leaked. The last time I talked to Jamie he was excited about some "profound breakthrough," and that this would be an extraordinarily bad time to close the door on their research. How often am I going to hear that one?

CRAD

Colonel Johann Solento sat at his desk admiring the framed photo of his promotion to Commander of the Vatican's Pontifical Swiss Guard. He looked dazzling in his white, ceremonial uniform, trimmed in gold. Pity he didn't have a photograph of himself being promoted to "Number Two" in the OVFS, the operational commander of the Order of the Vampire Final Solution. He would also like to have a nude picture of his girlfriend, Tanya, on his desk. He grinned at the thought. The clerics would be appalled even though a few of them had girlfriends of their own tucked away. His files contained some choice surveillance on a few of the more liberal ones. That might come in handy one day, along with the final testament of the late Cardinal Loconi who disappeared and was never found. His was the only non-vampire head in the OVFS chamber. Well, there is that waitress. . . .

No time to rest on my laurels, he thought. Cardinal Manlocara is leaning on me to wrap up the operations against Morgan Summers and her husband. That idiot, Andre Suroccan—a dolt like Father Hemming—had failed to deliver, and Johann had decided to pull out the sharpest knife in the box. The Mafia guy, code name Dante. He was, in the vernacular, a "hit man." Bloody expensive, but he had performed flawlessly in his two OVFS commissions to date. Well, the Mafioso should arrive in Cambridge within the hour.

Dante would finish what Suroccan had dithered away. Then it would be time to take out Suroccan as well. Fortunately the OVFS chamber has ample room for a few extra heads.

I am the real power now—not that bulbous cardinal. When this operation is over, I'll have to select an appropriate decoration to be awarded me by the Vatican. Over the years he expected to wear a chest full of ribbons and medals, not to mention a bulging secret Swiss bank account, a villa in Saint Kitts, and the services of several younger versions of Tanya, who had just informed him she was pregnant. Stupid woman.

Johann groaned. How was he going to convince Tanya, a staunch Catholic girl, to abort?

CRAD

Dante and NT sat in an old GMC van a block and a half from the Catholic Church, in a handicapped parking slot. No doubt one of the meter maids would soon ticket them. The van was stolen, of course, and would be dumped in a couple hours if their plan unfolded without any setbacks. With luck they would see Morgan enter the church before they had to move the van. They would carry Morgan's body out of Saint Paul's wrapped in the rug lying in the back.

Neither had paid the slightest attention to a battered car parked a block behind them.

28 - Gunfight at the Okay Cathedral

The mutant spore goes down and deep
Its toxins scourge the human form
No mere mortal could hope to dwell
From faith and love and family torn
Thus doomed to wander like his kind
Through all the ages, deathless worn
Without a soul, without a love,
Without a watchful angel above
Till the day that commeth so clear and still
From which he gathers the strength of will
To climb that one last desperate hill
And bare his breast for the Aspen Kill
The pulsing beat forever stilled.

The bag lady crept toward the side entrance to St. Paul's. She wore two moth-eaten sweaters under an ancient Navy pea coat she'd found in an Army-Navy surplus store. Fingerless wool gloves and a black watch cap pulled down over her eyebrows accented her disguise. Faded denim trousers almost reached her ankles, which were covered by clunky, brown boots. She pushed a squeaky grocery shopping cart piled high with her possessions. The few people she passed averted their eyes, which made her disguise even more effective. At the side door, she stopped, leaned against the brick wall, and grimaced. How long was this supposed to take? she wondered. Out of habit she glanced at the coats of arms on either side of the door: Pope Benedict XV on the left; Cardinal O'Connell on the right. She shrugged. Who cares about them?

A non-descript black Chevy van pulled up at the side entrance. The driver killed the engine, and after a couple minutes got out and walked around to the bag lady leaning against the church wall, trying to smoke a cigarette despite the drizzle.

"Hey, lady, how 'ya doin'?" No response, but the bag lady crouched as if she were about to run. "Look, I need a favor. I can't leave the van, but I'm almost out of cigarettes. Here's ten bucks. I want you to go buy me a pack of Pall Mall menthols. Keep the changer. Can you do that for me?"

She nodded once, snatched the bill out of Helen's hand, and pushed her cart as fast as she could away from the van. She would have to change clothes and get back to the church as fast as she could, but where to change with students filling the Harvard Yard? She spotted a Port-a-Potty near a construction site across Mt. Auburn Street. She would leave the cart behind it. Shit. She'd have to come up with a Plan B while she changed. I've *got* to find another way to get into the church without attracting any attention, she thought.

Fortunately, she had a black wig in the cart. When nobody was looking she opened the door to the Port-a-Potty and squeezed inside. Several minutes later she emerged, dressed in a shoulder-length wig, ankle-length cheap brown skirt, badly worn pink Reeboks, wrinkled white, long-sleeve shirt, and a costume necklace with matching earrings. She would wait at the front door until someone, or a couple, came along and join them, chatting as if they were old friends, as they entered the church. It would be risky, but she had to get in, and quickly. Gretta had said Father Hemming was in grave peril.

Ah, wonderful, she thought, spying a group of tourists standing around their tour guide at the church entrance, beneath a large rose window. A stone frieze adorned the central door, depicting Saint Paul. Morgan sprinted toward the group.

⊂ℨ℞⊃

"Did you see—" NT pointed at the running woman. Before Dante could respond, the woman tripped and hit the ground, her wig nearly coming off. Blonde hair straggled out before the woman could snatch the wig back on. Two young ladies from the tour helped her up, obviously concerned.

"That's our target," Dante said, his voice sounding like the slide on his semi-automatic Glock 23 with silencer, as he racked it back to insert a hollow-point round into the chamber. After checking the magazine, he placed it in a custom holster inside his trench coat, pulled his rain hat low over his eyes, and got out of the van. "Give me three minutes, then move up right in front. I'll come out walking briskly but not running. We walk in with the rug, stuff her in it, and then make tracks for the other car and ditch this one. Keep your gloves on. If anything should go wrong dial me using the phone I gave you last night. And don't put the number on speed dial. Then I'll find another way to meet you at the backup car. Got all that?"

"Yeah," NT nodded.

"Just don't fuck up on me. I don't want to have to add you to my list." Dante opened the door.

"Don't worry. Just get going." NT flicked his hand as if to dismiss Dante.

◆◆◆

Strange, Morgan thought, as she listened to one of the workers telling a tour group that both the transept and the altar were off-limits today due to some electrical wiring that needed repair. Why would the new secretary, Phyllis, set up a tour right through where some repair guys were going to be working? Bending down, she rubbed her skinned right knee. Her head snapped up. Unless they weren't really repair guys. They might be OVFS agents. That's what Gretta was trying to warn me about. Morgan edged away from the tourists, who were grumbling as they were being herded out by a very unhappy tour guide. She crept toward the door that led to the hall linking the church proper with the classrooms and administrative offices, including Father Hemming's.

A woman—who didn't look like an electrician—crouched behind the altar, and Morgan dropped down, crawling under a pew not far from the hall door and pulled her phone out of her skirt pocket. She turned it on and pressed the app that would send Lamar a silent emergency signal. It automatically activated GPS and fed the coordinates to Lamar along with a small area map. Hal had installed the system on their phones the day after Judeland had the photos delivered to Jamie Heller.

The two behind the altar failed to see or hear Morgan as she slithered from one pew to the next, getting ever closer to the side door. But she did not escape the sharp eyes of one man who stood behind a pillar, wearing a trench coat and hat pulled low, holding a Glock semi-automatic pistol.

If she makes a break for the door he could easily take her out with two quick ones to the back of her head, but the colonel said absolutely no damage to the head.

Lamar's phone vibrated; two long, two short. Morgan's emergency signal. The church. He turned right on Auburn and hit the gas. It should only take me a couple more minutes to get there. He pinged Morgan the response code: "Warning received; on my way."

CR&O

"How much longer," Helen whispered to Jake.

"Shit, I'm workin' as fast as I can. The two incendiaries are wired and one of the smoke bombs. I'll finish the last smoke bomb in about two more minutes—if you don't keep hurrying me. I told the boss how long it would take. I won't go over my time by more than thirty seconds or so."

"I'll tell her," Helen said, pulling out her cell and poking out a text message.

"Church is wired," Judeland read, her smile toxic. Father Hemming and his new secretary, Phyllis, stood, hands tied behind them. "One wrong move from any of you and I press this button," she pointed to her cell, "and the light show will begin. Now we are going to walk calmly out the side entrance and get into the van I have waiting. Charlotte is already in the van. We picked her up on the way over here. I'm sure she will be pleased to have company. Maybe she can tell you, young Phyllis, about being crucified on the church cross and other pleasantries we shared over a year ago. Move." She gestured to the office door with her pistol.

Father Hemming's jaw muscles were flexing; he was anything but eager to turn the other cheek.

CR&O

"Sir! Lamar!" Robert shouted, his heart hammering, face red as he sprinted through the rain. Lamar turned back, half way up the church steps. Robert, wheezing, bent over, hands on knees, handed Lamar his father's vintage .45 semi-automatic. "It's loaded," he gasped. "I have the .38. Best we use stealth, sir. And be ready for the worst case. I got a call from Father Hemming. He was obviously being told what to say. I suspected you were headed for the church unarmed. Bloody glad I caught you before you went in." Lamar grinned, punched Robert on the shoulder, and racked a round into the chamber of the .45. Robert handed him two more full magazines. "I do wish we had a Tommy-gun."

"What, no hand grenades, Robert?" Both men grinned briefly as they slipped into the church while the last of the tourists emerged, raising their umbrellas.

NT peered through his binoculars. Even in the gloom he could make out Lamar. The other guy must be his man servant. His jaw dropped as he saw the exchange of the .45 and Robert draw a .38 revolver from his belt. He had no time to think. Fortunately he had already screwed the silencer onto his Glock. He leaned out of the window, took careful aim . . . and cried out as his Glock suddenly became red hot. He dropped it onto the pavement, flipping his hand violently. "What the fuck?" he yelled. "How could—" he choked as if he had been garroted. Grabbing his throat he fell out of the driver's seat strangling and gasping, desperate for air. His vision began to narrow, but not before he saw a figure standing over him, pointing at him, arm quivering, eyes feral, lips pulled back. He was dressed like an old-fashioned parson.

The figure whirled in time to see Lamar and Robert enter St. Paul's.

೦೩೮೦

Morgan watched, helplessly, as Judeland pointed her handgun and marched Father Hemming and his new secretary toward the side door. She could hear two voices, one a woman, working behind the altar. Oh, God. It could be a bomb, and I'm only three pews away from it.

"Lamar, please hurry," she whispered.

Helen stood up. Her phone was buzzing. "Yeah. He's almost finished the bomb. Give him a few more—"

"Tell her it's done." Jake said, leaning over to grab his bag. A flash of light lit the sanctuary, followed in a millisecond by a jarring blast. Jake screamed and crashed into the altar, as chemical flames ate his clothing and filleted his skin. He ran up the aisle screaming. Two muffled pops caused Jake to pitch back, sprawling over a pew. His forehead showed two small holes; the back of his head was nearly gone. The pew began to burn as Dante stepped behind a pillar.

A second detonation preceded billowing smoke that began rapidly filling every part of the sanctuary. From a distance the sounds of more detonations added to the cacophony. Heat, smoke, and fire fought for ascendancy.

"Morgan! Where are you?" Lamar yelled. Was that her coughing?

As Lamar yelled again he heard a zinging sound and bits of marble fell onto his head. He dropped to the floor a second before a fusillade passed through the space where he had stood. Smoke was roiling up toward the entrance. He could no longer hear Morgan. "Robert, cover me, I'm going in."

Yanking his handkerchief out of his back pocket he dipped it in the baptismal font then hunched over and walked down the center aisle trying desperately to hear Morgan above the crackling fire, hissing smoke, and converging sirens. Concentrate. He had to find her fast. Though his throat was parched he continued calling her.

Dear God, help me. He sagged to his knees and slumped to the floor desperate for some air. His last thought was of Morgan reaching out to him.

Lamar, where are you?

❦

Time to bail, Dante thought. They're not paying me enough for this gig. She'll die in the fire in any event, along with her husband. They'll owe me the second half even if they died in a fire. To hell with the heads. Dante stepped out from behind one of the pillars just as two firemen with breathing tanks began pulling a hose down the center aisle. One of them gestured vehemently for him to get out. As he passed the last pillar two .38 rounds careened off of it, just above his head. Four more rounds dug holes in the back of the pew Dante had rolled under. Rolling on his back Dante squeezed off three rounds.

"Agh. I'm hit."

Dante stepped out from behind the pillar closest to the door and took two running steps before stopping abruptly. Robert stood, smiling, directly in his path, his revolver leveled at Dante's heart. As Dante frantically tried to get his weapon clear of its holster, Robert pulled the trigger.

Click.

29 - Click

*I must be willing to give up what I am
in order to become what I will be.*

Albert Einstein (1879-1955)

Only an amateur doesn't count his shots. And amateurs don't live very long, as you are about to discover." Dante raised his weapon. The wail of police and fire sirens grew louder, and Dante glanced out of the open front door. A figure was silhouetted against the gray light.

"You weren't paid to shoot the man who stands before you," the figure said, his voice measured, almost languid. Dante side-stepped and fired two rounds, hitting the figure in the chest. Robert threw his revolver, hitting Dante in the face and charged, but Dante side-stepped again and slammed the Glock's grip down on the back of Robert's head. Robert fell to the floor as the figure in the entrance walked toward the gunman.

"The next round goes in your balls—"

"I think not. Your arm is useless. Numb to the bone."

Both men watched Dante's Glock fall to the floor, his limp arm hanging uselessly. In that moment a fireman emerged from the dense pall dragging Lamar and laid him just outside the door. The fireman kneeled and began giving CPR. In a few seconds Lamar began to breathe, though coughing so hard he couldn't speak and gestured frantically into the roiling smoke.

Suroccan whirled and dove into the gray curtain that had begun to stream out of the open door. The wail of sirens grew.

"Hey, you. You can't go in there—" the fireman kneeling beside Lamar yelled. Suroccan passed another fireman carrying out Jake's badly charred and still smoking corpse.

"Rich, did you see anyone else in there?" the fireman beside Lamar yelled.

"Far as I could tell there's only the lunatic who just went back inside. You got more air than I do. Go see if you can drag him out. I'll call the chief. We need the bomb squad. I think this place has been fire bombed."

Suroccan knew he had to find Morgan and quickly. He heard a voice, clear but faint.

Ye be finding her near the altar. Count twenty and one pews then turn left. At the far end, look down under the pews.

Suroccan counted as he moved rapidly through the billowing clouds of smoke. Close to the altar he could see an opaque, orange glow from the burning fire bomb. The intensity of heat grew with each pew he counted. At twenty-one he turned in and raced to the end of the pew. Two firemen, also wearing breathing tanks, directed a stream of water at the altar. Hissing steam further diminishing visibility all around him.

Nothing! "Mother of Charna," he shouted. Did I miscount? Impossible. "Speak to me again," he yelled. Suroccan crumpled down on the pew holding his hands over his watering eyes. He had never been at a loss before. Not in over 750 years.

෴

Stunned, Dante watched the bizarre figure who must be wearing body armor bolt into the roiling smoke. He stooped and picked up the Glock with his left hand, awkwardly shoving it into the holster inside his trench coat, and walked out into the drizzling chaos.

Firemen were pulling more hoses into the church while shouting commands at one another. Lamar, desperately trying to plunge back into the church, was being restrained by two firemen. None of them saw Dante as he slipped out of the entrance and walked back to the car. He found no sign of NT, but the keys were still in the ignition. With difficulty he drove out into the traffic scrum and was immediately waved down a side street by a Cambridge police officer. He checked his watch while inching along and decided to call the colonel. The feeling in his right hand was gradually returning.

෴

His throat raw and his right hand burning, NT clutched a glass of

Pepsi filled with ice. The place was packed with students, most of them babbling about the fire at Saint Paul Church. What the hell had gone wrong? he wondered. And who was the guy that attacked him?

∞

"The bomb went off while he was still working on it," Helen sobbed. Judeland glanced at the detonator she still held and shrugged. "First Monty and now Jake!" Helen cried. The rain was thrumming down harder, the windshield wipers whacking away as fast as they could go. Helen was shaking so hard she could hardly steer, and her tears made it that much harder to see. Judeland was in the back with the hostages: Father Hemming, his secretary, Phyllis, and Charlotte, who was acting like an escapee from an insane asylum. All three had their hands tied behind them, lying on the floor of the van. Phyllis was crying, Charlotte singing, and Father Hemming grim but silent.

"Faster, Helen. Get us as far away from here—"

"I can't see, I can't see. It's raining dog shit."

"Do I have to do everything? If you can't move this thing just stop, and let me drive. I'm surrounded by idiots and assholes." Judeland looked to heaven as if for confirmation. The van lurched forward, its rear tires spinning.

The occupants heard the ear-shattering horn blast a moment before the fire truck tee-boned the van, which bounded across the intersection landing on its side. The van was a mass of tangled metal, its horn blowing, glass fragments littering the impact area, a section of running board lying on the sidewalk, along with one headlight. Radiator fluid and gasoline formed a lake around the mangled vehicle. Firemen pulled a battery cable, stilling the horn and quickly foamed the area before it could ignite. It took them about five minutes to crowbar the back doors open. Inside they found a war zone. Bodies were tossed around, blood all over. One of the occupants was moaning, one screaming, and one singing. The first responder that crawled inside was baffled to find three of the victims had their hands tied behind them. He cut their restraints. One, a priest, appeared to be unconscious.

"Hey, Bernie. Give me a hand with this one. She's bleeding from the mouth. May be a head injury. Let's stabilize her neck and head," an EMT called from up front.

"I'm on it." The crowd was growing, and police officers were having a hard time keeping them back.

One woman crawled over a body and out the shattered drivers-side window, hobbling over to the sidewalk. In another twenty minutes the other occupants of the van were being transported to Mass General. But when the first responders looked for the woman who crawled out of the window, she was gone. Two onlookers said she had headed down Grant Street, but others disagreed, saying she'd walked over to Dewolfe. Or limped.

CRBO

When the incendiary bomb exploded Morgan heard a man scream as he was enveloped in flames. He knocked over the burning altar as he ran up the aisle, still screaming. His head suddenly snapped back with two small holes in his forehead, and he fell into a pew. An instant later the smoke bomb detonated. Morgan had a moment to see a woman run for the side entrance and scrambled after her, staying just ahead of the unfolding dense clouds of light gray smoke. The woman had slammed the side door, and it took Morgan several tries to yank it open. When she finally did, she saw the van a block away, the rear tires spinning, creating a boat wake.

The rain felt like a cleansing balm, cooling and cleaning her lungs. Shelter. She needed shelter. She was freezing. And soaked. Her mind swirled like a puddle that had just been stomped. She felt hollow. Drained. And she was shaking. She needed to lie down somewhere. Somewhere that didn't have any sirens. Somewhere like Miss Lillian's. Her head hurt, and it was hard to focus.

The cabbie let her off two blocks from Miss Lillian's, who ran a boarding house that had become a safe house for Lamar and Morgan when they were battling the OVFS last year. Miss Lillian, in her late sixties, had done favors and provided "comfort" for quite a few Cambridge and Harvard gentlemen in her earlier years. If she ever needed someone to go her bail, a line would immediately form that likely would stretch the length and breadth of Harvard Yard. She felt as close to Morgan as a loving mother could. And Morgan reciprocated. She smiled as she walked through the rain and up to the back porch, using their secret knock, and in half a minute the door was flung open.

"Lan' sakes, Morgan, I was about to think you'd outgrowed me. When was the last time you came for a visit? A peck of Sundays I mind. Well come in and dry off. Hasn't that fancy husband of yours bought you an umbrella? You're soaked to the bone. Come in, come in. I've got a fire going in the living room. But first, you go up to the room you always use; it's empty. I keep it that way just so you can use it. Now take off them wet things and hang 'em in the bathroom. Put on the bathrobe in the closet, the one you use when you come, and then come back down. I'll have the wine ready and some Gouda cheese and crackers. It don't look much like that fellow you married feeds you near enough. I been cookin' a pot roast all day, which is just what you need some of. So git. Git!"

Morgan smiled wanly and hugged Miss L. then trudged upstairs to "her" bedroom. Good old Miss Lillian. Why am I so cold and so totally wiped? She sat down on the bed—just for a moment. She felt the fetus squirm. She lay back and closed her eyes.

⚬⚭

Miss Lillian looked at the clock. She's been up there two hours, poor thing. Fortunately, she'd turned the heat way down on their pot roast.

30 - The Unraveling
May

Shadows we are, and like shadows we depart.

The King's Deception, p.84, by Steve Barry

N T shook his head in disgust. Judeland had asked the cabbie for a cheap bar in Boston, but the cabbie had overachieved. The Branson Hill Pub was anything but a pub, at least the kind he'd frequented in London. It was crowded, loud—the chatter drowned out the music—had no discernable décor, the lighting was harsh, brick columns propped up a sagging roof, and the crowd was mostly teeny-boppers and twenty-somethings. It did serve cheap drinks and food. He pulled the last Fatima from the pack and crumpled it, sweeping it onto the floor. Judeland scowled and pointed to a no smoking sign over the bar. He scowled back and put the cigarette behind his ear.

He was only here for the money she owed him. Once he got paid he would disappear. As he often did, he thought about the Caribbean.

He looked at the group standing near his table. Tee shirts hanging out, baseball caps worn backward, dirty jeans, and cutoffs. America's youth has become a pack of degenerates. No wonder the ragheads are taking over. He finished his beer and looked at Judeland, who was nursing a glass of wine—probably Annie Green Springs or some cheap box wine. She ignored him, so he got up, wedged into the bar, and ordered his second Sam Adams lager. At least you could still get a decent beer in America. When he returned to the table Judeland was gone.

"Son of a bitch!" She's gonna stick me with the bar tab. And she hasn't paid me yet. The hell with it, I'm getting out. He paid the tab and hailed a taxi. He didn't dare go back to Cambridge for his things. At least he had both guns and several spare magazines, along with his passport and money. Maybe the Caribbean. He had a couple contacts down there. But getting through the TSA screening with my hardware would be tricky. He'd hire a boat; that would be much easier. He wondered if the OVFS was looking for him. Another thought intruded. If he could locate Judeland he might sell that info to the OVFS for a nice piece of change. *If.*

The news anchor on WBZ Channel 4 reported the accident, confirming two dead, two in the hospital, and one missing. The police chief took a lot of flak over allowing one woman to disappear from the scene. The chief asked for help, repeated the hotline number, and promised to search for the missing party.

Wonder if Morgan got toasted in the church? And maybe her husband? NT needed a cigarette.

CHEU

Flossie set the vase of hospital gift-shop flowers on his side table and took Father Hemming's hands in both of hers. They felt cold. "Hi, preacher man. Why don't you let me take you away from all this?" She smiled and waved a hand to indicate the whole hospital.

"Go pull your car around front, and I'll be down if I can disconnect from all this stuff," Ed Hemming mumbled through swollen lips.

"Well, well. Why weren't you this easy back when we were seniors?" Flossie leaned over and kissed him on the cheek. "I didn't kiss you when I came in what with your nurse fiddling around. Seriously, though, they told me you have a couple broken ribs and a punctured lung. What happened to your forehead?"

"Judeland had our hands tied behind our backs. My head slammed into something. I'm lucky not to have a fractured skull or a concussion. And lucky to have you come and visit."

"Luck had nothing to do with my visit, Ed. You *were* expecting me, right?"

"Yeah, I sort of thought you might stand in the door and ask me if I was okay."

"I've been standing in your door asking that question for half a lifetime."

Ed groaned. "I know you have. And it pains me to think of all the time I've wasted."

"My dear," Flossie squeezed his hands, "you are a damn good priest. Don't put yourself down."

"Flossie, just look at the record. All hell broke loose at Saint Paul last year, and now it's happened again, but with a lot more damage. We had to beg on the streets for enough money to repair the damage from last year. This year's toll will be five times that. Bob Shackleford, Chairman of the Building Committee, has been after my scalp since the day after I arrived. And in between the two wars fought inside Saint Paul's sanctuary, I went to Rome and fell flat on my face. So I reckon that my time is up. If I stay on, I'll get shunted out to Cut Bank, Montana, population three thousand. So I'm going to turn in my collar.

"And even if none of those things had happened, I'd quit the cloth anyway. Our time together at Old Orchard Beach sounded the death knell for me as a celibate. I can only thank God for your patience."

Tears coursed down Flossie's cheeks, and she choked, unable to speak. She leaned down and gave him a lingering but light kiss, then grabbed a Kleenex from a box on his bedside table and wiped her eyes, then his face.

She had anointed him with her tears.

ೞ೮ಶಲ

Dante used the special phone Colonel Solento had given him. It was to be used for all contacts with the commander of the Pontifical Swiss Guard. It had one pre-programmed number and could not be used to call or receive calls from any other number. The colonel picked up on the third ring.

"Yes?"

"Have you been following the events?"

"Tell me everything you know."

"I have no idea where NT is. He was not in the car as I'd instructed him to be when I got back and has made no attempt to contact me." Dante paused to light a cigarette. He'd grown quite fond of American cigarettes.

"Go on."

"I followed the primary target into the church and was about to take the subject out when the number two target arrived along with his valet, both armed. His valet provided covering fire while target two raced into the church obviously trying to find target one. I was about to finish the valet when a very strange-looking man, dressed like an old-fashioned preacher arrived and surprised me. He took two shots to the chest, and it didn't faze him. Must have been wearing body armor. The valet rushed me and I dispatched him. The strange guy in body armor suddenly ran into the church.

"In quick succession there were two explosions behind the altar. One was an incendiary device, the other a smoke bomb. The man who was installing them must have made a mistake, because he incinerated himself. The smoke masked everything in the church. I hid near the entrance and watched a fireman pull target number two out and begin CPR. He revived the target."

"Why didn't you off the two of them?"

"Other firemen were swarming in with hoses, so I left. Police were converging from every street in the city. I was lucky to get away."

"And what happened to target one?"

"I couldn't tell, the smoke was so thick, but I could tell target two hadn't found target one. There's a very good chance she died of smoke inhalation or the fire which consumed the altar and at least several pews, and some other stuff. They also set off a pair of bombs in another part of the building I heard one of the firemen say.

"The group that installed the bombs apparently came to a bad end when their van got hammered by a firetruck three blocks from the church. The early news said two were DOA at Mass General Hospital, and two were in critical but stable shape, whatever that means, and one apparently walked away from the wreck in the confusion. No names were released pending notification of kin. One news report said that the Catholic priest and his secretary were among the injured, and the driver and the woman who used to be the church secretary were pronounced dead at the hospital." Dante flexed his wrist. It seemed to have returned to normal. No way he was going to tell the colonel about that, however.

"Any chance target one was in the van that got hit?"

"I have no idea."

"Well find out!" the colonel yelled. "I'm not paying you to be a god-rotted *observer*. You are still under orders to take out both targets. Do that. And report to me within twenty-four hours."

"I will need a partial payment—Shit." The line was dead. Screw you, colonel. What I need is a nice room, hot shower, good dinner, and a full night's sleep. All that will be added to my expense account, which you, colonel, would be very wise to honor.

⋘⋙

Chief Special Detective, Cordell Peyton, Cambridge Criminal Investigations Unit, and his subordinate, Detective Blanton McConnell, stood quietly at Robert Diamond's bedside at Mass General. The doctor had said they could have five minutes and not to excite his patient, who was suffering from a concussion and smoke inhalation.

Robert sensed their presence and opened his eyes. His smile was weak. He nodded, and pain creased his face.

"We seem to only see you in the hospital over the past year," Detective Peyton said.

"I am decidedly too old for this sort of thing I discovered yesterday, to my profound regret. I intend to submit my retirement papers on the morrow."

"We only have a minute before the doc escorts us out. Can you give me a description of your assailant?"

"Probably not a very precise one. The explosions, fire, smoke, and exchange of gunfire were more than a bit distracting. He was about five eight, medium build, maybe 160 pounds. Very quick reflexes. Dressed all in black, including gloves, hat, leather trench coat, jeans, and rubber-soled boots. Exceptionally pale complexion, black hair, maybe dyed."

Detective McConnell, who had been taking notes, chuckled. "For all the distractions you observed a lot."

"For a moment there I was a dead man. It rather sharpens one's powers of observation."

"Anything else you can add that might help us, Robert?" Peyton asked.

"When I pulled the trigger and the gun just clicked, I kissed my arse goodbye, but the assailant side-stepped to shoot at a man behind me. I hurled my weapon, the .38 you held for evidence last year—did you recover it by the way, Inspector Peyton?"

Cordell looked at Blanton and raised his eyebrows. Blanton shrugged. "Somebody got it and will turn it in to us, no doubt," Cordell said. Robert grunted, his doubts obvious.

"Oh, one more thing," Robert said. My .38 hit the black-suited guy in the face, knocking him backward a step. That's when I lunged, but he was too quick for me. Next thing I knew I was here. I'd suspect the guy hit me with the butt of his gun, which, I think, was a Glock."

"Who was the guy behind you?" Cordell asked. Robert shook his head and winced.

"Sorry, gentlemen, but time's up." The nurse smiled and gestured to the door.

"Thanks, Robert. You have been very helpful," Detective Peyton said. His partner nodded in agreement. "Get well old sod. I plan to send you tickets to the next policeman's ball."

Robert's grin was more a grimace as he closed his eyes.

CRBO

Morgan felt groggy and looked at her watch. Oh, grief, she thought, realizing she'd been asleep for over two hours. What a hell of a way to treat Miss Lillian. She started to get up and felt something warm trickling down her legs. Blood! By all the gods, did I get shot in the church? She tore her clothes off. The legs of her slacks were drenched, as were her panties. Her stomach lurched, and she just made it to the basin in the guest bathroom and retched. Then she felt so dizzy she had to sit down. More like falling down, she thought. Her head spinning, she heard Miss Lillian knocking.

"Morgan, I'm coming in." Miss Lillian screamed when she saw the blood-soaked clothes at the foot of the bed. "My God, child, what's happened? Why didn't you tell me?"

Morgan groaned and doubled over in pain. It was the fetus. And paybacks were going to be hell. Going to be? She groaned again.

"Lordy, lordy, Morgan, are you having a miscarriage?"

"I can only pray that's true. Help me into the bed. Find some towels so I don't—"

"The hell with towels. Here, I'm gonna lift you up from behind, under your arms." She managed to get the half-naked Morgan onto the bed. The bathroom and bedroom looked like they had hosted a knife fight. Both women heard the front door open and close.

"Who are you expecting, Lillian? Quick, close the bedroom door, and get rid of whoever it is."

"Done." Lillian reached for the door knob but too late. The door was wrenched open.

"Morgan! What?— Who did this to you?"

"Suroccan? How come you to be here?" Morgan asked, her voice beginning to weaken.

"Marta Sorrel."

"Who is that?" Lillian asked, her eyes wide as she realized they knew one another. And Morgan seemed to suffer no distress about being half naked in front of him.

"Andre, it's the fetus. It never dissolved. I think it has torn something loose inside me."

"I'll call 911," Lillian said.

"NO, you won't. I will restore her, but I'll need your help. I want a basin of hot water, clean towels, and camphor. Do you have any?"

"Uh, camphor. Yes, I think so. I'm sure I do."

"Get it. And hurry." Lillian ran out and down the hall stairs.

"Andre, I'm scared. Help me." Morgan put her hands on her stomach and moaned.

"Trust me. I can handle this. I am going to deliver your fetus and make of it an offering to the Great Serpent. You have bled copiously, but not too much. First I will staunch the bleeding." He gently removed her blouse and bra, tossing them onto a bedside chair. "Lay out, and still your mind. Say your mantra. Pay no attention to what I'm going to do."

Suroccan pulled a small stiletto from his belt, stared at it until it glowed red, and then allowed it to cool. He rubbed a place on her right forearm until it grew completely numb, and with a quick slice, opened a vein in his right arm, then the corresponding one in hers. Speaking in an ancient tongue he caused the arms to be bound together. Blood from his vein began flowing into Morgan's. He watched her breathing become slower and deeper, as she sank into meditation.

The door opened and Lillian stumbled in, arms laden with towels and a very old bottle of camphor oil. "I'll run back and take the water off the stove. It won't take me—by all the saints in hell what are you doing to her?" Lillian's voice shook as her hands covered her mouth.

"Saving her life. Now *go get the hot water.* And I need bandages for both our arms. Hurry!" Lillian dropped her load, whirled, and ran out. He heard her clomping down the stairs. By his calculations he had transferred enough blood to stabilize her; he needed to get the fetus out quickly, before it could do any more damage.

"Good. Thank you, Miss Lillian. Hand me the bandages and place the hot water on the floor next to the bed. Then I want you to go downstairs again and make her a hot toddy with an ample shot of rum—or whatever you've got."

Breathing hard, Lillian headed back downstairs. Andre bandaged both of their arms tightly. With his knife he sliced a piece of pillow case into a long strip, dipped it in the water, and squeezed it fairly dry. He took the bottle of camphor oil and saturated the strip, then folded it into the shape of a cigar. Using the handle of his stiletto, he carefully inserted the camphor bundle into Morgan's birth canal. Her eyes opened.

"Andre?"

"I'm here my dear one. Try to relax. I'm going to induce the fetus to leave its nest. The fetus cannot long withstand camphor fumes." He dipped two towels in the hot water and positioned them beneath Morgan's hips. "Once the fetus is out, we will call 911 and get you to a hospital." Suroccan placed a hand on her forehead and nodded. "No fever, there's a blessing."

"Lamar! Someone has got to tell him where I am. Where they take me. Probably Mass General. He must be frantic, he must—"

The pain felt like molten lava had been poured into her belly.

"Andre!" she screamed. He placed both hands on her abdomen, intoning an ancient call for direct intervention by the Serpent of Charna. Then he focused on easing the pain. Morgan continued to whimper, but it sounded more like fear than pain. She became aware of movement. Lots of movement in her lower body.

"Andre?"

"It's coming. Close your eyes. It is imperative you not look upon the fetus. Remind yourself of the story of Lott's wife. Close them. NOW!"

She felt its flailing arms and legs and heard a diabolical keening sound that made her rigid. She squeezed her eyes tight shut and pushed with all her remaining strength. She was aware of Andre doing something in the basin of water, though his back was turned to her. A spasm of fear swept through her as she realized her eyes were open, and she squeezed them shut so hard it sent lesions of pain across her forehead.

"I will take my leave of you, Morgan. And I will return Morgram to the Great Serpent."

"*Morgram*? You have named it? It will live?"

"You must rest. Stay in bed till the first responders arrive. Miss Lillian has made you a hot toddy. Drink it slowly. Try not to move very much. You have sustained some damage internally and may need the care of a surgeon. I will be watching your progress, although you may not be aware of it. Marta can keep me advised. I communicate with her better than Gretta."

"How can I thank you, Andre? You saved my life."

"By recovering, my dearest." And he and Morgram were gone.

Miss Lillian, mouth agape, watched him walk out the door, holding something wrapped in bloody towels. She climbed the stairs slowly, as if her shawl were made of lead, and entered the guest bedroom and set two hot toddies on the bedside table.

"Lan' sakes, Morgan, I don't know who needs this the most."

She drained half of hers before Morgan swallowed her first sip.

31 - Lost and Found

A lady vampire sets the church ablaze
Her victims writhe within a maze
Their conflict of an ignoble sort
As they stand before the vampire court
But now it's of a late late hour
To know what is within her power
We play our roles as royal consorts
Conjuring chaos of every sort.

Lamar's phone buzzed, and he yanked it out of his jacket pocket. "Yes?" the tension in his voice obvious.

"Lamar, this is Miss Lillian. Morgan has been here the past few hours—"

"I'm on my way."

"No, wait. She's not here now."

"Is she okay? Where did she go?"

"She was taken to Mass General. She's a strong woman, and she'll be just fine."

"What happened to her?"

"Best she tell you that. Hang up, and get going. She needs you."

Lamar had about clicked off when he added, "Oh, and thanks. You're an angel."

"Nobody else ever said that to me . . . except maybe in bed." But he was already gone.

CR&O

"Mr. Bradford, would you give me your date of birth and last four of your Social?" Ms. Allred, receptionist at Mass General, studied the man in front of her. He looked like an unmade bed—her favorite cliché—and was breathing hard.

"Sorry. I ran in from the parking lot. I just learned my wife is here. I need to see her."

"Your last four and DOB?"

"Uh, right. 5175, February 13, 1974."

"Thank you. Ummm, I have a note for you: Doctor Margrove, her attending physician, wants to talk to you first. I'll call him. He said he would take you in to see your wife immediately after he explained some things you need to know." She began to dial.

"Please hurry," Lamar drummed the fingers of both hands on the receptionist's marble counter.

"Hi. Margie here. Mr. Bradford is here. Would you please tell Dr. Margrove right away? Thanks." She looked up. "He's on his way." She smiled, but it wasn't returned.

Lamar jumped and turned when a hand was laid on his shoulder. "Mr. Bradford?"

"Yes."

"Let's go grab a cup of coffee while I fill you in on your wife's condition."

"I'd much rather see her right now."

"This won't take long." He glanced at his watch. "I have a couple more hours on shift and badly need some caffeine." He started off, and Lamar followed. Coffees in hand they sat at a table in the all-night cafeteria.

"Mr. Bradford, your wife has undergone some major trauma. I'll keep my explanation in layman's terms. First, she has sustained a shock, although she is no longer *in* shock. She saw a grizzly scene while visiting Saint Paul Catholic Church yesterday, and she was almost trapped in a burning building. I understand a man was burned to death and ran right past her engulfed in flame. There is always the chance that that event could cause a degree of PTSD, but it will take some weeks or months to know if she has any significant residual psychological effects.

"More importantly, she has suffered some internal trauma, and we are not altogether certain what caused it. Some of her symptoms suggest she had a badly managed abortion that created all manner of internal damage. She is out of danger for the moment, but it will take us some time to discover the full effect and decide what treatments are called for. I have rejected the results of her blood study and sent it back to the lab to be reworked. The initial results were bizarre—off the charts so to speak. Either the blood study was badly compromised, or she has blood dynamics the medical community has never seen before. Can you shed any possible light on that? Has she ever had a blood transfusion? Has she traveled to 'exotic lands,' way off the beaten path? Has she been experimenting with any drugs or herbs? Was she pregnant? Can you think of *anything* that would create such a problematic blood profile?"

Oh yeah, doc, I can. But I'm not about to tell you. "Nothing springs to mind, doc. If she was pregnant she hadn't told me. I believe she has traveled before we met, but I don't really know the details. Have you asked her?"

"Not yet. I was hoping you could provide a lead or two to get us started." Doctor Margrove blew on his coffee and drank several swallows, never breaking eye contact with Lamar, who remained silent, continuing to stir his coffee. And fidget.

"One more thing, Mr. Bradford. Do you know her blood type? This is the first case I've had where we couldn't determine a patient's blood type."

"No, sorry. May I see her now, doc?"

"Almost there. It looks very much like she will never be able to become pregnant again. Further, I'm afraid some of her internal trauma may require surgical repair. That is going to be a very hard decision if we can't type her blood, however."

Lamar's head dropped into his hands, elbows on the table. "You sure about her not being able to conceive?"

"I'm sorry," Margrove said. "We will know more after our detailed internal examination—I've ordered more scans—so don't take all I've said to the bank just yet."

"Can I see her *now*?"

"Yes, but keep the drama down. She has been sedated, and we don't want her to go back into shock."

"I understand." Lamar's breath gusted out as he stood, trembling.

◌◌

His stomach tightened as he saw in the subdued light all the hardware surrounding her, heard the soft pinging, and watched computer symbols flit across monitor screens. He hated the antiseptic smell. Her eyes were closed, her breathing even. He reached for her hand. It felt cold and lifeless. But her eyes opened.

"Lamar?" Her voice sounded scratchy.

"Right here, my dearest one." God, she looks so weak.

"Have you been here long?"

"No. Just a couple minutes. How are you feeling?"

"Like a train wreck. And you look like one. How are *you* feeling?"

"I'm, uh, okay I guess. I got pretty upset in the church when it filled with smoke, and I couldn't find you. How did you get out?" Lamar asked.

"Followed the woman who was working with the man who . . . who—"

"You don't have to explain that. Where did the woman go?"

"Out the side exit. She slammed the door so hard I couldn't get it open at first. When I finally did, she and some others—probably Father Hemming and his new secretary—were driving away in a van. It was raining hard by then. I just stumbled down the street and fell into a cab. Ended up at Miss Lillian's. She put me to bed when I started to bleed."

"Yeah, she called me. Why the hell didn't I think of Miss Lillian's? Stupid, stupid, *stupid*."

"You were upset, my love. Both of us were." Taking a deep breath, she sighed.

"They will shoo me out of here in a minute, Morgan. Before they do can you tell me what happened to cause you all the, the uh, trauma?"

"My water broke, and it was bloody. The fetus was definitely a vampire, and while it was fighting to get out it hurt me inside. I would have died if Suroccan hadn't come. He got rid of the fetus and saved my life."

"*Suroccan!* Hell's fire, why don't we just give him a room at Coleson Manor?" Lamar's voice was bitter.

"Lamar, please. He saved my life." Tears slid from the corners of her eyes.

"Mr. Bradford, you must leave now," the duty nurse said from the door, giving him a black look.

"Morgan, I'm so sorry. So sorry." He leaned over and kissed her forehead, wiping away her tears with a tissue from a bedside box. "I'll be back soon." She waved, and he kissed her hand, then turned and walked out, head down, shoulders slumped, eyes burning.

Suroccan. Always Suroccan.

32 - The Healing Hand

Come lay with me fair maid and learn your lessons sweet
In the gathering dusk inhale the musk that proclaims a special treat
For lust abounds mid whispering sounds escaping from neath the sheets
You have no choice but to rejoice and nestle in your heat.

Pale, gaunt, Morgan lay, mindlessly watching the TV with the sound muted. Lamar's visit that morning had been exhausting in every way: mentally, morally, and physically. How could he understand when she lived in a kaleidoscope of indecision? What did she owe Andre now? And her husband?

She told him she'd lost the baby, and that it was a vampire. She felt like a soul tossed overboard, flailing in the water, grasping for life preservers as they floated by but always out of reach. The fetus was gone, a blessing from the gods, but why, then, did she still have the old vampire sensations? The signals were unmistakable. The urge to go hunting was growing by the day. Those kinds of feelings should have dissipated when she disgorged the fetus. Her appetite had lapsed again, but she was desperate for red wine. She rejected the notion that what she really wanted—needed—was blood. No, that was not possible. Not acceptable.

Suroccan had saved her life. She would have bled to death. But what about his blood now coursing through her? Unresurrected vampire blood. Was it overpowering her mortality? She would talk to Wally. Maybe there is a way to separate my blood from Suroccan's. Maybe Wally could filter her blood.

CRRO

She felt the vibrations, and the sub-conscious tone, the primeval sound the Universe makes when all other sound is muted. And then the scent of Absinthe descended around her. He was near. It couldn't be anyone else. She knew his DNA as if it were her own. She squinted. Why was the light fading?

"How are you my dear?" Though standing by her bed, he looked like a silhouette. Dark, indistinct. He reached for her hand. She could feel him pulsing in the way vampires said hello.

"Andre? How did you get in? Lamar told me that Harvard Security had placed a list of approved visitors at the front desk, and I'm certain you're not on that list."

"I inserted the thought to Ms. Allred that I *was* on the list. And when I reached your door the nurse who was about to enter suddenly became convinced that she had to go get rid of some contaminated medical supplies, and she promptly left. Vampire trade craft of course. Surely you used it during your active years as one of us? Oh, my dear," he blurted, frowning deeply. "You have been more grievously attacked than I had at first realized. What have the doctors told you?"

"They need to do more lab work. My blood work came back a complete shambles, no surprise. They can't even type my blood. The first round of x-rays didn't look good. A lot of internal damage. They think my reproductive organs are beyond repair." Morgan sobbed. "They're discussing surgery but not right away as I've lost a lot of blood, and, they can't type me. They're pumping me full of plasma, antibiotics, and meds to help with coagulation. Maybe some other stuff, too, that I don't know about. Andre, I feel so . . . so bad. It feels like I'm reverting to vampirism. That or maybe I am going to die."

"No, Morgan, you are *not* going to die. Nor will you require surgery. Dr. Suroccan will take charge of your healing. It will take three visits, possibly more, but in the end you will be healed. I will pay special attention to your reproductive tract such that it will bear fruit in the fullness of time, if that be your desire."

He frowned at the door for a long moment. The snapping sound of a thumb lock being turned echoed through the room. "There, that should buy us the time I shall need."

"But there are no locks—"

"Ah, quite right. None that can be seen that is. I am going to lay healing hands above your distressed areas. I want you to relax, go into deep meditation, and trust me with all your faculties, all your energies. Together we will put to rights the scars left by that charnel fetus. We begin now."

Morgan began to relax: deeply, quietly, in harmony with the rhythm of mother earth. She heard the earth tone as if a crystal chime had been lightly struck. She could feel the warmth of his hands over the areas of distress. In the furthest reaches of her mind she was aware of the fragrance of Absinthe. Pain intruded, ebbed and flowed. While aware, she merely observed it without concern. The crystal chime sounded louder, and the pain receded, gradually disappearing as her mind gave up all pretense of functioning.

CS&O

Morgan leaned into the wind, sand stinging her legs. The sky looked like rotting liver streaked with a vein of dull orange fat just above the horizon. Waves hissed up to her feet, depositing jagged lines of kelp. The water was cold, stunning her feet and ankles. She staggered in a sudden guest of wind, aware of the moaning that rose and fell as if from the combined voices of all who had perished at sea. She had to find shelter. But where?

She heard a baby's cry and stopped, as still as a portrait. There it was again. She saw a red glow just on the other side of the dunes that formed the lee side of the beach. The wind paused, as if to take a fuller breath. She heard the infant's cry again and set off for the dunes. The red glow increased in intensity as she drew closer. As she crested the dune she saw a round fire pit surrounded with large stone. Flames danced frantically in the wind, smoke billowing, then being torn apart.

The infant screamed. The flames parted to reveal a fully formed fetus pointing at Morgan. Its lips were pulled back, revealing two rows of canines. Morgan sank to her knees, her mouth open. She tried to speak but could make no sound. The fetus began to laugh. Maniacally. Growing larger, it rose with the smoke and looked down on its mother.

Mother of Charna, Morgan thought. Does it want back inside me? She could feel its malevolence, feel it clawing at her womb, hear its hideous laughter. She ran toward the breakers, her insides on fire, and plunged into the closest wave. It knifed through her with savage cold. She sank into the brine, into the blackness. She would add her voice to all those lost souls crooning from the deep.

"Quick, call Dr. Rouse. Code Blue! This woman is freezing. And her blood pressure has dropped to eighty over fifty." The nurse watched for a moment as Morgan twisted from side-to-side, moaning, then began piling blankets on her while the other nurse dashed out of the room.

CℨEꝃ

She smelled the antiseptic, heard the monitors pinging, even though her ears felt as if they were stuffed with cotton. She felt a hand on her shoulder. When she opened her eyes, the light seared her dilated pupils, and she quickly shut them.

"Mrs. Bradford, are you okay?" the nurse asked.

"Ummm. I'm okay, I think. In fact, I'm hungry. Any chance you could hit up the kitchen for a filet, medium rare?"

The nurse's eyes widened. "A steak? I think I'd better call Dr. Margrove. I'm sure he'd want to hear this." She glanced at the IV bag and frowned deeply.

Someone had turned it off.

33 - Spontaneous Remission

The healing touch from a vampire shorn
of love and care from his birthright torn
Yet has he evolved from the denizen's night
To cure and heal and cause torment's flight?
One woman whose unborn babe doth writhe
A quest to emerge from its unwelcome hive
Reviling she who bears the unholy stain
Of a vampire's life on the barren plain
Will it fight the woman who gives it life?
Becoming the source of everlasting strife
The mother who wraps it in withering hate
Who carries the mantle of a darkening fate
The fetus despoils its hostile home
And lives for revenge. May the gods dethrone

D r. John Margrove clasped his hands behind his head and leaned back in his swivel chair. "So what do you think, Ed? Thanks for coming by the way."

Ed slowly shook his head. "Damnedest blood chemistry I've ever seen. I talked to a couple hematologists over at Auburn. One asked me if I was trying to pull a practical joke; the other wanted to know where we unearthed a Neanderthal. I would like to meet your patient if you don't mind. Maybe that way I can be considered a consultant on the blood study of the century—maybe the millennium." Dr. Ed Childress closed the cover on Morgan's file. "You come up with any ideas, John?"

"I've had her lab work done three times. The last time I stood over the techs. If I were to give a three-year-old a computer filled with blood chemistry elements, along with a pot full of stuff we've never seen in anybody's blood, the kid couldn't come up with a worse conglomeration than Mrs. Bradford's. I swear I'm beginning to believe the nut cases that say we've been visited by ETs who mated with earthlings. This just has to be one of those. It is so bizarre I'm afraid to even consider publishing it."

"Don't talk to me about peer review," Ed said. "I doubt you could find anybody worth listening to who would lend his or her name to any article on this . . . this whatever. I'd think long and hard before going public."

"And that's not all. Look at these x-rays." John swiveled his monitor around so Ed could see it and poked in an address. Dr. Childress studied them in silence for two minutes. "Whose are these?"

"Hers! Two days later. Yesterday evening." Dr. Margrove shook his head and threw up his arms palms up.

Ed leaned forward and squinted. "John, these have got to be from some other patient. The fallopian tubes looked like tangled spaghetti on the first set. Now look at 'em. And the uterus, not to mention lacerations to the liver here and here," he pointed. "The colon on this one looks like it was machine gunned. And the bladder. Jesus. Any chance the Late JC of Nazareth visited her in between x-rays?"

"Brother. That's the only one I hadn't considered," John said. "We've all studied the placebo effect, but she hasn't been here long enough for that. Then there is spontaneous remission. We've all seen a little of that, but it's one-in-a-million. But if you give up Neanderthal, ET, and JC, what are you left with? Her healing has happened so fast we are talking about a miracle. I don't know about you, but Duke's School of Medicine didn't teach miracles."

"So what are you going to do, old buddy?" Ed glanced at the wall clock and stood.

"Watch her like a hawk. I'm going to put an intern on her twenty-four/seven.

"Look, call me. I'm interested. That's an understatement. Good luck." The two men shook hands. As Ed turned to leave he said, "Oh, and call me when I can visit her."

C3&0

"Andre, what have you done to the intern and the nurse? They can't see or hear you, am I right?"

Andre smiled. "And how is my patient today?"

"I can't believe how much better I feel. Other than a sense of heaviness, the pain is all but gone, and I feel like I am getting my energy, my strength back. Whatever you did, I'm up for some more."

"Since we may not have much time let's use it wisely. Go back into your deepest meditative state, and trust me to do the rest. When you awaken I may be gone, but fear not, my dear, the healing is going better than I expected. By the end of my third visit you will be free to choose your path—the old one or the new one. Now lie back. No more questions."

She heard the earth tone and then the chime, finding herself on a beautiful beach, surf pounding, a stiff sea breeze, and bright sunshine baking her nakedness. The ocean swirled around her ankles, cool but not cold. Cormorants and sea gulls swooped and cried at her in a welcoming swirl. The pull of earthly life fell away, and she knew lightness, freedom, joy, and a strong sense of self.

Plunging into the waves she rode one back and stood, allowing the sun and wind to dry her. She laughed aloud as she found a beautiful pink conch shell and put it up to her ear, grinning like a child. Dropping it she waded into the surf but was jolted by the sight of Lamar, who seemed so far out—beyond the breakers— his head just above the waves. He beckoned, and she heard him calling.

"Come to me, Morgan. I love you. We will create another child. Here. Now. I can make you happy . . . and no one else can."

She started to swim toward him, then stopped. How could he be so sure? Why wasn't she? She had been so sure until Andre. He'd saved her life and has renounced any connection with the vampire killers. He would go through resurrection if she demanded it. He is so powerful in bed, attuned to my every need, every desire. She turned back toward the shore, but the receding tide held her in its grip.

Andre stood, naked, at the water's edge. Smiling, he motioned for her to join him. He glistened in the salt spray, glints of sun rebounding from his flawless body. She lunged forward.

"Morgan! Wait!" She turned. Lamar was wading through the surf. He was closer now. A lot closer. She froze. Torn. She wanted them both. No. I must choose. God help me.

God?

☾☙☽

"What do you make of that, Beverly?" Bernard was on his third month as an intern. He began writing on the old-fashioned clipboard form.

"You should get used to making your comments directly into her computer record. I was just watching the BP drifting down. Her heart sounds just fine. Normal. Much better than night before last. Here, have a listen." Nurse Beverly handed the stethoscope to Doctor Bernard Eversol. He listened for a minute.

"Wish mine sounded that good," he said.

"And her respiration is better. A lot better. She's been off oxygen since this morning after first rounds. What could account for that? It's like her body is repairing itself with no help from us, and at breakneck speed."

"Well, the human body is built to do that. Most of the time a physician's real job is to get out of the way, and let nature do the real healing." Bernard handed the stethoscope back to Beverly.

> *Quite right, Andre said, knowing they could neither see nor hear him. Morgan, I bid you good evening. When you are ready just float back into your body. I am so proud of you. See you tomorrow for the final tune-up, as the automobile people would say. He let himself out as the intern and nurse stood, sight riveted on the monitors whose readings continued to improve.*

☾☙☽

Morgan lay rigid and mute, afraid to say anything for fear it might cause the doctors to keep her in the hospital even longer. Dr. Childress had listened to her heart, tested her reflexes, studied her latest x-rays—as well as the earliest ones—and slowly shook his head. "This patient has got to be the mother of all spontaneous remissions. If I were to need hospitalization, I'd ask for this very bed. It must be under some esoteric medical spot beam."

"Mind if I quote you, Ed?" Doctor Margrove asked, grinning.

"Damn right I mind. John, you can't keep her much longer unless she consents."

"I don't consent," Morgan said, sitting up. "You have all the records, and you can always call me. I live locally." The two doctors looked at one another and then down at the floor.

"I'll sign the release forms, Ms. Bradford. Thank you for being patient with us. It's rare for a doctor to see a one-of-a-kind medical condition. Yours really should be written up for the journal—"

Dr. Childress coughed loudly, interrupting his colleague. "Let's have a cup of Java before I have to leave. While we are doing that your nurse can disconnect all the sensors." The two men walked out.

"I trust you will return my clothes promptly, Nurse Beverly?"

"Of course. It will take me a couple minutes to retrieve them," and she walked out. Morgan thought about Suroccan's third and last visit yesterday.

Andre smiled at her. "And how is my patient this morning? You look like a goddess."

"Oh, right. My hair is a rat's nest, I need my nails done, I'm starved out of my mind—a good sign wouldn't you agree?—and I need a long soak in a Jacuzzi. Do I really need any more healing, Andre?"

"Just some fine tuning. And an opportunity for me to inspect your system to make sure we didn't overlook anything."

"I guess you want me to go into meditation again."

"A necessary part of the process, my dear, but it won't be for long."

Morgan sighed, lay back, and closed her eyes. Her breathing slowed and became deeper as her awareness faded. The Earth Tone and the Chime sounded. She was soon there . . . wherever "there" was.

Once again Morgan found herself on a sunny beach filled with ocean smells, the raucous cries of birds, a buffeting wind, and the crash and hissing sigh of the endless waves. She enjoyed walking along the water's edge and wished she had a dog with her.

A shadow fell across the beach and she looked up, surprised at the sudden appearance of a fast-moving bank of dark clouds. The wind began to whip across the sand, sending it in stinging surges around her ankles. It would rain soon. She spotted a dilapidated shack just past a bank of dunes on her left and veered toward it. Any shelter in a storm, she thought.

The door was partly open, walled in place by wind-blown sand. She squeezed inside and looked around. Holes in the roof would admit considerable rain. Most of the few window panes were broken, leaving jagged shards of glass, almost like bared teeth. She jumped when a shutter began banging in the wind, and a low whistling sound caused her heart to race.

There was no furniture, she noted, although she smiled at the horseshoe nailed above the door on the inside. A set of stairs probably led to a sleeping loft. She might as well investigate. Each stair creaked, and she wondered if it was all that safe to continue.

Upstairs she was startled to find a full-length mirror hanging on one wall. As she approached it, she stared at her own reflection, frowning as it began to dissipate. She reached out and touched the glass. Her hand went through it, and she yanked it out. Her strangled cry filled the shack.

"You will come to no harm, Morgan." She froze. Andre! His reflection began to materialize in the mirror. "I have come to offer you a lifetime of wedded bliss, of adventure beyond your wildest imaginings, of discovery, and of love."

"But you will not accept that offer, dear Morgan, for you are my wife, my love, my life." Lamar's image materialized in the mirror next to Andre. "You are trothed. And you are in love with me. I can give you mortal babies. He can't. So come to me. Now."

A blinding flash of lightning followed by explosive thunder brought Morgan to her knees, her hearing and sight obliterated. For a long time she cowered, lying in the fetal position. Slowly the ringing in her ears ebbed. She could hear the ocean, the birds, and finally opened her eyes, squinting against the sun's brightness. A small black and white dog sat watching her, just out of reach. She looked around.

There was no trace of the shack.

CRBS

"Mrs. Bradford. Wake up, dear. I brought all your things. Sorry I took so long—we had an emergency. What would you like to wear home? Your husband brought several of your outfits. He's in the waiting room." The nurse tucked some loose hair back behind Morgan's ears. "I just can't get over how fast you healed. We were sure worried about you just four days ago."

"Was there a full-length mirror in this room?" Morgan asked.

"No, I don't think there's ever been one, other than the small one over the sink in the bathroom. Why?"

Morgan sat up, swung herself into a sitting position, and a moment later stood. She grinned. "I feel absolutely wonderful. Wait till I tell Andre."

"Who?" the nurse asked.

"That is, wait till I tell Lamar."

The nurse frowned.

Morgan looked down, her face flushed.

34 - Shock and Awe

Finders Keepers, Losers Weepers
True Love floats above the fray
Dream her back through deepest sleepers
No exceptions, it's the only way

The clock chimed twice. Then nothing. Just what the doctor ordered for these old bones, however, Robert thought. After inspecting the tall case clock, he walked into the library, took off his suit coat, draped it over a corner chair, and flopped into Lamar's favorite wingback. Turning the pages of the Boston Globe he spotted an article on recent genetics discoveries. "Well, well. It seems like many of us are directly related to Neanderthal Man. I've long suspected as much." Calvin meowed as he squeezed behind Robert's ankles. Oxnard sat on top of the baby grand piano, tail flicking from side to side, watching.

A cup of coffee wouldn't be amiss, he thought. He headed for their new Keurig one-cup machine. As he reached the kitchen the door chimes sounded. "Hmmm. Not expecting any deliveries." Robert often talked to himself—an old habit he'd found impossible to break. He moved to the window lights on the right side of the front door, but the person was standing too close to be seen. "Yes?"

"Robert. Don't be a prig; open the door."

"God's teeth, what could she want now?" He opened the door, and there stood Nancy Worthington, dressed in a one-piece black jump suit that had to be monstrously out of style, the front zipper pulled precariously low exposing way too much cleavage, black spiked heels, black pocketbook hanging from a long shoulder strap, short black hair (he recalled she had been a sandy blonde when last he had cast eyes on her—all of her). He coughed as a wave of perfume wafted over him.

"Well. What can I do for you?" He raised his eyebrows.

"Oh, balls." She pushed into the entrance foyer and delivered a vigorous hug before he could back up. Robert clenched his hands into fists and pursed his lips.

"I do not respond to people barging in. Why are you here?"

"Really? You must have a very short memory. For openers, how 'bout we share a glass of wine and talk?"

"I don't believe we have any—"

"And before I go you can return the garment I left here last time we were, uh, engaged." She smiled sweetly and winked at him.

"What sort of garment—"

Nancy opened her pocketbook and withdrew a pair of flesh-colored Bikini panties. "The mate to these, dear Robert. I believe they were inadvertently left under the sofa in the library." Robert's jaw dropped. "Let's have a look, shall we?" Robert, seemingly unable to move or speak, watched. In a moment she was on the floor looking under the sofa. "Do be a dear and get me a flashlight."

"Damn and blast. If your cleaning crew were up to the standards I expect, one of them would have found the bloody thing long ago."

"Humor me. Just go get a flashlight." Robert stomped out of the library. Nancy quickly placed the Bikini panties in Robert's coat pocket.

When he returned, the black jump suit was draped across one arm of the sofa, the shoes had been kicked off and were under the piano bench. She lay on the sofa wearing naught but a smile. (An evil one without question.) The flashlight fell from his hand, and both cats raced for the lowest bookshelf where they could hide behind the encyclopedia volumes. Unbidden, his eyes traveled the length of her, pausing where absolutely required. Her requirements were quite generous, making his inspection overly time consuming.

"If you don't get dressed immediately I shall call security." Robert glared, his lips white.

"Rubbish. Just FYI you can find their speed dial number under the heading: R A P E."

Robert ran a hand through his hair and groaned. "Did you find the bloody pants?"

"Does it look like I did?"

"Look, Miss Worthington—"

"Nancy."

"Look, Nancy, you can't just barge in here whenever the fancy strikes you and disrobe. What if someone else arrives? Lamar and Morgan could come home any minute." He glanced at his pocket watch. "And besides, you could find a fortnight full of eligible younger men who could satisfy your, uh, your special requirements. I could almost be your father." He remained standing, trying desperately to hold eye contact. His hands were clasped behind him in the posture of military parade rest. "Could we negotiate something a little less precarious?" Anything to get her dressed and out of Coleson Manor.

"Yes, I suspect we could my *old* friend. How about Friday night. My place. I'll cook us something nice. You bring the wine. Red please. Are we okay with that?"

"Yes, yes." He gestured toward the pants suit then grabbed it and handed it to her.

"Fetch me my shoes, old boy." Her smile exposed teeth that were white and even. He muttered as he handed over her shoes.

After closing and locking the door, he groaned. Standing in the foyer he became aware of perspiration on his forehead, upper lip, and under his arms. Reaching for his handkerchief he saw a piece of fabric sticking out of his coat pocket and pulled it out. Flesh-toned Bikini panties.

"Oh my god, not again."

35 - Searching for Judeland

See the Cosmos crack, the gods quail, the Tree of Life upended
As vampires clash, the Furies weep, the pulse of Life suspended
Nature's fierce cry, its terminal roar, is stilled within the deep
The bombards signal from peak to peak
Compounding the epic torment
Will not the gods send down their grace
Before all life is spent?
Bear witness then as time is quenched
and destruction is heaven sent

The cardinal was expecting a head. Morgan's. Suroccan would give them a head, but not the one they expected. It would be Judeland's. They could consider it a down payment. Hopefully that would buy him some time. He had endured endless time as a vampire. Now he had just forty-eight hours to mail a head to the Vatican.

Suroccan stared at the two candles on his coffee table. Bram Stoker's book lay between them. He would slay Judeland Bundaeker. Call her out. She would have to answer or become a pitiful outcast, barred from the company of all vampires, the red "O" for outcast branded on her forehead. He would have Number Three lay the challenge at her feet: the black feather and the red rose. Final death for one, victory for the other.

But first he had to find her. It was a good deal harder to find a vampire than a mortal human being. Vampires were unusually expert at hiding.

It would be a mistake to underestimate her, Suroccan thought, even though she had acquired her powers no more than a year ago. She was cunning, diabolical, and remorseless. She was also alone. Three of her gang were dead, and one—NT—had vanished. If he could locate NT he might convince him to reveal Judeland's bolt hole. Where would NT hide? An occult voice echoed in his memory: Use your powers. . . .

Suroccan blew out the candles and drew his cloak around him. He stood in front of a full-length mirror repeating the mantra that summoned his preternatural vision. He focused his mind, and as he did so his reflection blurred and finally vanished. In its place he saw a shabby hotel, the Brookstone, on Atlantic Ave. The Universe had given him Number Three.

CRXO

"Room service." Suroccan affected a teenage voice.

NT vaulted out of the threadbare overstuffed chair and drew his automatic in one fluid motion. He pushed the chair against the door and stood to one side, holding his breath. The Brookstone hadn't provided room service since the 1960s, and he hadn't ordered anything.

"I would like to hire your services, Number Three. If you would look in the envelope I just slid under the door you will find a handsome compensation for a short conversation."

NT located a broom and used the handle to pull the envelope to him so he didn't have to expose himself in front of the door. Inside was a card printed in French except for the name: Andre Suroccan. The envelope also included three one hundred dollar bills.

"You might as well holster your gun and open the door. I could have opened it in any event, as your friend Monty discovered."

The door opened, and the two men stared at one another. NT slid his 9 millimeter back into his shoulder holster and squinted at his visitor. Finally Suroccan raised his eyebrows, and NT stood aside. "Shall we sit?" The vampire pulled up a kitchen chair and motioned Number Three to sit and waited while he lit a Turkish Fatima and took a deep drag.

"I need some information. The money in the envelope is yours regardless of the outcome of this meeting. In fact, I'd like you to work for me. The pay will be quite satisfactory." Andre glanced around the room. He'd been in better flop houses. NT said nothing but watched the vampire intently. "First, I need to find Judeland. Second, I need you to deliver something personal to her. And third, I need a courier to deliver something to the Apostolic Nuncature—the Vatican's embassy in Washington. I guarantee to protect you from Judeland, the Vatican head hunters, and from the local police. It wouldn't surprise me if Judeland owed you some money you will never see, and that you are unable to safely withdraw funds from one of your accounts overseas because they are being monitored. Am I right?"

NT grunted and nodded, flicking a long cigarette ash into an ash tray on a side table next to a small lamp with a torn shade.

"Let's start with her location."

"No idea. Last I saw her we were having dinner. I walked up to the bar to get a drink, and when I came back she was gone. The bitch even stuck me with the tab. Believe me, if I knew where she was I'd tell you."

"Any ideas where we might look for her?"

"She has three safe houses scattered around Cambridge. She wants to take down the GenLab, starting with Doctor Heller, so you might keep an eye on him. He might be the bait you need to find her."

"*We*, Number Three, we. Right?"

"Sure. But the minute you make a wrong move, I'm out. Game over."

"It occurs to me," Andre said, stroking his chin, "that you manage to change sides whenever it suits you. Let me warn you against that habit. If the Vatican finds you, you are history. If Judeland gets her hands on you, you face unspeakable horror. And if the police get you, you will be a very old man before they let you go. I offer protection from all those players, and I can line your pockets with hundred dollar bills. Are we clear on all that?"

"Yeah. Clear. Let's agree we have a contract. But when the gig is over, we separate, and that's the end of it." NT lit another cigarette.

"These safe houses. You know where they are?"

"Um hum. Which is why she may no longer use them."

"At least it's a start." Suroccan stood and gestured toward the door.

"I'm hungry," NT said.

"Okay. I'll buy you lunch, and then we search."

NT picked up two spare loaded magazines out of the side table drawer for his Glock, wriggled into his sport coat, and nodded. Locking the door he wedged a piece of clear plastic between the door and the frame. "Ready." He scanned the hall.

A cat stretched and yawned at the other end of the corridor.

"Damn cat," NT said. "Pisses all over the carpet."

"Maybe it's emulating some of the tenants."

NT rolled his eyes.

36 - The Triumph of Evil Over Evil

Can you think of life eternal save for the stake and severed head?
Can you decry the endless lust, while denied love's words unsaid?
Fear not for you are vouched an ending
Life and Love and Death ascending
We vampires know no second birth
Doomed to a living death on earth.

Judeland, her face pinched, stared at the red rose and black feather lying on the coffee table. She examined the envelope, sniffed it, and then tossed it aside. No matter who delivered it, the challenge could have only come from one vampire: Andre Suroccan. Or whatever his real name is. He had challenged her to a duel, a "Last Man Standing" fight. Each party to the duel was required to bring an aspen stake, a hand maul, a sack, and a saw. The stake, driven through the heart using the maul, would administer the death blow. The saw would be used to cut off the loser's head, placing it in the sack. A summons to a duel carried a time limit. It would start no later than forty-eight hours after receipt of the feather and rose. There was no provision for seconds, or judges—only winners.

Suroccan had been won over by Morgan; that much was clear. Judeland wondered what Morgan had promised in order to turn him. Couldn't be money. Rumors had it that he had amassed a fortune, that his Swiss bank accounts were bulging. Was it sex? Not likely. He was a battering ram and had sniffed the skirts of half the remaining European royals, along with other members of the rich and famous. Could Morgan be carrying his get? Maybe threaten him with an abortion? Although the loose lips around Countess Amberglass's leather goods shop agreed that Suroccan had only made one girl pregnant in seven and a half centuries . . . and that had ended badly. For some reason the mighty Vampire

Suroccan was smitten with Morgan. No matter; she had to make ready for the fight. By long-established protocol she would choose the location and the exact time. She glanced at her watch. In twenty-four hours one of them would meet Father Death. Hmmm. She had to finish one task first. She reached for the note to her father and reread it.

> *Dearest Daddy,*
> *I have just given birth to your granddaughter. She looks so much like her father, your late son, JJ. We shall come see you soon. In the meantime, here is a photo suitable for framing. Can't wait to see you.*
> *Your Bastard Daughter, Jude*
> *P. S. Did I mention that JJ's daughter chewed through her own umbilical cord? Oh, yes. And I have sent her to the Serpent of Charna for her elite education. You are invited to her graduation, of course.*

All lies, but artfully told nonetheless, she thought. I shall send roses of my own. To decorate my father's hospital room. They will be a deep red when received. A nurse will put them in a vase. But when she leaves, the roses will turn black.

CR&O

Suroccan grimaced. It was just like Judeland to pick a place with no poetry. A roadside dive called Pirates Rock. A most fitting nom de guerre. He parked Old Oxidation next to Judeland's SUV. Fog hovered just above ground level. It was unseasonably cool and damp, he thought. Probably less than an hour's daylight remained. He would announce himself.

Stilling his mind, he focused on transmitting a single thought: I am here.

In but moments he received a reply: So you are. I await you in the back room.

Andre strengthened his force shield. How clever the producers of Star Trek thought they were. Yet for the previous seven hundred years he and many other vampires had been employing force shields.

The front door opened and two burly men walked out wearing lumberjack shirts, each carrying a bottle of beer. "Well. Here's a weirdo if I ever seen one," the taller of the two said, pointing at Andre. The other one guffawed.

"Let's give him a shoe shine," the second one said. He walked over to the vampire and was about to pour some beer on Andre's boots when his own burst into flame. "Ahhheee. Gawdamighty," he yelled, bolting for a puddle of water a few cars away.

The taller man squinted at Andre. "How'd you do that, man?"

"Would you care to have me demonstrate again?"

"Hell, no," he mumbled and walked briskly over to his buddy who was soaking his stockinged feet in the puddle. Steam was rising off his boots.

Andre stepped inside and blanched at the smell of stale beer, rancid fat, and body odor.

"Howdy, Mister. What'll it be?" the bar tender asked.

"Draft beer." He slid a ten-dollar bill over the bar. "Any chance you know where I might find a woman who is expecting me?"

"That would probably be Jude. She a friend?"

"Not particularly."

"Not surprised. She is one weird broad. Keeps to herself. Rents the back room. See that door. I'd knock first if I was you. Need any change?"

"No."

"Thanks." The bar tender began wiping glasses he pulled out of day-old, cold, soapy water.

Andre paused at the door, and embraced the vampire combat mode. As he reached for the door it swung open a few inches. He took a deep breath, exhaled half of it, repeated his Serpent of Charna mantra, and burst through the door, springing to his right. The room was black. A single spotlight focused on the stuffed remains of JJ, late son of Dr. James Heller. A split second later the light was extinguished and ear shattering ghostly laughter filled the room accompanied by clouds of silver-gray florescent smoke.

Andre heard a snap followed by an instant whooshing sound. He lunged to his left just before a sharpened stake slammed into the pectoral muscles where his heart had been milliseconds earlier. His breath burst from him as he crashed backward into the wall. How had she penetrated his force field? Pain pierced through him, but it also cleared his mind. He saw Judeland at the other end of the room wearing a gas mask and night vision goggles. She was reloading a device that looked like a spear gun. He yanked out the partially embedded aspen stake and hurled it at Judeland, causing her to drop the stake she was trying to load. Blood flowed down his shirt. Fortunately he had not taken off his thick cloak, which blunted the impact of the stake. His right side was already beginning to go numb. Had she covered the tip with poison?

Andre laser-focused on Judeland's night vision goggles. In a couple seconds she threw them aside and hurled a pain bolt at him. Suroccan realized that his weakened protective shield would allow Judeland's bolt to penetrate the opening. A moment later he sank to his knees, clutching the pain site with his left hand. He knew she would follow with a second bolt that would rapidly diffuse through his entire body and affect his mind. He had to seize the initiative—and fast.

Springing forward into the roiling smoke, he fashioned a double blast, one aimed at her eyes, the other at her birth canal. Taking several seconds to strengthen them, he became aware of two rows of flames, racing to encircle him. He let go his blasts just before the flames reached him.

Judeland doubled over and screamed. Her protective field had not held against the strength of Andre's double blast.

As Andre fought the flames he saw Judeland pouring beer into her eyes. The pain from the surrounding fire sought out and penetrated the opening in his force field. He coughed and retched, trying to catch his breath. He felt weary, his sight dimming. "Charna, help me," he breathed.

Use your powers. Do it now. Leave your body.

Marta? Marta Sorrel? Andre's voice was weak.

Do it NOW, Master Suroccan!

Andre turned inward, cloaked the pain as best he could, and called up the most difficult invocation he had ever studied—the transfer of self to another. But transfer to whom?

Finishing the invocation—speaking in ancient Vedic Sanskrit—he began to lift, his consciousness separating from his body. Having only seconds of untethered existence before he would dissipate, he flung himself at the only alternative.

As Andre fled his body, he was aware of continuous lightning bursts outside and pounding rain that fell with near hurricane force. Water cascaded into the room, damping the fire around his body, changing it into a cauldron of hissing steam.

Ah, Marta, you have done well. Where did you learn to conjure a storm?

From the one true witch of Old Salem, and that would be you, my dear Gretta.

For a brief instant two voices cackled across the timeless void, blending with the continuous lightning bursts and thunderous cannonading.

Judeland overcame her pain. Grabbing her aspen stake and her saw, she advanced on the body of her enemy.

"Judeland!"

She whirled. There stood JJ brandishing a stake and a maul.

"You can't be—NO! It's not possible!"

Summoning every volt of his psychic strength, Andre lunged. Seeing JJ "alive" had caused Judeland's force field to weaken. Andre's stake cleaved her heart, stanching the cry Judeland made during the instant she realized how JJ could be attacking her.

Andre made it through the reverse transformational sequence and found himself back in his own body. Though staggering with pain he severed Judeland's head and dropped it into his burlap sack. Minutes passed while Andre focused on his most powerful pain relieving mantra. The sound of his groaning was muffled by the storm. He found a back door and sizzled the lock. With JJ's body slung over one shoulder and his burlap sack dragging the ground, Andre, nearly bent double, stumbled through the driving rain to Old Oxidation. Then he went back for Judeland's body. The stench of burned flesh made him gag. He would have to work on self-healing.

Andre stuffed the headless body into the trunk, tossing the burlap sack into the passenger-side footwell. JJ, drenched, was splitting his seams extruding crumbling bits of damp Styrofoam over the back seat.

Andre drove away in a daze, rain beating against his car, lightning flashes and bone-crunching thunder obliterating all other sounds. Locking the car he dragged himself up to his apartment.

Opening the door he collapsed . . . into Morgan's arms.

◌ЗꙨ

Morgan disinfected the shoulder wound with some whisky, closed it with eight stitches using a sewing needle and dental floss, and bandaged the wound with long strips cut from a sheet. Then she treated his burns. She had no idea how much blood Andre had lost but coaxed him into drinking a glass of red wine before he sank into a stupor. She sat beside the bed, taking his pulse every fifteen minutes, all the while invoking the vampire's healing mantra.

Lamar found her by Andre's side. A sheet covered Andre's nakedness. His bloody clothes lay strewn at the foot of the bed. In one corner, unnoticed, lay the burlap sack with its grizzly cargo. Judeland's body was stuffed in the closet.

Lamar groaned.

Suroccan!

Again.

37 - Dances with Vampires
June

Can Green Street be the womb of love?
Made sweeter by the gods above
Who'd see the shackles of wisdom rent
And witness passion both earned and spent

Tired, Morgan sank back in the car seat, and breathed deeply several times. She'd only been released from Mass General two days ago, and her head was in turmoil. Why had Andre asked her for a . . . a what? Well, call it what it is: a date. She had met him at her old apartment. He had opened the door and guided her back out to his parking place. "Andre, I don't think we should do this," she said, staring out of the rain-smeared window of Old Oxidation. "Where are you taking me?"

"That will be my surprise. I think you will enjoy the evening."

ᘓᘔ

Morgan looked around at the posh interior. She had never been to Green Street, a favorite with the Cambridge locals. Lamar wasn't a big fan of cruising the bars, but she had enjoyed taverns, ale houses, pubs, saloons, bistros, military and private clubs along with dives and gin mills over the centuries. She smiled at the recollections of some particularly rowdy times she'd spent in 1940 at The Plough, drinking Royston Ale with RAF pilots from Duxford, Fowlmere, and Bassingbourn.

The room felt alive—and above all, friendly. The band was playing *Stardust*, and several couples were dancing. She inhaled deeply. Something smelled delicious. The maître d' guided them to a corner table that had a rather private feel. Green Street boasted the finest bartenders and the widest assortment of drinks to be found anywhere in the state. It was home to serious drinkers, and the breeding place for the birth of many strange and wonderful drinks. Andre had ordered Zombies, a mix of light and dark rums, Orchard apricot liqueur, and fresh pineapple juice. She sipped it and smiled. "Ummm." She decided it would be wise to restrict herself to just one. She looked up. He was studying her, as he always did.

"Andre, I don't want you to go," she said, her voice soft and breathy. He had ditched the turn-of-the-century clerical garb for a Brunello Cucinelli gray pin-stripe three-piece suit, with black Florsheims, a Martin Grant linen off-white dress shirt with a gray Burberry silk tie flecked with blood red spots. His hair was slicked down with a small pony tail at the back of his neck. She all but swam into his knowing dark eyes. By all the gods in the Cosmos, this was a man. She detected the faint aroma of Absinthe and flinched. She wasn't supposed to be able to detect that after her Resurrection booster shot. Andre smiled.

"What aftershave are you wearing?"

"The usual." He lifted his drink and clinked with her. "To the good life."

"No. I'll toast that you find the woman of your dreams." She examined her drink as if looking for something, blinking rapidly.

"I already have." His voice was so low she had to strain to hear him even in the Green Street's subdued ambiance.

"You know what I mean."

"And you know what I mean," he replied.

Morgan took another sip of her Zombie. "This is really good. How did you find out about it?"

"The original was created by Donn Beach for Donn the Beachcomber restaurant in Hollywood back in 1934. Since then it's become a crapshoot with every bartender using whatever fruit juices and rums he had on hand. But this one is made by a gentleman who follows the original recipe to the letter. I'm glad you like it. Sort of creates a foundation for dinner. By the way, you can't beat their Dover sole; I highly recommend it. We shall pair it with a fine Grand Cru Chardonnay."

"But Andre, how can you eat like that? You haven't been through Resurrection."

"Ah. How perceptive of you. Well, I have provided special instructions to the chef for very small portions for me. For both of us, actually."

"I should have eaten dinner before they brought the Zombies. I can feel mine already."

"You have lived with an incredible amount of tension for a long time. Let us cast our troubles to the winds and live large . . . if just for a few hours."

Morgan frowned and shook her head but finally smiled and clinked her Zombie with Andre's again. She could feel the tension begin to untangle. Both turned to look at a quartet that began to play the 1930s tune, *Memories of You*. Great start, Morgan thought and groaned inwardly. Tonight was going to be hard. "Why do you have to disappear forever?"

"You know the answer to that, dear heart." They fell silent until the band began the next tune.

"May I have the pleasure?" Andre stood and held out a hand.

"You want to dance?" Morgan raised her eyebrows in surprise. They had never danced before.

"We can pretend we are at the Court of Versailles. Guests of Bonaparte. On second thought maybe not, for he would steal you away from me, just as Mr. Bradford did."

"No Andre, he won my heart before you first introduced yourself." They glided across the dance floor as if performing for the Emperor himself.

Morgan felt a spreading warmth in her chest followed by a wave of heat that dappled her neck and face. Why am I acting like a bloody school girl? This is Andre Suroccan, master seducer. Once again she was aware of the faint aroma of Absinthe. Dammit! Other physical reactions were warning her as well. Better sit down. What has happened to my control? "Andre, you're making my head spin. Let's sit out the rest of this one."

He seated her and she reached for her Zombie and gulped it. No, no. I need some coffee, not any more of that. She blinked several times trying to clear her vision. Everything seemed to have a diffuse aura. That was an unmistakable sign. She was over her limit, but how could that be? She looked at the drink; it was still half full. How could—

"Ah, my dear, I hope you haven't spoiled your Dover sole. It should be out in just a few more minutes."

"I need a walk and some fresh air. Tell them to hold our dinner for another ten minutes." Morgan pushed back and stood. For a moment she swayed and put her hands on the table to steady herself. As she turned to leave she glanced at her drink. It was three-quarters full.

Damn him and his parlor tricks. I have got to clear my head.

She breathed deeply. The cold air felt like a jolt of electricity. By all the gods, I can't remember getting from the table to the sidewalk. And I'm wearing my coat. She felt thud-footed. Each step seemed to jar her face. If he put something in my drink I'm going to knee him in his squishy part. She felt his hand on hers. "Andre, if you have worked a spell on me—"

"That really hurts, Morgan. Do you think I'd spoil our last night together by using the crass tricks of a first-year vampire? I respect you—and myself—too much for that. I think you owe me an apology."

Morgan took a deep breath, held it, and exhaled. "Okay, I'm sorry. I guess the drink hit me like the roof fell in. Walk me to the next intersection, and then we'll go back and enjoy our dinner. I'll skip the wine, however." And the after-dinner liqueur too, she thought.

The band was playing *Smoke Gets in Your Eyes*, and Morgan wondered if it had been a request by her host. Something had gotten into her eyes. Everything looked opaque, and the colors seemed to blend as if created by a child finger painting. And that damned Absinthe. He must be pumping the stuff out like a steam engine.

Louie cleared away the dessert dishes and Andre nodded for the check. "Would you care for an after dinner—"

"Absolutely not. I'll just have a few more sips of this Wolf Man."

Andre smiled. "I think you meant to say Zombie." The band began to play *Laura*, sounding a lot like Dave Brubeck's group from the 1950s.

"What are you doing, Andre? I've been drinking all night and the damn thing is still over half full. Reminds me of that Christmas movie, *The Bishop's Wife*. Remember? Cary Grant is an angel, and he keeps refilling the professor's bottle of wine. You're doing that. Don't try to deny it."

Andre frowned, looking like the proverbial kid caught with his hand in the cookie jar. "I just wanted you to relax, and let your real self emerge. And no, I didn't spike your drink or use any kind of a spell. The feelings you have experienced have been your own, all the way back to your asking me not to go."

"You never really answered that question."

"It seems like that's all I've been doing. I can no longer be around you and keep my hands off. If I can't have you, my dear, I've got to leave. And don't ask me why we can't be friends. We will always mean more to one another than friendship. The temptation for me to use my powers against you would soon become overwhelming. Does that answer your question?" He sat back, breathed heavily for a few moments, and smiled wanly.

Morgan reached across the table and took one of his hands in both of hers. Both stared at the temple they had created. Tears shimmered in Morgan's eyes. She started to speak, but her voice broke, and she started over.

"The first and only time you have taken me I was under the influence of a highly erotic drug. The second—and final—time will be different. We will act out our love with no resort to drugs or spells or anything beyond the bounds of mortal love. And for as long as we both shall live we will have the memory of the one time we . . . we," she faltered. Her eyes closed.

"Don't get your hopes up, Andre. I plan to have Lamar's babies and become his soul mate. But there will always be a corner of my heart that hides the love we have created, shared, and said farewell to. Is that clear to you? And are you willing to abide by that which dictates our separation as strongly as the love that compels us to want to share it physically?"

Andre sighed. "I have no choice. I will spend this night with you in body and countless other nights in memory. I will draw a cloud over Lamar's memory so he will not wonder where you were for so long. And should the day ever come when you no longer have him, I shall return. And trust me, I will take care of the OVFS.

They walked out into the cold night.

Old Oxidation was waiting at the curb.

38 - A Feast Finely Served

How cunning the gods who invented sex as icing on the cake
To watch the fulsome chaos reign as lust became our lot
There be no better yeast than desire our mindless needs to slake
Oh joy of joining! Cast out our morals for they muddy up the plot

Morgan felt as if she were in a dream state. Her emotions were tumbling yet they seemed to be doing so in slow motion. She felt safe with Andre; as safe as one could be, yet she knew she was taking the biggest risk of her 360 years. She was married and loved Lamar with all her heart.

Oh, really? The etheric voice was challenging.

Well, but this will be a one-off joining. We owe this to one another . . . and to ourselves. After all, he saved my life, and I'm still not out of danger until Andre destroys the OVFS. The only other time we made love—or was it had sex?—oh, I don't know. I was under the influence of a powerful aphrodisiac.

And that's no longer true? Gretta's dry chuckle made Morgan angry.

"Well. My body aches for him, but I've fended that off before. A part of me loves him, Gretta, I admit that, and this will be my special—and only—gift to him. And to me."

Ye be gettin' good at rationalizing what you want, and the better you gets the more likely this won't be once and never again.

"No, you're wrong. I will hold to my pledge for the rest of my life, or the rest of Lamar's."

Ye be sounding like a solicitor now.

"You could try to be a little understanding. Andre and I became soulless mates, something you wouldn't understand. More than sex, we have shared a wanting that, for a vampire, lies between sex and love. We are vampire bonded." She heard Gretta snort.

That be a good ways down the road to love, my dear one. That's what this is all about. The sex is just icing on the cake, be that not true?

"All right, I admit it. I love him. I can hardly control my feelings."

Of course, after tonight those will go away.

"He will leave. Forever. Like him, I'll have memories, but that's all. I'll get over him."

And, of course, you won't ever put the two of them on the scales to see which one is best.

"This has gone far enough. Are you intentionally trying to spoil tonight?"

CŽƋ

Andre pulled Old Oxidation into its parking place and smiled at Morgan "I have deeded this place to you, my dear, effective tomorrow. You may use it as your private hideaway if and when you need one. Or it can be a private getaway pad for you and Lamar, whatever you choose. And yesterday I gave the formula for my Jekyll and Hyde potion to Dr. Wally. That should give him a leg up on his research."

"That's so sweet, Andre. Thank you."

Arm-in-arm they climbed the steps to the front door. He gave it a hard look and it unlocked. After they were inside the door closed and locked itself. He hugged her and then held her head with both hands, inhaling her fragrance. The shampoo, her soap, perfume, and one other: the wanting. The last scent was one Morgan couldn't detect, but it brought another smile from Andre.

"I have decided to lay aside my powers, Morgan. Just for you."

"I don't want you to do that, Andre."

"No? I am surprised." He stepped back to better see her face in the pale wash of light from the street. He hadn't turned on any lights in the apartment. "Why?"

Morgan looked down, her voice timid. "I want you to have all your sexual powers tonight."

Andre's laugh was rich. "Then, my fair wench, have them ye shall. Give me a moment to reclaim them." He picked her up and carried her to the bedroom. She kicked off her shoes en route. He lay her on the bed and kissed her neck as he removed her scarf and unbuttoned her blouse. "Ah. You have dispensed with that silly undergarment that stifles your beautiful breasts. How thoughtful." He made quick work of the rest of the undressing until she lay before him in a red string Bikini. He studied her as if she were hung in the Louvre.

Andre undressed with speed and elegance. Morgan murmured something and nodded, arching her back as he relieved her of the final garment. She reached up and suckled one of his nipples.

"Ah. I see your education is not entirely lacking."

"Methinks you need a bit more of a demonstration before reaching any conclusions," she said.

Andre laughed again, and Morgan joined him. It was the sound of a Vampire joining.

ೞ

Exhausted, she lay on a sheet soaked with perspiration. Her voice was pensive. "Andre, all the stories I've heard have underestimated you. After the past hour, how can you still be, uh, ready for more?" She reached down and touched him to confirm her observation.

"You asked me to keep my powers tonight. I hope you haven't changed your mind."

Morgan rolled over on top of him, made an adjustment, and they were, once again, coupled. "Do I act like I'm ready to nod off?"

"No, but soon I recommend we shower and cool off. Have you ever made love in the shower?"

"La," she said, beginning to move on him with a slow rhythm, "I don't intend to share all my secrets."

"Why not," he laughed, "you've shared just about all of them by now, surely."

"You are an egotist as well as a glutton and a chauvinist."

"Ah, dear Morgan, I am considerably more than those." He increased the pace of his thrusting. Soon Morgan was breathing in gusts and bursts, making small noises in the back of her throat.

"Andre!" She went rigid, twisting her head from side to side and groaning. Finally she slumped on top of him. "How can you keep doing that to me?" she gasped.

"You don't expect a vampire to share all his secrets, I trust," Andre replied.

She poked him in the ribs. "I am hot and thirsty and more than ready for that shower." She slid off to one side, mumbling something about the room being unstable. She could still feel the echo of the throbbing that had all but claimed her sanity.

"We have some Champagne on ice. You go start the shower; I'll bring our beverage. The combination of tepid water and ice-cold Champagne will restore your libido."

"By all the gods, Andre, I wish I could recall my old powers. A couple more big Os and you will have to convey me home by ambulance."

"To paraphrase your Admiral John Paul Jones, we have not yet begun to love."

CR80

Morgan shook her head and stepped into the shower.

Some idiot had cracked open the Venetian blinds allowing a slice of morning sunlight to dissect her head. Rolling over, she decided on the instant that sex, Champagne, and showers were meant for people younger than 360 years.

He was not in the bed. She wondered what time it was and reached for her watch on the bedside table. There was a note lying under it. She sat up, and the room became unstable. She waited a few moments and then opened the note and squinted.

> *No words can express the love and joy I was blessed to share with you. All of it makes our parting—for me anyway—a bitterly sad event. I've never been good at partings, even though I have had centuries to perfect the art.*
> *If you should ever need me, send a thought form, and I will burst forth from a dense cloud amid great flashing and rumbling.*
> *I forgot to mention, I have titled Old Oxidation to you as another farewell gift. The keys are on the table by the door. I think it may need some transmission work, as I never got the hang of gear shifting.*
> *This morning, while you slept, I cut a curl of your hair. I plan to find a suitable locket with a gold chain that I may keep it close to my heart forever.*
> *Go back to him, Morgan. Love him and make a wonderful life. Forget me if you can. I did not use any of my powers to help you forget, for that should be your choice, not mine.*
> *You will always be my Love, my Lover, my Friend . . . my soulless mate.*
> *Andre*
> *P. S. I will attend to the OVFS before disappearing completely. When that task is completed, I will send you a secret message to that effect. A.*

"Oh God." Tears fell on the note, smearing his words.

39 - One More Head

Hickory Dickory Dock
The vampire looked up at the clock
Tis time to go hunting in bright-colored bunting
His victim is in for a shock

Cardinal Manlocara spent the early morning hours on grooming, beginning with a long hot tub bath. He washed what little hair he had remaining, almost one strand at a time. He applied his favorite pearl-handled straight razor with infinite care so as not to inflict a single nick. He lavished his face and neck with his long-time favorite "after shave splash"—Chanel Pour Monsieur. He had canceled two appointments to create the time for his extended ablutions.

Today, he must look his best. For today he planned to roast the Holy See's Commander of the Pontifical Swiss Guard. Today was the last and final day accorded to Colonel Solento to present the "grand gift" to the Cardinal, supreme leader of the OVFS. Morgan Bradford nee Summer's head was to rest forever in the OVFS chamber of vampire heads. Or the colonel's. Three times the Cardinal had extended the due date for her head. There would be no more extensions. That fop, Johann Solento, would soon become an eternal guest of the chamber, alongside his first supreme leader, Cardinal Loconi. Few things in life would give him more pleasure than to permanently rid himself of that marionette. He had been wise to put Dante on a yearly retainer.

The tall case clock struck ten times. "Late as usual." Manlocara glared at the clock as if it were responsible for the colonel's slovenly habits.

He heard the gentle knock and growled permission to enter. His pimply-faced acolyte edged through the door as if ready to bolt back out into the hall. He bowed deeply. "Colonel Solento to see you, Your Most Reverend Eminence."

"Show him in."

"Good morning, Your Eminence." Solento strode briskly to the cardinal's seat and bowed, placing his attaché case at his feet. "You look quite resplendent this morning, if I may be so bold."

Manlocara looked puzzled, as if he were studying a rare species of butterfly. The silence descended like a gentle rain. Solento brushed the front of his immaculate uniform, with its three new medals. "Why are you here, Colonel?"

"At your request, Eminence. The note I received did ask me to report to you this morning."

"And at what time?"

Solento frowned and glanced at the tall case clock. "I believe you asked me to present myself at ten o'clock."

"So where were you at that time?" Manlocara's eyes had become slits.

"Why, speaking with your acolyte just outside your door."

"Rubbish. You were two minutes late."

"Hmmm, might I ask when the last time you had that clock serviced? It could be running a bit fast."

"That clock has been correct since the turn of the 15th century."

Solento raised his left eyebrow and returned the Cardinal's stare, precipitating another extended silence.

"Well?" Manlocara finally said, his voice like a scythe on a stone sharpening wheel.

"If you are inquiring about the head, it has been received and processed."

The Cardinal jerked back and his eyes widened. "Processed?"

"Yes. It resides in its canister in the OVFS chamber in the Necropolis."

"God's death, fool, I know where the chamber is. When did you receive the head?"

"In yesterday's courier with the usual dispatches."

"You are certain of the identity?"

"Absolutely."

"From now on I want to see the heads before they are processed. Have you received the operational report on how the task was accomplished?"

"Not yet, sir, but I expect it this week."

"I want it in my hands the moment you receive it. And I shall require a guided tour of the chamber. Make the arrangements. Dismissed."

Solento bowed, picked up his attaché case, turned, and walked to the door, ramrod stiff, his smile not visible to the cardinal. Not far from the cardinal's rooms he ducked into an alcove and sank onto a marble bench below a statue of the Madonna. Pulling out a large white handkerchief he wiped the sweat from his brow, not trying to hide his smile. Oh, he had been quite honest with the cardinal; he had received a head in the courier pouch—one belonging to Judeland Bundaeker. She was definitely on their list, just below Morgan and Lamar. He doubted the cardinal would ever actually visit the chamber, never see the empty canister reserved for Morgan.

He drummed his fingers on the attaché case. He would have opened it if the cardinal had somehow learned the truth. He would have given the cardinal a copy of Cardinal Loconi's final confession, which revealed the whole history of the OVFS, including the names of all who had served its grisly mission. That was his ace-in-the-hole, one he would hold until needed.

Solento knew that if he'd gone into that meeting empty handed his days—his hours—would have been numbered. Through his cunning he had bought himself more time.

He needed to make plans.

So little time.

40 - Now Dash Away, Dash Away, Dash Away All

Each Christmas Tide at the stroke of ten
The headless vampire rides out again
From Dracula Hollow cross frost-bitten snow
He rides on a mission to deliver a blow
To the wretched villain who done him in
The vengeance he swore was a mortal sin
Some say he alighted for a pint of their best
At the Boar's Head Tavern to take his rest
Though the aleman fainted quite dead away
At the sight of a body whose head wouldn't stay
Twixt the blades of his shoulders atop the neck
Best hurry your departure when a black shadow falls
From a headless vampire who wanders the halls
And was heard to exclaim ere he rode out of sight
Where have you hidden? Come out and fight

Andre absently patted the suit coat pocket that held his passport. "Dr. Jene Claude Vompre," a name he hadn't used until recently, since the early 20th century. On the other side he had a wallet with a driver's license, credit cards, AARP, and others.

He thought about his night with Morgan and smiled, unaware that he had. She wanted me to retain my powers; she wanted a night of vampire sex. It will take a couple days for her to recover. In a way, she never will. Nor will I. He sighed. But I will get her back . . . someday.

The Airbus A 330 lurched once but resumed its smooth flight. Alitalia Flight AZ-615 had departed Boston's Logan International at 10:45 p.m., right on time, and should land at Leonardo da Vinci/ Fiumicino International in Rome at 12:45 p.m. local. Very civilized. He recalled earlier flights in first class in the venerable 747, but business class would do.

The plane lurched again, and the fasten seat belts sign came on, followed by the normal blather from a flight attendant.

Andre thought of the bon voyage breakfast he'd shared with NT. Odd, he'd never found out what his real name was. He'd come to like the rumpled old Cold War assassin and had given him a generous start on a new life in the Caribbean, beginning with passage on a private yacht belonging to an old friend and fellow vampire. Andre had obtained a full set of credentials for Number Three from one of the best in the business, a brand-new Glock 17 Gen 4 pistol with customized grip and a supply of cartridges sufficient to start a small war, a cell phone to be used only between themselves, and finally a $175,000 retainer. NT would be on call to support Andre whenever and wherever that might be required.

NT had been a big help the previous couple of weeks. First, he'd delivered the feather and rose to Judeland and later had her body cremated, the ashes dumped in the Saugus land fill. No one had ever treated NT with kindness, and he found it extremely hard to say thank you. Finally, NT reached into his jacket pocket and retrieved an envelope and handed it to Andre. It contained a camera memory chip.

"Judeland had me take some surveillance pics of Father Hemming and one of his old flames getting it on at a beach cottage. Never made any prints." He watched as Andre melted the chip into a liquid mass.

While not given to nostalgia, Andre felt a twinge of regret at their parting. They shook hands. Andre said, "Good luck"; NT mumbled something, and both turned and walked away from one another. Neither looked back.

Just before going through airport security Andre received a code word message from Countess Amberglass confirming that Morgan's fetus had been safely transported to the Serpent of Charna. He had been stunned when Madam Amberglass informed him that Judeland had aborted her fetus prior to their combat, having made arrangements for its transport to Charna.

Andre was jolted. The two fetuses could grow up and form a dynasty. Interesting. His future might be more complicated than he'd earlier thought. And from this moment he had to energize his vampire powers to the fullest if he was to outwit and survive this trip. No more romantic memories.

This would be his only trip to the Vatican, and it would seal the doom of the OVFS. He would make his first-ever withdrawal from the bank vault of the Banca Monte dei Paschi di Siena: gold Spanish Colonial Doubloons, minted around 1650. He had deposited them in the late 1600s; they were now worth approximately $ 2.45 million.

He would use doubloons as the bait to lure Cardinal Manlocara away from his safe haven.

ೞ

His favorite room in the five-star Inn at the Roman Forum faced the Coliseum. The Inn was the only accommodation in Rome that included ancient Roman ruins as part of the architecture. From the entrance a passageway wound down to a cryptoporticas—a stone gallery bearing engravings over two thousand years old. The city provided a rich collection of archeological wonders that were all considerably older than himself, which he found to be comforting for reasons he'd never quite diagnosed.

Having ordered a bottle of Valpolicella, a single-vineyard red, he twirled it around in his glass, held it up to the light, inhaled it deeply, and tried a sip. Magnifico! He retrieved a fountain pen, linen writing paper with matching envelope—no logo—and penned a note to Cardinal Manlocara.

In the year of Our Lord, 2013

I have long appreciated your vast knowledge of ancient gold coins and wish to share some of my collection with you. I desire to place a substantial portion of my collection at your disposal in return for your intercession on my behalf with the Master Creator. You see, I have not led a life of purity, faithfulness, and adherence to the Church's canonical requirements.

I wish to do penance for past deeds and to bask in the peace of forgiveness. For reasons that need not be stipulated here, I wish to conduct this transaction outside the shadow of the Church. None need know of it but the two of us. As I wish to keep my personal life veiled, I ask that you take no action to have me traced or vetted. Such action would prompt me to find another mentor who would fully respect my wishes in this regard.

Included with this missive are two coins from my collection. I will give you three days to have the coins valued. If you associate with a reputable coin dealer he will inform you that each of these coins, in uncirculated mint condition, is worth just under 12 thousand dollars. Should you for any reason wish to bypass this opportunity please retain the two coins for your time and consideration . . . and your continued silence. I'm

certain that we both have substantial reasons to honor
silence on this and other matters of mutual concern.
You may contact me in person, by hand-carried
message, or by I-Phone.
It is with great anticipation I await your reply.
Sincerely,
A Friend of the Church
Room 18, Inn at the Roman Forum, 06 6919 0970
I-Phone:617-244-0409

Andre re-read the note, enjoyed a satisfying swallow of wine, then placed the two coins in the center and folded the note into a package. He addressed the envelope, sealed the note and coins inside, pulled off his surgical gloves, and shoved them into a side pocket of his satchel, then slipped the pen in with the gloves. It will be a crowning accomplishment to put an end to the murders of my brothers and sisters. He offered a toast to all whose heads lay in wait for the vengeance they had so long deserved.

CReap

Colonel Johann Solento flipped through the listing of travelers into Italy, starting with those who entered Rome. He was indebted to a colleague in INTERPOL for supplying him with timely listings of such travelers. For the past fourteen months he had been scanning the listing that was compiled and forwarded electronically to the Pontifical Swiss Guard. He had tracked his own OVFS operatives, members of the Vatican's hierarchy as they traveled, known or suspected criminals based on tipoffs from INTERPOL, and a few special cases, like that American Priest, Father Hemming. The software program highlighted unusual or interesting cases, or ones that fell outside of the program parameters. Solento was about to toss the list when he spotted a name on the "outside parameters" listing. Dr. Jene Claude Vompre.

Why does that ring a bell? he wondered. For the next ten minutes he ran the name through a variety of files the Swiss Guard maintained. No hits. He was about to give up when it occurred to him to look in the OVFS files. They were pen-and-ink files locked in the chest in the head chamber. "God's death, I hate that place," he said, unaware he'd spoken aloud.

"Do you need me?" his secretary called from the adjoining office.

"No, no. Thank you." I'll have to go tomorrow, he thought, glancing at his watch. He did that a lot since he'd bought a brand-new Oyster

Perpetual Day-Date 40 Rolex 60th anniversary model, with its signature olive green face and pink gold case and expansion band. He wasn't supposed to buy luxury items until he retired, but he couldn't resist this one. The vice president of the Vatican's bank, Banca Monte di Siena, was wearing one a couple weeks ago. It looked like the finest watch he'd ever seen. He shuddered at the price, not that he couldn't afford it, but he hoped Cardinal Manlocara was no longer monitoring his OVFS Swiss bank account.

"Colonel, it's the cardinal's secretary on line one. Says the cardinal wants to see you right away."

"Merda! Tell him I'm on my way."

C820

The colonel was shown into the cardinal's study. A swatch of strong sunlight through a single window lit his desk as if by a heavenly decree. From the deep shadows, the cardinal spoke. "How long does it take you to get here, colonel?" his voice finely edged.

"No longer than usual, Your Eminence." He glanced at his watch, as did the cardinal.

"It may have cost you some time as you stop periodically to admire your new time piece." Manlocara scowled. The ticking of a mantel clock, previously silent, sounded like the echoing sounds of a Chinese gong.

The cardinal stood, one eyelid fluttering. "I have a matter of urgent business, one which will call me away from the Vatican's walls. I want you to pick six of your best men to provide protection for me as I pursue that business. Can you have your men ready by tomorrow noon?"

"Without fail, Your Eminence."

"All of them need to wear regular street clothes. I do not wish to draw any attention to myself."

"I understand." Why would a six-man SWAT team draw anyone's attention? How little these red caps understand the real world.

"You have received the operational report from our operative in America?"

"It arrived yesterday, Your Eminence."

"And have you transcribed it into the codex? Finished all the paperwork?"

"Yes. All is as it should be."

"Good. As I said at our last meeting, I would like to inspect the vault. I've been remiss in not doing so earlier."

The colonel knew the cardinal had never inspected the vault. Well, Loconi will be delighted to welcome you and introduce you to our collection. That should make your day.

"After the noon meal we shall perform our inspection." Solento's eyebrows rose.

"As you wish." I'd wager you won't keep your noon meal down very long. The colonel bowed stiffly, saluted, executed an about face, and marched out of the study.

As the door shut he glanced at his Rolex. Again. "Damn." That was going to be a difficult habit to break.

41 - Return to the Necropolis

Gold gleams in the eyes of all mankind
Who search the mother lode to find
They paw the earth for gold nuggets rare
But rarely find any solace there
For the richest treasurers are to be found
Within their hearts—not in the ground

A nd how many of these coins," Manlocara held out the two he'd been given, "did you say you wished to place with the Church for safekeeping?"

Oh you toady, Suroccan thought. The greed is extruding from you, and it has the stench of a sewer. "I would like to hope that one hundred would provide the intercession with the One Eternal Spirit that I need in order to pass by the gates of Purgatory and enter into the Eternal Kingdom without experiencing any form of purification."

"Umm, I quite understand. It is a tall order, though, one which might require the intercession of the Holy See himself. Such penitence would encounter many administrative hurdles and could be quite time consuming. Were we to have additional resources, many—perhaps even most—of these Gordian knots could be bypassed." The two candles on the table flickered as their waiter carted off their dinner plates and silver. The cardinal had cleaned his plate; Suroccan had nibbled around the edges of his, which, no doubt, would draw the ire of the chef.

"My collection is not limitless, Your Eminence."

"Keep your voice down. We don't want our identities revealed."

Suroccan glanced at the nearby table that held four big men, all dressed in black. Two others had been detailed to cover the entrance and exit. Martin, the name Suroccan had chosen, had laughed aloud as the phalanx of men jumped out of a black SUV, which all but shouted to the universe that it was the conveyance of a very senior official, or perhaps a senior Mafioso.

"What would it take to acquire Papal intercession on a timely basis, say this year?" Suroccan offered a cigar to his dinner companion, who accepted. They lit up from the candles. A waiter rushed over with a large ash tray, and in a moment, another provided two Espressos.

"Ah. I haven't enjoyed one of these in a very long time. After coffee perhaps we could enjoy an aperitif?"

"Most certainly," Suroccan replied, sipping his coffee and puffing grandly. "You were about to consider my question—"

"I am all but certain that doubling the offer of vintage coin would guarantee a most timely absolution for your soul, my dear Martin."

Suroccan gasped as if he'd been shocked. "You place a most exorbitant price for such a diminutive soul."

The cardinal gulped the last of his wine, puffed vigorously to reignite his cigar, then sat back with a sigh. "I am never surprised that those on the outside believe that there is some Papal magic wand that can be waved that would cut through centuries of red tape. With the right person and sufficient funds, much can be accomplished, dear Martin. Much. But take away either of those two ingredients, and the bread will not rise."

Suroccan sat hunched, hands folded in his lap, a deep frown creasing his face. At last he, too, sighed. "I have so enjoyed your company and your wise counsel, Your Eminence. But alas, I must seek another venue. Bless me and those like me. I am deeply disappointed, but perhaps my expectations were excessive. I must leave you now, older and wiser." Suroccan slowly rose from his chair, his face a mask of despair.

"My good man, not so fast. Please be seated. We haven't exhausted the subject, surely." The cardinal vigorously waved him to sit, and Suroccan settled back down like a balloon that had lost its air. "To what extent could you increase your contribution? Be aware I'm not trying to condemn anyone to penury." The cardinal smiled and spread his hands out on the table as if rendering a blessing.

"One hundred twenty-five. That would exhaust my holdings."

Cardinal Manlocara's eyes narrowed as might a poker player trying to determine if his opponent were bluffing. Suroccan's eyebrows rose as if he were calling the bluff. "I think we can work with that my good man. When could you arrange to transfer that sum?"

"Half now, the second half upon the final absolution of my soul."

"HALF—" The cardinal's face flamed.

"I trust that won't be a problem, Your Eminence."

The cardinal coughed into his napkin but nodded. They relit their cigars and ordered cognac.

∽

Suroccan arrived at the cardinal's office precisely on time. He carried a leather satchel that clinked occasionally when he moved. They waited five minutes for the colonel. Introductions were brief. The colonel led the way, carrying a long flashlight; Manlocara carried a second one.

The cardinal had debated revealing the OVFS chamber to Martin, but after that queer duck delivered the second payment, he would find his eternal rest along with Cardinal Loconi. He would have to trust Martin—and the colonel—for a little while longer. The OVFS chamber was the only truly safe place to store the gold, all of which would soon belong to Manlocara. Another body or two in the vault would hardly matter.

The colonel blocked everyone's view as he pulled the brick out, opening the door to the vault.

"This is the vault?" The cardinal scrunched his face. "It smells like a . . . only Satin knows what. The air is putrid. How can you stand . . . ?" his voice faded.

The colonel lit two oil lamps and turned to see the cardinal staring at the coffin propped up in one corner. Cardinal Loconi's dead eyes stared back. Manlocara quickly crossed himself and looked away. "So this is where my predecessor will spend eternity," he mumbled, turning his attention to the six rows of vampire heads, sixty in all, floating in the containers filled with the ancient brine, each showing a different emotion. The flickering light made the heads appear even more hideous. The vault was surprisingly large, measuring about twenty-five by twenty-five feet with an eight-foot ceiling. It was damp, and the rock from which it was hewn glistened.

It felt slimy, the cardinal thought. And while he'd never encountered an atrophied body, the stench reminded him of death and decay, and he pulled his large handkerchief from his sleeve and held it to his nose. His eyes began to burn, and he had the beginnings of a dull headache.

"This, Your Eminence, is the first head in the collection. Dated 1925. From Ireland. All the heads are in date order. On the shelves opposite are our empty containers, waiting to be filled. You look a bit unsteady. Here do sit down on the bench."

The cardinal slumped down, his eyes darting around the room.

"Who else knows of this place, colonel?"

"The two of us, and now your guest." The colonel glanced at

Suroccan.

"Good. Good. We must take no chances, colonel." In the silence that followed, both looked at Suroccan.

A slow smile spread across Suroccan's face. "I trust you do not plan to have me become a permanent guest?" he asked, nodding at Cardinal Loconi. "That would complicate our transaction, wouldn't you agree, Your Grace?"

"No, no, no my dear Martin," the cardinal replied hastily, his voice a pitch too high. "The shriving of your soul will be based on absolute trust between the church and you, kind sir. Eternal absolution will depend entirely on your taking our secret to your grave. Any violation of our trust would result in eternal damnation . . . and would require physical purification as well. I'm certain none of that will be necessary, of course." He turned to face the colonel.

"Now, Solento, show me the records of these vampires," Manlocara commanded, breaking the tension. He watched the colonel open the old sea chest in one corner and retrieve the vampire codex. It had been scrupulously kept by the first two cardinals and more recently by the colonel, who placed it on the table. The two sat shoulder to shoulder, peering intently as Manlocara turned the pages.

Suroccan backed slowly to the door so that the coins in his satchel made no sound. He looked up and identified the brick that activated the door and pulled it out. The door opened about three feet. "Your Eminence I am convinced you will need sufficient time to study the OVFS records in depth. I am prepared to grant you that time."

Both men turned toward Suroccan. "Whatever do you mean by that, Martin?" The cardinal raised one eyebrow and fixed the vampire with a commanding look.

"No. NO!" The colonel lurched toward the door.

"I must leave you now. I no longer require Papal intervention."

"You what?" Manlocara's eyes widened as he saw the vault door open. How . . . why. . . ?" His jaw hung slack.

"Gentlemen, I bid you adieu." He slipped through the door and activated the brick on the other side.

"Cardinal, you fucking idiot!" Solento screamed as the door closed.

Suroccan transfixed the activator brick with a powerful focus, causing it to melt, jamming the mechanism.

"And may you both rest in peace amongst all the vampires who will soon become your eternal companions." Suroccan nodded once, his face grim, and began the long trek back.

"Holy Mother of God," Manlocara bellowed, racing to the door and pushing on the brick, which was still warm. He redoubled his efforts, finally turning to the colonel, his face ashen. "Do something, you ass! Get us out of here."

The colonel slumped across the table and sobbed.

Cardinal Manlocara mindlessly pounded on the brick with his fist.

42 - Coleson Manor
November

The vampire left with heart so shorn
A new life again would have to be borne
What despair was his to live on a far shoal
For she had breathed new life into his withered soul
And she loved him still though there was another
Who for this lifetime would be her mate and lover
He must endure and await her return
For his love and passion would forever burn

The afternoon sun, reflecting off a thin glaze of ice covering the garden, sent flashes of sunlight through the library, dappling the leather-bound tomes of the famous and the forgotten works of men trapped in the corridors of musty history, their mute voices a cacophony of silence. The window lights carved the intermittent sunlight into oblique squares, suggesting the antiquity of ages past.

Lamar hung his sport jacket on the back of his chair, pulled down his tie, tamped more Billy Budd into his pipe, and flicked his gold pipe lighter. Dust motes glinted on and off like a coven of midnight fire flies. He rattled the cubes in his twelve-year-old scotch: The Ancestor—John Dewar & Sons—Striving for perfection since 1846. The cubes rattled again as Lamar took another sip. He rather liked the sound—like the bones of Coleson Manor's ancestry announcing their continuing presence.

Oxnard's tail flicked from side to side as he studied the drifting smoke. Calvin slept.

Lamar returned his attention to the family codex. His fingers traced the delicate Celtic scrollwork surrounding the opal embedded in the center of the green leather cover. He marveled at the parchment, which appeared not to have aged. The gilded page ends and the lavish illustrations further enhanced this eight-hundred-year-old masterpiece. Was the faint scent of Absinthe his imagining, or did it actually cling to the manuscript? Lamar shook his head. "Humbug. Bah!" He chuckled. Rather like Dickens, he thought.

Opening to the bookmarked page he stared at the ink splotch. Was it intended to guard a codex secret? Or had the scribe upset the ink bottle carelessly left on the same copying stand as the manuscript itself? A rookie mistake. Yet the richly endowed sketch of a monk working in the scriptorium, with a baleful cat watching him from the window ledge, and the many pages of illustrated script, testified to art of a high order. Then why the spill? Had the Brother Scriber appeared unexpectedly and was about to read what his subordinate had just written?

Lamar patted the envelope in his sport coat pocket. At long last he had received a reply from Dr. Dorrel, director of Harvard's graduate history program, who had managed to extract some of the text under the ink blot with the help of a focused UV spot beam. Lamar had resisted opening the envelope in Dorrel's office, but why so hesitant now? With shaking hands he unfolded the letter and began to read.

21ˢᵗ September 2013

Lamar:

A portion of the writing covered by the ink blots resisted all efforts to decipher. I was able to recover most of the missing text, as you can see, but you will find a few words/phrases that stubbornly remain illegible. I have offered my best guess on some of the resistant ones; I wonder if you might be able to supply a few more based on context?
I wish to discuss the codex—and its meaning!—with you, at your earliest convenience.
Transcription Follows.

J. Dorrel

What role hath the vampire within the Kingdom of God?
Mayhap he be a disciple of Lucifer, the prince of fallen angels with powers to corrupt the soul of the unwary, those who attend not to their salvation. And what hath our Lord Jesu to say about this abomination?

The holy words under this _____(inkblot?) will reside, for

millennia stretching forth, the message meant for but one man, he
who pierceth this veil of ink. The universal secret, long hidden, lies
forsaken neath the blot . . . until now.

Lamar frowned and relit his pipe.

But of even greater import, the prelates have ground to dust the
reality of reincarnation—the fact that all souls travel numberless
lifetimes as they seek to attain spiritual mastery. Life is hard,
brutish, and short. Would an all-loving God demand that
we _____(learn everything?) in one roll of the dice?
Mankind demands better of its gods.

Reincarnation? Hmmm. Lamar added to the pipe smoke that hung
over his desk. What's so secret about that? It's been around since the
dawn of religion. The notion of reincarnation makes controlling the
masses a bit harder, of course. He took another sip of his drink and held
the cold glass to his forehead.

And so, my fair shade, I am writing to myself, a self who will
live in a lifetime yet to unfold. It be foreordained that the later
version of me, known to his fellow members of society as Lamar
Bradford—

"Jesus H. Christ," Lamar yelled, leaping to his feet and knocking the
chair back against the wall. "This can't be!" He shook as he bent over and
squinted at the passage.

—will find this codex and will plunge beneath the darkness of the
_____ (ink blot?)—a rather perfect analogy for life—to find
the truths that form the salt of our being.
You are eternal. We all are, even those who do not carry the evil
spore of the vampire. Alas, the vampire curse will blossom in
you, my dear one, casting darkness upon your soul, but you will
overcome that terrible affliction to _____(become?)
the fountain of healing for others like you, _____(who
suffer the?) malicious scourge of vampirism. One day you will lead
those lost souls into the sunlight, to the vast relief of all mankind.
_____(?) Then one
day we will _____(?) yet unconceived, yet
unborn, yet unknown to the gods.
_____(Signature?)

Lamar carefully placed his pipe in its holder. How, according to all the gods man had ever breathed life into, had he survived vampirism only to find himself chained to the wheel of life, to endure one lifetime after another, almost as if he were still a blood brother of Andre Suroccan and his lot? Was reincarnation a curse or a blessing? Would Suroccan know the answer? Would anybody?

Some nameless monk, circa 1200 and something, just had a little chitchat with a future version of himself. Me! Does that make me a helpless pawn on some cosmic chess board?

A chill swept through him as he stared at the codex. Elbows on the desk, he slowly lowered his face into his hands. The silence was oppressive.

Morgan opened the library door. "Lamar?" She saw him flinch.

"Sorry, I didn't mean to startle you. It's such a beautiful brisk day I thought we could go for a walk. We need to move our bones."

Lamar shrugged into his sport jacket, jammed the letter in his pocket, and followed her out. They set off hand in hand.

It really was a beautiful day.

Robert closed the codex and carried it off.

Epilogue

ndre sat by the fireplace watching the flames, searching for a message. The Mangy Moose Saloon, with its iconic moose head, had attracted flees for over a half century. It looked about like he felt: ancient, bedraggled, and forgotten. He stirred his coffee the way Morgan had, round and round till the coffee cooled. Doors opened for breakfast at 7 a.m. unless you were a vampire. He slumped with a mug of coffee, unaware of the wait staff as they prepared for the morning breakfast scrum.

It was snowing out, but he hadn't noticed as he walked from his villa to the saloon. That was a singular "talent" as Jackson Hole in the winter was a tableau for Currier and Ives or Norman Rockwell. The snow fell softly, its oversized flakes coming straight down. The cold morning hush reflected his mood.

He thought about last night. What was her name? Linda? No, Susan. She'd almost finished her RN at the Denver College of Nursing. They had skied—he was mortally tired of skiing—had dinner—she ate like a starving moose while he barely touched his plate—and had shooters at the bar. She joined him in a private hot tub where they had sex. He tried so hard to pretend she was Morgan. But that never worked.

⊙≋⊙

Lamar had fallen asleep in five minutes after they finished. It had been good; it mostly always was. Still, she felt alone, taken for granted, left out somehow. She had given up trying not to think about the one night she had made love to Andre. She tried to shout down her wicked self who wanted (needed?) another night like that. Oh, Andre. Where are you?

Andre lunged toward the fire, spilling his coffee. He had seen her in the flames. She was calling for him. No, to be brutally honest she had wanted to know where he was. He adjusted his mind, his will. I am here, dear heart. Are you calling for me to come to you?

Morgan felt a shock. Her eyes widened and her nose flared. The scent of Absinth seeped into her awareness. She hadn't been aware of that scent during the past five years since he'd left. Was he here? Impossible. She hadn't called for him to come. Had she? He wouldn't come unless she called for him to come. Surely he hadn't misunderstood?

She eased out of bed, shrugged into her bathrobe, and picked up her slippers. Her bare feet would make no noise on the stairs. A pocket flashlight provided enough light for her to slip into the library. A bed of coals glowed in the fireplace. She missed seeing the single yellow rose on the coffee table as she walked over to one of the windows and pressed her nose against the cold pane. It was snowing.

She sighed.

"Oh, Andre."

Acknowledgments

My wife, Jenny, wore several hats: research assistant, editor, collaborator with my publisher, and darn good cook. She kept me going when the Muse was on vacation.

The late Professor of English, Libuse ("Libby") Reed, spilled gallons of red ink on my compositions while I was an undergrad at Ohio Wesleyan University. I can still feel her proverbial ruler across my knuckles. Over the years I sent her many manuscripts, and she treated me like the student I'd once been. At one point she asked me if I "owned a cliché machine, or was I making them all up myself?"

All the members of a string of critique groups, especially the last two: Novel Experience and Wren Writers.

A succession of writing partners including: CJ Cooper, Cindy Young-Turner, Cyndy Kelly, Pat Ryther.

TJ Turner, consummate writer, warrior (three deployments to Afghanistan as an Air Force officer), patriot, and good friend. We've traded war stories and manuscripts. Good therapy that.

Jeanne Johansen, the boss of High Tide Publications, Inc. Fixer of all problems, morale builder, developer of web sites, marketeer, trainer, and pure grace under fire—she does it all.

And to all those who ever stomped or flitted through my life leaving a residue. I've used them to cobble into many characters that fill these pages and the pages of other books yet to grace the shelves at B & N.

Dare I leave out the Muse?

Hardly.

About the Author

Born in Washington, D.C., Charles V. Brown wrote his first Fiction short story in the fifth grade. He still has it; in fact, it is reproduced in his as-yet-to-be published memoir, *Sleeve an' Me*.

For years a fiction dabbler, he allowed a thirty-year Air Force career and an advanced degree, along with raising two daughters, three horses, breeding English Setters, playing innumerable Dixieland Jazz gigs, and a tour in Vietnam to get in the way of writing.

His second novel, Viking Lady, won grand prize in the Maryland Writer's Association's annual novel contest, and then he got serious about writing.

After seventy-two years as Marylanders, Vic and Jenny moved to Williamsburg, Virginia and rescued a cat—Crickett (with two t's!)

Vic still plays jazz and writes and critiques and basks in the warmth of a mighty-nice place to live: Windsor Meade.

Sample Excerpt

Vampire Resurrection

1

1

Apocalypse Revealed

November 25, 2011

The greatest trick the Devil ever pulled was convincing the world he didn't exist.

Charles Baudelaire,
The Generous Gambler, 1864

Lungs heaving, Lamar leaned his forehead against the brick wall, willing the dizziness away. His hands ached from the cold. "Where's my trench coat?" he mumbled, unable to see much in the dark alley. As his breathing slowed, he began to retch. The stench of urine, garbage and vomit was overpowering. He tasted iron and touched his right cheek, which was burning."

Blood dripped from his chin. I've been cut. Or clawed?"

He found his handkerchief and gently daubed his face, then frowned, not sure what to do with it. Lamar looked down. It took a moment for him to recognize the peculiar shape at his feet: a cat.

Dead. Mutilated. He bent over. The cat was still warm.

What could have done this? He heard footsteps running toward him. I need a weapon. Something. Anything. He spotted a broken whiskey bottle and reached for it but lost his balance and fell against the wall.

"Mr. Bradford. Are you all right? Here, let me—" the man's voice trailed off as he looked down. "Oh, God. It's started. Sir, put your arm around me." He pulled Lamar upright. The street lamp at one end of the alley cast grotesque shadows that reached for them with long bony fingers.

"Robert?"

"Here, sir. Lean back against the wall for a moment." Robert produced a handkerchief and began wiping Lamar's face, patting his right cheek. "We'll get you home and sorted out." Robert took Lamar's bloody monogrammed handkerchief, balled it with his own, and looked around, then jammed them into his topcoat pocket. "Can you walk now, sir?"

"Yes, yes, I'm sure I can." His voice sounded hollow, and his mouth tasted foul.

As the two stumbled through the alley, Robert found Lamar's trench coat and wrapped it around the shivering younger man. Within minutes they were in the warm backseat of an Ambassador cab.

"The Jaguar."

"I'll collect it in the morning," Robert said.

"Robert, did you see the dead cat that was at my feet?"

"Cat, sir? I don't seem to recall one, no. Wouldn't surprise me though. The way that alley smelled, all manner of vermin must have crawled in there and died."

Lamar took a deep breath and exhaled. So much for seeing The Hound of the Baskervilles, he thought. He remembered Robert dropping him in front of the Cambridge Central Square Theater, a favorite with Harvard students, and driving off to park the Jag, then that strange sensation, almost like falling. It reminded him of the seizures he used to have as a schoolboy. Then nothing until the cold bricks against his forehead. He felt exhausted but with a strange sense of exhilaration. His head sagged, and his chin rested on the knot of his tie, which Robert had pulled down. It was shredded.

Oh, God. It's started. Lamar bounded out of bed, trembling. Robert's voice echoed like the fading chime of the ponderous clock downstairs.

"What's started?" The large, opulent room swallowed Lamar's voice; all the rooms in Coleson Manor were opulent. One of seven colonial mansions in the heart of West Cambridge's Brattle Street District, the homes were still referred to by some as "Tory Row," 230 years after the Revolution.

Why couldn't he remember what happened in that alley? Damn and blast. A burning sensation on his right cheek reminded him of the scratches from last night, and he touched the gauze pad and bandage. The recollection made him dizzy.

Lamar never thought of himself as handsome. Everything about Everything about him was average, even his age—thirty-seven. At five-ten, one-sixty-two, trim and in fair shape from his twice-weekly visits to Harvard's Malkin Athletic Center, he looked reasonably good. In an average sort of way. A few gray hairs announced the fading bloom of youth. In a few more years he'd be totally gray, like his father had been at forty-two.

His pale blue eyes—this morning they were red, with puffy eyelids—turned almost black when he was angry. Or frightened. At least that's what his mother had said. With perfect white teeth he could make a TV commercial for Aquafresh, but this morning his mouth tasted like the stink from the alley, and he reached for his toothbrush and the Listerine.

Still somewhat dazed, Lamar felt a chill draft and wandered into the bedroom to shut the window. A mocking bird was blasting through its entire repertoire on the limb of a nearby white birch. "Damn stupid bird," he shouted, slamming the window. Neither shouting nor slamming was recommended, Lamar discovered. His scalp tingled, reminding him of Robert bending him over the sink, scrubbing for God knows how long to get the blood out of his hair.

His stomach rumbled.

He glanced at his wrist. No watch. Nor was it on the bedside table. Where the hell's my watch? Maybe Robert took it off when he was scrubbing me. He could have left it beside the bed, damn him. And why is my clock radio unplugged? Whatever time it is, he's overdue with my morning coffee.

Gripping the banister he slowly descended the staircase. When he reached the landing that joined the two flights of stairs, he called, "Robert! It is way past coffee time." Nothing. The house was silent save for the ticking of the eighteenth century English longcase clock in the hall. Strange. As he reached the first floor he noticed a card, folded like a tent, on the Queen Anne handkerchief table next to the clock.

Mr. Bradford,

I am off collecting the XKR. It needs an oil change according to the Jag maintenance manual, and I've booked it for next Thursday. Your watch took a beating, and I shall drop it off at the Swiss Watchmaker on Church Street. A pot of coffee with two croissants and honey await you in the kitchen, along with two Advil, which I suggest you take. The Times and Globe are in the library. I also plan to stop at Formaggio's to replenish the wine cellar a bit. Do rest easy until I return. I'll fix your favorite Eggs Benedict and champagne brunch. By the end of the day you will be back to being a regular old sod.

Robert

Lamar read the note a second time and shook his head. Good old Robert. A peculiar man. As much a part of my lifeas my shoes. Put them on in the morning and never think aboutthem the rest of the day. I get up, put on Robert, and don't much think about him either. Indispensable yet rather intrusive. Extremely helpful but to a fault. Doesn't seem to have any vices. Doesn't have a life other than looking after me and this cavernous old haunt. In spite of a slight paunch, he seems unusually agile for a man his age. Maybe sixty? I ought to ask. And quick-witted. Bloody man insists I dress for dinner as if we were part of a large, turn-of-the-century Victorian family, and there's only the two of us.

He grew up in England, but I don't even know where for sure.No family apparently. Butler, valet, chef, nurse, tutor, estate manager—the man does everything but pee for me. Faithful as an old hound dog, but I don't even know if he likes me. Watches me like a mother hen,even more so of late. Especially last night. Can't imagine what would have become of me....

Wonder what my father's trust fund pays him? Couldn't fire the man if I wanted to, not that I would. Besides, he's the only person in the world I can talk to.

Ah, Robert Diamond, you are a world-class chamberlain. It might behoove me to find out—crap, I'm even using words like 'behoove.'

Lamar scowled and walked into the kitchen, poured a cup of coffee, and swept the two Advil into the disposal. Ignoring the croissants, he headed for the library.

Robert had made a fire. Lamar added a couple pieces of apple wood from the neatly quartered and stacked logs in the brick arch next to the fireplace. Dull gray light from the windows cast a pall throughout the dark, wood-paneled room, and Lamar turned on the electrified candle stand lamp, settled into his favorite leather wingback chair with matching footstool, opened the Globe, and read the weather forecast. Hope Robert gets back before it startssnowing.

Almost an hour later he spotted an article about the annual Dedham antique car rally to be held in July. Antique cars had been a secret passion of his since early boyhood, and he recalled pouring over the 1911 edition of the *Encyclopedia Britannica* and marveling at the Stanley Steamer, the Baker Electric, the Reo Runabout and other early automobiles. He had always longed to own an antique car. His all-time favorite was the 1929 Stutz Bearcat two-tone, dual-cowl phaeton with the LeBaron chassis. A hot car during Prohibition, it could outrun the Feds any day of the week. He'd even seen one once that had a bullet hole in a back fender. Ah, for the Roaring Twenties. He sipped some coffee and smiled, wondering if he could find the Stanley and the Baker again.

The bottom shelf of the floor-to-ceiling bookcase held a long row of thick, gray-green volumes, covered with a light film of dust, notwithstanding the cleaning crew that came once a week. He would mention that to Robert. That'll wilt the starch in his collar.

Crouching down, he extracted volume A. As he did, the longcase clock began striking, and, as he had all his life, he counted the number of chimes. Twelve? It can't be noon. Lamar looked athis wrist, grimaced, and then peered at the library mantle clock, which showed ten forty-four. "What's wrong with you, old friend?"

He recalled it had only been a couple of months since the guy from the Swiss Watchmaker serviced it. "Damn and blast."

Gathering volume A, he was about to return to the wingbackwhen he noticed another book lying behind the row ofencyclopedia. Pulling out two more volumes, he retrieved anobviously old, leather-bound book almost two feet long, nineinches wide, and a couple inches thick, with gilt-edged pages.

He walked to the kneehole desk that had been his father's and placed the strange book, with its dark green leather spine and thick covers, on the desktop. He switched on the desk lamp, pulled open the lower left drawer and retrieved a half-full bottle oftwenty-five-year-old Chivas Regal and an eighteenth centurytavern glass, both left there by his late father. He poured thescotch and sniffed it, then took a sip. Drinking in the morning.

What's to become of me?